Praise for Losing Brave

"If you love mystery, suspense, a touch of romance, and a plot that will keep you guessing from the start, pick up *Losing Brave*. It's a great read for all ages!"

CANDACE CAMERON BURE, actress and author

"I was on the edge of my seat with each twist and turn, and the ending blew me away. Pick up *Losing Brave* and prepare yourself for a late night of reading, because you won't be able to put this book down until the very last page."

CHLOË GRACE MORETZ, actress

"I very much enjoyed reading *Losing Brave*. Bailee Madison and Stefne Miller have crafted a story that unfolds in surprising ways, and the character of Poe will stick with you long after the book ends."

—MAIA MITCHELL, actress

"Bailee Madison uses her unique observation of human behavior and environment, that she's used so beautifully as an actress, in this collaboration with Stefne Miller, to create a richly detailed, haunting world that keeps you turning the page with anticipation."

—CHRISTINA HENDRICKS, actress

"*Losing Brave* is an engaging story that will keep you on the edge of your seat. The mystery of Dylan's disappearance, and how it affects her twin sister will keep you guessing with each twist and turn along the way."

—ALLY BROOKE, Fifth Harmony

"The Southern setting, suspense, touch of romance, intriguing characters, and the mystery surrounding what happened to Payton's sister add up to a book that ticks all the right boxes. I highly recommend *Losing Brave!*"

—MARCIA GAY HARDEN, actress

LOSING BRAVE

BAILEE MADISON
& STEFNE MILLER

BLINK®

BLINK®

CHAPTER 1

August 11, 2017

6:20 a.m.

"Payton? Are you all right?"

Payton opened her eyes and peered up at her father. The previously dark closet was now slightly illuminated by soft orange sunlight that streamed in through her bedroom's large, eastern-facing window, and she could once again see the colorful clothes hanging around her head.

"Um . . ." She lowered her eyes and realized she was crouched down, her toes tightly curled into the carpet. And based on how white—and numb—her feet were, she'd been in that position for some time. "Um . . . I'm good."

She stood quickly, and tried to act like she'd only taken a slight detour from her morning routine. The sudden blood rushing through her body made her light-headed, and she felt herself tip into the sweaters overhead. She forced a bright smile to flash across her face as she surveyed the closet, wide-eyed and basking in a sea of options while the latest Top 40s pop station played loudly in the background. "What's a girl to wear?"

His eyes narrowed into a confusion-filled squint. "You were hiding out in the dark because you weren't sure what to wear?"

"Girl problems."

The squint disappeared. Like he usually did whenever she or any other female confounded him, Daddy seemed to accept her answer with a casual but uncomfortable shrug. He then swept his hand toward the bedroom in a formal invitation for her to leave the confines of the dark closet.

Now fully composed, Payton tiptoed out of the closet, walked over to her dresser, picked up her hairbrush, and started to run it through her long hair. Back to her normal routine: fifty strokes. She glanced over at her daddy, noting his hair's contrast to hers.

She'd always preferred the color of his hair. It reminded her of the fizz that perched atop her faux champagne every New Year's Eve. It was a happy color, unlike the curse she was left with: a mopey shade of brown that was more day-old coffee than the café macchiato hue her friends called it out of kindness. Each morning, she was tasked with trying to apply enough shine and color to her cheeks and eyelids to detract from the depression that circled her face.

He disappeared deep into the bowels of her closet much like someone entering unknown territory and chopping their way through a dense forest canopy. "I don't know how you can find anything in here." His voice was a little muffled, as if the cotton, cashmere, and denim fabrics took him in and smothered him under their weight.

"Daddy?" Being from small town Mississippi meant that even if Payton were ninety-seven years old, she'd still refer to him as Daddy. If she or her friends ever called their parents anything other than Mama or Daddy, they'd be accused of rejecting their Southern roots. "Daddy?" she asked a bit louder. "You okay in there?"

Another muffled response from the closet. "I'm fine. Just lookin'."

"Lookin' for what?"

"Umm . . . pink. Your mama wants you wearing pink."

"You shouldn't have to search very hard. It's everywhere." Payton smirked at her reflection, although she could only see slivers of herself between the many photos taped to the perfectly shined surface. "Why pink?"

"It's happy." He reappeared with a simple pink pouf dress that was sure to make her look twelve years old rather than seventeen. "This screams happy."

Payton scrunched up her nose. "I think I wore that to one of Mama's Women's Club teas back in middle school. It was ugly then and it's even more grotesque now."

She carefully placed the brush back on the dresser, walked to the closet, swung the door completely open, and walked back into the cramped quarters.

"Is that light out again?" he asked.

She hung up the atrocity and inspected other options with an intensity she usually reserved for shopping online. "It burned out a few days ago," she muttered.

Daddy reached up and slightly twisted the bulb. It immediately resurrected and illuminated the space. "Nope. The bulb's fine. Must be a wonky socket."

"Weird."

"I'll make a call. Get someone out here to look at it."

"No." Her heart raced and she felt her face flush. She placed her hand on his forearm and squeezed. "Don't do that. I don't want anyone in here."

"Payton—" He stopped himself, and then slowly nodded.

"Anyway . . ." Her voice trailed off as she collected herself, smiled again, turned toward the pink section of her closet, and pulled out a blush-colored halter dress. It was much more Marilyn Monroe than Shirley Temple; and the only reason she knew who those 1950s starlets were was because Nana made her watch their movies every Sunday afternoon, and had for as long as she could remember.

One time, while the three generations of Sassy women watched *The Seven Year Itch*, Payton's mama moaned over the fact that Nana prayed and prayed for a daughter like Shirley Temple, but she got stuck with a Marilyn Monroe.

Payton couldn't even fathom it. In Payton's estimation, Laurie Sassy-Brave was the most straight-laced woman this side of the Mason-Dixon Line, and the only thing that proved there was ever a time when that wasn't the case was the fact that she'd become a single mother five months after her sixteenth birthday.

Her mama's more outgoing Marilyn Monroe phase was obviously short lived.

Daddy parked himself at the foot of the twin bed that sat under the window. It was piled high with so many clothes that he could hardly find a spot to sit. While one bed was a night-mare in the making, the other bed, which sat on the opposite wall, was neatly made and covered in enough throw pillows to make her daddy see putrid.

Since David Brave wasn't a fan of the frilly stuff but had no say in the decor in the upper floors of the house, when he had the funeral home portion redecorated a few years before, he'd made a point to request furniture with clean lines—and any time her mama so much as placed a throw pillow on a sofa, it up and disappeared with absolutely no trace of having existed.

Although she'd never caught him in the act, Payton believed that he shuffled them out of the house, and they eventually found their way to the incinerator where he performed cremations. The next day, a brand-new pillow would suddenly appear, and the cycle would repeat itself until her parents found a new territory to silently fight over.

"Lady Bug's full of gas and waiting for you," he announced as he scanned the room and scratched his head. Daddy pretty much always looked like he was lost or missing something. Sad truth was, he never seemed to find whatever it was he was looking for.

"And Brody got her all shined up for you. He found her all caked in mud. Said maybe you somehow took her four-wheeling or something." He stood quietly, and watched her brush her hair. "Did you?" he asked in a half-serious tone.

"Did I what?"

"Take Lady Bug four-wheeling?"

"Course not. That thing can hardly drive over a pothole, so I'm pretty certain it wouldn't ever survive muddin' terrain." Payton grabbed her makeup bag and kissed him on the top of the head on the way to the bathroom. "Thanks for the gas, and I'll be sure to thank Brody for cleaning her up." She arrived in front of the bathroom mirror and started to lay her makeup out on the spotless countertop. "I saw you bring someone in late last night. Who passed away?"

"Mrs. Humphrey. She fell off a curb and broke her hip."

Payton cringed. More from seeing her bare, slightly freckled face than the news of the broken hip. "She died of a broken hip?"

"No. She died during the surgery to fix the broken hip. Nothing uncommon for someone her age."

Lilac eye shadow floated across Payton's eyelid as she quietly digested his words. "I suppose the most important piece of information is that she's no longer with us, and the children of Cornwell can rest assured that they'll never again get toothpaste in their trick or treat sack."

"That woman did have a thing for clean teeth," he muttered.

She smiled, then tilted her head toward the overhead light and carefully applied shadow to the other lid. Most girls would never be able to get away with purple eye shadow, but Payton wasn't most girls—at least not as far as they were concerned, anyway.

"I best go take care of Mrs. Humphrey. I wouldn't want her to get lonely down there." Daddy stepped into the hallway and walked to the top of the stairs. "Come say bye before you head off."

"Yes, sir."

Moments after Payton finished putting on her face, Mama's voice rumbled up the stairs. "Payton Brave, breakfast is ready!" Her mama's announcement pierced the eardrums, but it was nothing out of the ordinary. For over a decade, the broadcast had rolled through the house at the same time every morning. In years past, if it went ignored, she would stomp up the stairs, walk to the doorway, and announce it in person, but her mama hadn't walked upstairs, let alone stepped into Payton's room, in a year, so the shrill voice now would echo through the halls of the Brave home over and over again until Payton made her appearance downstairs.

"Yes, ma'am. I'll be right down." Payton slipped on a pair of sandals, grabbed her bag, and raced down the steps as she coated her lips in a slick, clear gloss.

Payton only had a few minutes a day with her mama before she left for work, and would miss her altogether if she wasn't downstairs promptly at seven. In fact, if Payton wasn't downstairs at seven ten to see Mama off, she got a passive-aggressive text message promptly at seven thirty.

I'm sorry that you weren't able to see me before I left. Or, I'm sorry you missed me. Perhaps you can make time this evening?

Of course, that wasn't a request, it was a not-so-subtle demand of Payton's time, and if she failed her twice in one day, may God have mercy on her pitiful soul.

Payton entered the vast kitchen, where an ungodly amount of wicker baskets hung from wooden beams on the ceiling. Like the throw pillows, they were one of her mama's decorating obsessions and Daddy's nuisances, and he was convinced that the rough basket surfaces did nothing more than collect the pollen and dust that caused his allergies to wreak havoc every spring.

"It's about time you got down here," Mama huffed. "I was just fixin' to leave. I have a full patient load today—seems like everyone's gettin' pregnant lately."

"Mus' be in the water," Nana said, her voice as breezy as the air that drafted through the open kitchen windows. Being an old-school Southern Belle, Nana wouldn't allow the air conditioner to run until the heat of the day. She'd always made her family spend the morning with the windows open so they could feel the breeze on their skin and take in the relaxing visual of the draperies blowing in the wind.

The family accommodated her wishes, which meant that in the hottest months of the summer they walked around in a perpetual state of stickiness due to the sweat that accumulated on their skin.

This morning was no different. Payton threw her purse onto

the counter, and walked straight to the bay window that faced the back patio and looked out over the cemetery. She stood with her legs slightly parted and lifted her dress above her knees so the breeze could cool her already overheated body.

"I'm beyond ready for fall. This heat and humidity can't be comfortable for anyone." She glanced over her shoulder and noticed Brody's head was stuck in the refrigerator as he scrounged around for food, and Nana sat at the kitchen table with a bowl of grits in front of her and sipping on a cup of coffee. The china she held gently between her fingers and supported in her hand had been passed down for two generations, and nobody but Nana ever touched it.

Brody emerged from the refrigerator with a hand full of cheddar cheese cubes.

"Don't feed Pugsley," Mama ordered. "I caught him with a half-empty bag of beef jerky this morning."

Brody covertly dropped a cube of cheddar onto the floor, then shoved several into his mouth. "A'ight."

"His sodium levels are probably through the roof." If Mama hadn't been wearing her white physician's coat, she'd look more like Payton's sister than her mother. Not a line on her face, and with her milk-chocolate hair styled into a high, effortless pony-tail, she could've just as easily been on her way to cheer practice instead of her newly opened OB-GYN office. "Payton. Act like a lady, please."

Payton let the hem of her dress drop back to below her knees and immediately felt flushed.

"What brings you here this mornin', Brody?" Mama asked.

"I've got some big news. A guy I met last night. Maybe wants to go into business with me on that club I was telling you 'bout."

"Oh yeah?" Payton asked, walking to the kitchen island.

"Yep. I wanna get your daddy's opinion."

"He's gonna tell you to wait until the shop's doing better. You know that," Mama said. "Best prepare yourself so you don't get your feelings hurt."

"But I've got an investor. It's gonna work now. Just wait. You'll see." He walked to the toaster, pulled out two newly browned pieces of bread, and started to butter them. "Big things ahead."

Brody Wynn was practically Payton's big brother. Ever since his dad died suddenly when he was a senior in high school—leaving him with no other family, and forcing him to drop out and run the family body shop—Daddy had taken him in as one of his own. Brody was one of the biggest talkers and dreamers she knew, but he never followed through with anything, so Payton felt instant sympathy for her daddy, who was about to have to hear another one of Brody's grand plans . . . and she was thrilled she wouldn't be around to hear it.

"Is David already downstairs workin'?" he asked.

"Yes. He's with Mrs. Humphrey."

"Really? What did her in?"

Payton caught his eye. "Broken hip."

"Let's have a little compassion, shall we?" Mama suggested while briefly eying Payton's dress. "Interesting choice of color." Her voice was a little chilled, and the r disappeared at the end of the sentence. Her mama's coastal Southern accent was stronger than most. Possibly even forced, since she couldn't claim to be a Southern Belle if she didn't actually sound like one.

"What do you mean? I chose it because you wanted me to."

"Me?" Her mother briefly shot Payton a raised eyebrow before going back to doing a million other things, including avoiding

13

a run-in with Brody as he simultaneously moved through the kitchen and grabbed any food item not already taken. Payton wasn't sure he'd even gone grocery shopping in the last two years. For the most part, he showed up at the Braves' for almost every meal, and when he didn't stay to eat, he raided the fridge and pantry and made off with whatever he could fit in his arms.

Payton scrutinized the pink dress, which now felt more like a garbage sack, and then eyed the bologna sandwich her mother was smothering in mustard. "Perhaps a little lighter on the condiments, please?"

She was actually more of a Miracle Whip girl, but due to the calorie count, her mama only let her have it on weekends.

Mama stopped herself, then took the opposite edge of the knife and scraped some of the yellow substance off the bread. "I'm preoccupied."

"With what?"

"I've got a sixteen-year-old girl having some complications. She's on edge, and I'm worried that the stress is gonna throw her into early labor."

"Stress can do crazy things to a person. Not that we'd know anything about that." That last part was muttered under Payton's breath as she grabbed a bag of Cheetos from the chip drawer and simultaneously kept an eye on her sandwich in case her preoccupied mama decided to add more mustard, or forgot to salt the slice of tomato. To Payton's relief, she didn't, and finally slapped a piece of bread on top and wrapped it in wax paper like it was a Christmas present.

"You sure you wanna choose those?" Mama asked while rinsing the knife, and the veiled order was so slick, it resembled the satin lining in one of the showroom caskets.

Payton held the chip sack against the now rancid pink dress, and cringed. "I suppose not." She tossed the Cheetos to Brody and then gripped a bag of Baked Lays, tossing it on the counter like an attorney throwing down evidence in hopes her client would be exonerated. "Were you talkin' about Misty McNeese?"

"The pregnant girl?" Her mama dropped the knife into the dishwasher, kicked the door shut, and turned her focus to cleaning the spotless kitchen counter with some Ajax. "Do you talk to her much?"

"Not really." Payton grabbed some fruit snacks and threw them in the paper sack with the chips before her mother could make another snide comment, such as *A moment on the lips is forever on the hips.* "Misty and I never ran in the same circles. She was more Dylan's friend."

The maneuvering between Payton and her mama was like a well-choreographed dance. They moved in unison while simultaneously talking without actually communicating.

"By the way, you missed your dentist appointment last week. I rescheduled for next Tuesday at three."

"I promise that my teeth are fine. I brush and floss every day."

"You've missed your teeth cleaning twice now."

"I keep forgetting."

"You're supposed to get 'em done every six months."

Payton walked to the hallway and pressed on the intercom situated at the top of the basement steps. "Daddy, please tell Mama to leave me be about the dentist."

A few moments later, her daddy's response crackled back. "Laurie, leave her be about the dentist." He sounded distant, which made Payton suspect Daddy's assistant, Maggie, was the

15

one who'd gotten up and pressed the return button so Daddy could keep working.

"Her teeth are gonna rot out of her head," Mama asserted.

"They will not rot, but Mrs. Humphrey will if you two don't let me finish this embalming."

Life and death. The reality of Mama and Daddy's occupations often amused Payton—one helped bring life into the world, the other helped to usher it out, or at least made it look prettier after it went.

Payton plopped onto the stool that sat at the top of the basement steps, but kept her finger firmly planted on the intercom button so her father could hear the continuing conversation. "I brush and floss twice a day. What more do you want?"

"I want you to go to the dentist every six months like normal people do."

She heard Daddy's footsteps approach the intercom. "Normal people don't go to the dentist every six months, Laurie. Obsessive people do."

"Quit taking her side!"

The two-story argument left some tension hovering in the floorboards below Payton's feet. More tension than being caught eating a bag of crunchy Cheetos, then chasing it with a Moon Pie and downing it with sweet tea ever could.

"Put it on your calendar."

"Mama, I—"

"Now. Please."

Payton pulled out her phone, entered the appointment, and held the phone in front of her mother's face. "Feel better?"

"Yes."

Payton laid her phone on the counter, grabbed another bag

of fruit snacks, and shoved them in her brown paper lunch sack while her mama kicked her routine into overdrive. "Okay, I best be goin'." She collected her briefcase and medical bag. As she turned back around, she did a once-over of the pink dress, pursed her lips, and then tore off down the hallway. "Add a little color to your cheeks," she hollered as she passed through the front door.

Payton picked up a perfectly polished silver serving spoon out of the drawer and tried to look at her reflection to check her foundation to blush ratio. "Looks fine to me." She dropped the spoon back in the drawer and slammed it shut with her hip.

Nana stood from the table, straightened her floral cotton dress, and grabbed her pocketbook. "All right. I'm off to the bus station."

Payton and Brody shared a quick glance.

Nana slowly strolled over, kissed Payton on the cheek and Brody on the forehead, then moseyed down the hallway and out the front door without another word. Pugsley waddled not far behind.

Payton rushed over, cranked on the air-conditioner, and then grabbed her lunch sack and purse, raced back to the basement steps, and pushed the button again. "Daddy, Brody's here. Says he has some news for ya."

"Great news!" Brody mumbled with a piece of toast hanging from his mouth as he started closing windows.

"I'll be up in a minute, Brody. Make yourself at home."

"He always does." She and Brody rolled their eyes at each other before Brody closed the last window and took another large bite out of his buttered toast.

"All right, bye, Daddy. See ya when I get home."

"Have a great day, sweet girl."

She removed her finger from the button, quickly ran her hands over her dress to smooth out any wrinkles, and turned to Brody with a large smile. "Best of luck with Daddy."

"Thanks."

"What about my blush situation?" she asked.

"Looks fine to me."

"I'll take it." She walked outside and onto the patio, where Nana now sat in all of her splendor. A regal woman, Nana was always impeccably dressed, and at the moment had her hands on her pocketbook and bright red lipstick applied in mass quantity as she waited on the porch for a bus that would never come.

Payton kissed her grandmother on the cheek and gently primped her over-teased silver hair. "Have a great mornin', Nana. Are you going to be okay out here?"

"I'll be jus' fine, Payton. Jus' fine. It's a little humid out. Hope it don't mess my hair."

"No, ma'am. Your hair looks beautiful, just like it always does."

"Well, I'll be. You're a sweet little bug, ain't ya?" Nana elongated every word as it left her mouth. A true Moonlight Magnolia drawl that could lure anyone into a trance.

"I try." Payton gave Pugsley a quick pat on the head, and then skipped down the steps. "I'm fixin' to head off to school. Do you need anything before I go?"

"No, sugar. Leave me be. I'm jus' waitin' on the bus."

"All right then, I'll be back later." Payton walked out into the yard.

"Payton!"

Brody hopped down the steps. "You were so worried 'bout your makeup, you forgot your phone."

She expelled a sigh of relief and clutched her hands to her chest. "Thanks, Brody. You're a life saver."

He shrugged, then wiped his nose on his shirtsleeve like a first grader before tossing her the phone. "Sometimes I think you'd lose your head if it wasn't attached to your neck."

"Sometimes, I think you're right. But Daddy's worse." She made her way to her bright red vintage Volkswagen convertible bug. "And thanks for cleaning Lady Bug. I'm not sure how she got so dirty."

He laughed. "You don't remember driving through about a foot of mud?"

"Not really." She tossed her book bag inside, then turned her attention to her cell phone.

Arguments with your mama first thing in the morning means no time for a stop at the coffee shop. Tragedy. she tweeted.

Payton took one more look toward the patio. "Bye, Brody. Bye, Nana!"

"Soar, Payton Belle Brave!" Nana shouted. "Soar!"

And soar she did. Right through Cornwell, Mississippi, a town she'd lived in her entire life. It was situated not far from the river and directly on the bayou—not to mention a hop, skip, and a jump from New Orleans. Cornwell, where the moss hanging from the trees was as heavy as the Southern accents. *And,* Payton thought, *the need for the townspeople to be considered among Southern elite.* The town was small enough to be quaint and large enough to matter, but if a person moved there hoping they'd blend in and go unnoticed, they moved out within a matter of months. She knew firsthand that anonymity was an impossibility. Everyone was in your business, and your business depended on it.

Like the Brave Family Funeral Home, stores were all family owned and operated, and had been for generations. While Payton and her friends dreamt of having a Starbucks, there was no way the town council would ever let something so common and trendy situate itself on Main Street.

With a sigh and another coffee-craving pang, Payton pulled Lady Bug into the Cornwell High parking lot, where students arrived for the day. Some walked slowly, clearly dreading the reality of school starting in a matter of minutes. Others seemed to almost tremble with excitement as they made their way directly into the school building.

She waved to passing classmates as she threaded Lady Bug through the rows of vehicles, straight up to the first parking spot. A sign perched in front read "Senior Class President." It was a title she'd won with hardly any effort. Perhaps because she never admitted that she only wanted the position for the primo parking spot.

Once the car came to a stop, Payton checked her makeup one last time in the rearview mirror, added a bit more blush and lip gloss, put a big smile on her face, and then climbed out. Grabbing her book bag in one hand and lacing the car keys between her fingers in the other, she slunk past Lady Bug and strolled into Cornwell High.

Payton hadn't made it ten steps inside the building before her best friend, Starr, rushed up to her with the giddy look on her face and her cell phone clutched in her hand.

Payton and Starr had been friends since sophomore year. They'd started off as adversaries when they both ran for freshman homecoming court princess, but after Payton won the coveted spot and somehow managed to survive Starr's catty attacks for the remainder of the year, she took Nana's advice and decided to befriend her.

As Nana always said, "It's safer to stand beside the bear than beside the honey."

Truth was, they moved up the social ladder faster together than either could have alone, and while the duo often had difficulty tolerating each other, Payton managed to find some things she liked about Starr and forced herself to focus on those. Plus, Payton was an eternal optimist and she truly believed that if they hung around together long enough, she could turn Starr to the nice side.

But so far, two years hadn't been long enough to get the job done.

"Guess what?" Starr squealed.

"You've found a boy who won't make it another day if you don't bless him by your presence?"

"How'd you guess?" Payton appreciated that Starr was often naive and optimistic, but she was also exceedingly arrogant and genuinely believed in her soul that any boy should, and would, be honored to call her "his girl." Of course, her soul wasn't the deep sort. It was more wading pool depth, so any feelings she did have were fleeting, and the joy of being some boy's girl quickly turned to a deep disdain for that same boy whose eyes and attention eventually wandered.

It was Starr's expectation that she should attract more attention than Payton ever could, that drove Payton up a literal wall. Sure, Payton was newer to the in crowd, but her struggle to get to the top was partially what cemented her in place.

Being born to a single mother from the wrong side of the cove hadn't made things easy. When Mama "conveniently" married David Brave—who was well-respected, from family money, and much older—it hadn't gotten a great reaction from Cornwell's upper society. In fact, the Braves were excluded from social events until Mama finished med school the summer before Payton and Dylan's freshman year. Suddenly, Laurie Sassy-Brave was a woman of her own making, and that gave Payton just enough of an opening to start her own climb up the social ladder. A ladder she'd scaled by honing her beauty, charm, leadership skills—as well as her mama's new connections with certain families—until she rose to the top.

"Payton Brave."

Payton turned to the voice that boomed through the double doors she'd just entered. "Ethan?"

The twenty-year-old, once a classmate of Brody's, stood halfway in the doorway, his ballcap facing backward on his head. Since he wasn't a student at Cornwell High anymore, he wasn't allowed to enter the building. "I got something for ya."

She held her pointer finger up to Starr, stopping her incessant rambling. "Pause, please."

Starr raised her cell phone to within inches of her nose and started typing. Seconds later, a notification pinged on Payton's cell, and she unlocked it to read Starr's tweet:

> @AStarrIsBorn00: Always a lady in waiting, never the queen. What say you, @PaytonBeBrave? #PassTheSceptor

She looked up to make sure a path was clear to the doors, and then started reading her friends' quick responses as she walked toward Ethan.

"Here." Ethan pulled a paper cup from behind the door.
"Triple venti, half-sweet, nonfat caramel macchiato."

She stared at the cup and couldn't believe what she saw. "I
didn't order that."

"Well, someone did." He thrust the steaming hot drink into
her hand.

"Who?"

"I don't take the orders, I just deliver 'em. See you around."
Ethan walked between the rush of bodies that approached the
door like salmon swimming upstream, and left Payton holding a
drink she hadn't ordered but desperately needed.

Starr's face contorted in utter disdain as Payton returned.
"You had coffee delivered? That's even a whole new level for you."

"I didn't." She held the coffee up, and spun the cup in her
hands, looking for a person's name or note. There was nothing.

"Shocking," Starr said. "Payton has another admirer."

CHAPTER 2

August 11, 2017

12:30 p.m.

Payton, Starr, and Lindy walked from the picnic tables outside the cafeteria, threw their lunch sacks away, and made their way back into the school building. Only thirty minutes of lunch meant that Payton was always famished by the end of the school day. Of course, this caused her to sneak several snacks before dinner. She'd never cop to it, though. It was best if homecoming royalty never admitted to wanting to eat their weight in chocolate, and it was even better if you didn't admit it to Mama.

"Hey, listen," Starr purred. "Spencer asked me out again for this weekend."

Payton conjured up a smile as she plunged straight through the mob crammed in the hallway, talking about the latest gossip and slamming their metal lockers with gusto. "Good for you."

"He asked if maybe you might want to come."

"On your date? No thank you. I'm not a big fan of being the third wheel."

"You wouldn't be a third wheel. We thought we'd invite Joshua to come along."

"Umm . . ." Payton nibbled on her thumbnail and furrowed her brow as images of being the odd man out rumbled through her mind to the soundtrack of her sister, Dylan's, not so shy or friendly thoughts about the boy.

In social terms, Joshua was just her type: perfect features, a nice car, polite speech, and top social standing. If the two of them got together, they would be seen as the most perfect couple at Cornwell and the one everyone had waited for. Everyone but Payton. And Dylan.

Mama tried to attach Joshua to Dylan once, and it failed miserably. Now, it felt like Starr was behind the scenes, forcing another pairing.

"I don't know . . ."

He seemed nice enough, but like Starr, Joshua's ego was the size of the Gulf of Mexico. Not that it was his own doing. His daddy was a big lawyer in town, and everyone knew he pushed Joshua to be the best in everything. Even when it came to choosing a girlfriend, which could be why he was working on his second Brave girl.

"Hey, Payton."

Payton's mood momentarily perked up as she smiled and waved to the blurred profile that quickly greeted her and disappeared, leaving the scent of obscene amounts of Axe body spray in its wake.

Starr nudged Payton in the elbow. "Well?"

"I don't think so, Starr."

"Come on. He really likes you."

The bell rang overhead, and the activity in the hall became frenzied as everyone rushed to their next class so they wouldn't be late.

"Honestly, he thinks you're the best-looking girl in school, and he's one of the few guys who's willing to overlook the fact your family's a little cuckoo for Cocoa Puffs—"

"Starr, we're not crazy. We're—"

"Right. Thanks to the funeral home house, you're more Addams Family oddball, with a nana who's off her rocker."

Starr's comment left an ache of truth in Payton's chest, but she quickly opened her mouth to object on principle, before Dylan's boyfriend interrupted and slid between the girls and into the Spanish room without so much as a hello. Aside from dating Dylan, he'd spent plenty of time at their house since his mama owned the flower shop that provided most of the flowers for the funerals put on by the Braves. And while he didn't mind Payton so much, he and Starr weren't fans of each other. They'd never been in the same social groups, and although Starr often told Payton that their distance was due to her superiority, the truth hovered more around the fact that Cole couldn't care less about status, privilege, or attention. He'd made it well known that he preferred to stay out of the spotlight and away from the constant drama that seeped into the pores of the majority of the town.

Starr kept right on talking. Seemingly oblivious that life existed outside her orbit. "So we thought that if all four of us went together—"

"I'd say yes?"

"Yes."

While it was true that a night with Joshua didn't quite sit right in Payton's psyche, the idea of time away from Starr suddenly felt liberating. "Unfortunately, I'll have to pass."

"Payton!"

The girls followed Cole into the room and made the turn toward their desks. "Joshua practically ruined Dylan's life," Payton said. "I feel an obligation to loathe him for all eternity."

"I don't see how it's his fault she wore a hoop skirt or that

Dylan, her skirt, Joshua, and his daddy couldn't all fit in his truck. I mean, really, who wears hoop skirts?"

"It was a costume party, and she was Scarlett O'Hara. The outfit was completely appropriate."

"Still."

"Starr, they stuck her in the back of the truck . . . alone. The least he could've done is ride back there with her."

"The truck had a camper cover on it. She was fine with the whole thing."

"Are you taking his side?"

"It was almost two years ago and she ended up landing Cole, so what difference does it make?"

Payton collected the skirt of her dress around her legs as she slipped into her chair so her sweaty legs wouldn't stick to the plastic seat. "It was the most humiliating night of her life."

"That's right. The most humiliating night of *her* life. Meanwhile, you're the only one holding a grudge."

"Nana's holding a grudge too."

"Yeah, well, your nana's a little—"

Payton looked over and issued a silent warning.

Starr course-corrected and added, "A little, sweet old lady."

"Anyway, do me a favor and find a polite way to tell Joshua that as soon as hell freezes over, he and I can go out. Just don't use those words specifically. It's unseemly."

"We wouldn't want that." Starr rolled her eyes. "You're unbelievable sometimes." She pulled out her phone and started typing with impressive speed. Much faster and with better accuracy than she would ever manage to type on a computer keyboard. And Payton knew she had the C- grade in Keyboarding her freshman year to prove it.

Payton spun in her seat and observed the classmates in the room around her. More than half were already suffering from the post-lunch lull and had their heads on their desks.

"Hey, Payton."

Payton turned her attention to the girl sitting just to her right. Kasi Plummer had been in at least one of Payton's classes every year since first grade, but the two girls weren't necessarily friends, or at least hadn't been in quite some time. They were now more friendly acquaintances than anything. "Hey, Kasi. How's it going?"

Kasi smiled, as she always tended to. The girl was nice to everyone. Even those who weren't always so nice back . . . and Payton hadn't always been nice back. "I'm really good. Thanks for asking."

Kasi's eyes beamed and her voice held a genuine appreciation for being talked to, so Payton did the proper thing and continued the conversation. "Are you ready for this test?"

The girl rolled her eyes and giggled. "I was up until well after midnight. I think I'll do okay."

"I'm sure you'll do great. Languages always came easily to you. Didn't you win the spelling bee every year in elementary school?"

Kasi's eyebrows raised and her eyes brightened. "Every year but the fourth grade. Dylan won that year. I came in second. Even though we were friends, I'm not sure she ever fully forgave me for beating her every year."

Starr loudly sighed a "someone look at me" sigh. "Look, Payton, if you don't find someone to date, you aren't going to have anyone to take you to homecoming. How can the homecoming queen not have a date to homecoming?"

Kasi smiled. "You've got my vote."

28

"Thanks." Payton started to turn back to Starr, but her line of vision swooped down the length of Kasi's khaki pants. Several staples held the bottom hem in place, and her brown flats were badly scuffed. Realizing she was now staring, Payton turned back to Starr and tried to provide her with the attention she obviously so desperately desired. "Homecoming? That's like . . . what? Three weeks away?"

"The Friday before Labor Day." Starr stared glossy eyed as she scrolled through her social media mentions. "A homecoming dance on Labor Day weekend," she huffed. "It's insane. Why can't we live up north, where school doesn't start until September? Who can look good in a formal when it's ninety degrees outside?"

"Not me, that's for sure."

Starr rolled her eyes. "You know you're gonna win."

"No, I don't."

"Yes, you do. You freakin' win everything."

"Atención, por favor."

Payton dutifully turned her attention to her Spanish teacher and watched the somewhat elderly woman distribute the test of the day to students struggling to escape their carbohydrate-induced comas.

"Veinte preguntas. Treinta minutos."

"Si, señora," the class moaned.

"Cuando termine, leer tranquilamente."

"Si, señora" had become the fallback answer to anything she said, regardless if they understood it or not.

Payton knew that, as second-year Spanish students, everyone else should've known exactly what Señora Ramirez was saying, but three months of baking their brains out at the cove meant most still couldn't remember anything school-related.

The girl seated in front of Payton swiveled in her chair, plopped two tests and Scantron sheets onto Payton's desk, and turned back around. Payton picked up the top printout and a Scantron, then turned and slipped them onto Cole's desk. "Good luck," she whispered.

He simply nodded and turned his full attention to the test, while Payton glanced around at the room of faces who now had their eyes on her. And it wasn't because of her watermelon-pink dress. As a matter of fact, within a couple of days, Payton knew good and well that watermelon pink would probably make a comeback in the halls of Cornwell High.

She slowly moved her gaze to Señora Ramirez, and waited for a new game of Solitaire to illuminate the teacher's computer screen. Once it had, Payton looked back down at her test and untucked the hair behind her ear as she read the first question:

1. ¿Cómo está tu hermano?
   a. Es de California.
   b. Yo como con mi hermano.
   c. Está mucho mejor.
   d. Mi hermano esta allí.

A second after she read the third option, she colored in the C bubble on her Scantron sheet, glanced up at Señora Ramirez to make sure she wasn't looking, and then with one effortless movement tucked her hair back around her ear, being sure to hold up three fingers while doing it.

As soon as the others saw the three fingers, they colored in the C bubble on their answer sheets, and quickly, but subtly, peered back at her in anticipation of receiving the next answer.

The only ones in the room who didn't watch Payton and worked the test on their own were Cole and Kasi.

Two years of Payton watching her sister and Cole's relationship bloom gave her plenty of evidence that he was more of a make-it-on-your-own-or-fail-on-your-own sort of guy. It was one of the things that Dylan noted liking about him. He'd never taken a dime from his parents to use to take Dylan out for dates; instead, he earned every penny himself by working at the flower shop. And even though Mama never approved of Dylan dating Cole, he'd never let Dylan lie about how much time they spent together or where they were going.

In Payton's eyes, he was a young man of integrity, which in Cornwell meant nothing but to her sister meant everything.

And for Kasi's part, everyone knew that she was a good girl who wanted to accomplish big things, and she seemed to accept the hard work needed to succeed.

Whereas many saw Payton as Cornwell High's Mother Teresa, only younger and with less-weathered skin; but she didn't see the harm in getting a little help now and then, since she so often gave it. And while she didn't have to help everyone—only Zoe and a few others deserved the favor—her willingness certainly didn't seem to hurt her standing in everyone else's eyes.

Once those eyes were back on Payton, she shook her head a bit to let her hair fall back over her face so the process could repeat itself for all twenty questions.

At the end of class, the victorious group turned in their answer sheets on the way out of the room. Zoe walked up beside Payton as they exited the room. She awkwardly reached her arm in front of Payton and Starr and offered Payton a few pieces of paper. "Sorry I didn't get these emailed last night, I got held up."

Starr rolled her eyes and chuckled. "So we heard."

"What does that mean?" Zoe whimpered, as her shorter legs scurried to keep up on their trek to Calculus.

"It means you and Simon Teel were spotted together out at the cove after midnight."

Zoe's jaw dropped and her cheeks blushed. "Is anything private anymore?"

"No," Starr said bluntly. "Nothing is private, and it never was. Someone's always watching."

"Who was watching?" Zoe asked.

"What do I look like, TMZ?"

Payton scanned the papers for a few seconds and then summoned every ounce of attention she could spare and gave them to the humiliated girl walking beside her.

"I'm ruined," Zoe whispered, tears on the brink of falling.

"No," Payton soothed, while giving her a sympathetic smile and a gentle rub of her arm. Living above a funeral home meant that she was always running into people who needed some sympathy. She excelled at giving it.

Starr, on the other hand . . .

"Ruined?" Starr snapped. "What century are we in?"

"Payton?" A deep voice interrupted their chatter as they walked into the room.

Alarmed, Payton quickly turned to face the front of the room. "Yes, Mr. McDonald?"

"One-to-one function. Explain it, please."

"Uh . . ." After only a split second of thinking, Payton quickly flipped through her Calculus book, desperate to find the correct page.

"You don't need the book. You know this. Come on. One-to-one function."

Her heart raced, and her chest tightened. Still standing at the front of the room, she felt all eyes on her. "One-to-one function."

The phone vibrated in her hand. As soon as Mr. McDonald's back was to her, she glanced down and read the text from Zoe out loud: "When no two values of x produce the same y."

"Correct." Mr. McDonald turned his attention to his next victim, and Payton rushed to her desk and cowered so far into her seat that the hem of her dress almost hit the floor. She placed the side of her hand over her brow like a visor then peered over at Zoe and mouthed, "Thank you."

By the grace of God, Payton was spared from being called on again. Finally, because he was either out of material or out of patience, Mr. McDonald awarded everyone free time for the remainder of the period.

Starr didn't hesitate to pick up where she'd left off before Spanish began. "Heading to the cove after school?" Starr asked. "Joshua will be there."

"I'm not sure."

"It's the championship."

"I know it's the championship, but—"

"You've gotta crown the winner."

"Why do I have to crown the winner?"

"Because Dylan won last year, and since she isn't here to crown them, everyone expects you to."

"Why?"

"She was your sister. It's what—"

Payton felt her jaw turn nearly rigid. "She *is* my sister," she managed to speak through gritted teeth.

"Right. That's what I meant."

Payton slid her textbook off the desk, jammed it into her backpack, stood from her seat, and quickly moved down the row of desks toward the exit. She escaped the room just as the bell rang out, and managed a few seconds of a silent hallway before classroom doors all through the hallway flew open and students burst forth.

Once at her locker, Payton worked on the combination. *Thirty-one . . . nineteen.* Her eyes moved to the locker next to hers.

Dylan's.

Being one of the few people left in town who still believed that her sister might come home and life would get back to normal, Payton begged the school to let her locker stay empty. Waiting for Dylan's return.

They obliged, and also allowed Cole to switch lockers with Shaun Bream since his sat just to the right of Dylan's.

When summoned to the office to discuss the matter with Payton and Cole, Shaun didn't put up much of a fight about the locker change because, well, who wants to be beside a locker that's become nothing more than a shrine to a missing girl?

On the first day of school, Dylan's locker was decorated from top to bottom with notes, and Payton received a lot of sympathy from her classmates, but a few weeks had passed and everyone had already moved on. Payton got the feeling everyone wanted her to do the same.

Not wanting to catch the attention of others and become the topic of conversation for obsessing over her sister's disappearance, she only allowed herself to look at the locker for three more seconds before she forced her attention back to her own.

. . . Twenty-three.

The lock popped. She opened the door, tossed her calculus book back inside, and pulled out *The Complete Tales and Poems of Edgar Allan Poe*. She took in the cover for several seconds and ran her hand over the slick surface. "Poe," she muttered.

"You okay?"

She didn't need to look his direction. She knew Cole's voice, his distinct speech. Unlike everyone else in town, he didn't have an accent. He carefully enunciated his words but always sounded as if he had a stuffy nose. The sounds came more from his throat than mouth and nose. And his manner of speaking was more formal. No "mama" or "daddy" from him. He addressed his parents as Mom or Dad. Dylan once told Payton that she wasn't sure if he spoke so formally due to his specialized training or if he thought saying Mama and Daddy was too childish.

Either way, it was just another thing that made him different. That and the fact that he suffered from an autoimmune disease and lost his hearing in the sixth grade. He spent his seventh-grade year away at the School for the Deaf learning how to live in an unhearing world. When he returned, he was more of an outsider than ever.

He didn't act like anyone else, and he didn't sound like anyone else. He didn't fit and he didn't seem to care. A concept Payton found both enticing and unattainable. Even foreign. And then there was the fact his voice recently started leaving her with an odd balance of feeling on edge but somehow comforted at the same time.

"I'm fine."

Out of the corner of her eye, she watched him open his locker, and then reach over and reaffix the tape that held his

35

note to Dylan in place. It read, "I love and miss you. Come back to me soon. —Cole." He then ran the tips of his finger over the tape on the four corners of Dylan's photo.

In the picture, her long brown hair was pulled into a tight ponytail, and she wore a slight smile on her face—almost more of a smirk. Dylan always hated picture day, and this photo was proof of it.

As they studied the photograph, a silence grew between them, made worse by the contrast of the hallway noise. "Do I go to the cove in her place?" she eventually asked, looking back at the book.

"Do you *want* to go to the cove in her place?"

"No."

He nodded, then shrugged, as if accepting her reality better than she could. "But you will."

She paused and choked down his response. "Yes." Payton slammed her locker shut and walked away without another word falling out of her mouth, but her mind swimming with them.

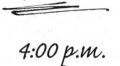

4:00 p.m.

The King of the Mountain Championship.

Winner takes all. A pot of cash, a gift card to the local coffee shop, free admission to all school functions for the year, and most of all, bragging rights.

It was quite the spectacle, and anyone who was anyone (and some who weren't anyone at all) were there. Even Payton, who'd finally accepted that it was her duty to be at the cove along with the others. Dylan was always the one who loved the beach and playing in the water. Payton only went on special occasions or to make an appearance from time to time.

Like everyone else, she and her friends staked out a section of sand with colorful beach towels, and peeled away any extra layers of clothing to reveal the bathing suits they'd changed into after last bell. As she glanced around, she noticed that, like always, everyone huddled in the same groups that collected in school hallways and sat by sections in the lunchroom on weekdays, or in church pews on Sundays. None of them showed any interest, or courage, to casually walk to a different group and strike up a conversation.

Payton watched Starr and Spencer frolic in the water several yards away from the swim platform. They took turns trying to dunk each other under the water's surface, but it appeared to Payton that it was more an excuse to put their hands all over each other than to actually submerge one another.

A shrill scream momentarily turned Payton's blood cold and spun her attention to the wooden platform in the middle of the water, where a senior lifted a sophomore girl above his head and threw her over the side and into the water with a violent splash.

"Payton!"

She twisted around enough to spot Joshua as he appeared out of the thick brush of the woods. The bright orange swimsuit he was wearing stood out against his tanned skin and his flip-flops tossed sand into the air as he walked her way.

"Why aren't you in the competition?" she asked.

"I've got nothing to prove." He slunk up beside her and observed the anarchy on the water. "That platform sure has seen a victim or two."

She laughed, surprisingly a bit charmed by his attention. "It does get pretty vicious." With her eyes hidden behind her dark sunglasses, she was safe to watch him sit on the edge of her towel and sink his feet into the sand.

He slid his sunglasses off his nose, perched them on the top of his head, and looked over at her with a half smile. "So get this. I checked the weather, and you aren't going to believe it, but hell just froze over."

Payton felt her body recoil. "Starr wasn't supposed to word it quite so harshly. I apologize."

"It's good for a guy to know where he stands. Even if it is in the pits of fire."

Trying to remain unfazed by his advances, she focused on the action in the water.

"Come on, Payton. Lay aside our differences—whatever they are—and give me a chance."

"They aren't differences so much as . . ." She pressed her lips tightly together, thinking it best not to bring up his atrocious date with Dylan.

"You'd have a good time. We have a lot more in common than you think."

"Like what?"

"I like . . ." Out of the corner of her eye, she watched him glance at her brightly colored bikini. "Red."

A bit unsettled by his leering, she cut her eyes back to the action on the water and tried to ignore the fact that the muscles in her neck were tensing up. "We live in the South. Everybody likes red. It's what we do."

"All of my friends are your friends. And my parents are friends with yours."

"I don't believe they are."

"Okay, so they're friendly. Sometimes," he corrected.

"You dated Dylan," she slipped. Her intention to avoid the topic failed miserably. "I— I think it would be odd."

"I didn't date Dylan. I went out with her twice freshman year. We were an epic fail."

She sighed.

"I never went out with her again. For some reason she wanted to be with Cole, and you and I both know it."

Yes, she did know. When her overbearing mama forbid Dylan to date Cole, they broke up for the whole first semester of freshman year. Her mama convinced Dylan that if she'd just be open to other options, Joshua especially, she'd realize that Cole wasn't all that she thought he was.

Mama was dead wrong.

Payton let her focus go beyond the participants. She couldn't watch anymore. It didn't feel right. Like nothing happened. Nothing was missing and life was back to normal.

"Did you by chance have coffee delivered to me at school today?"

"Why?"

"Somebody had one delivered, but whoever it was didn't give their name."

"Maybe someone is priming you up so they can ask you to homecoming."

"I don't want to go to homecoming."

"What do you mean? Isn't homecoming a high school girl's ComiCon or something? Girls like you live for that stuff."

She closed her eyes and pictured herself under glowing lights, wearing a beautiful dress even her mama could love. "Yes. I suppose we do."

Hot sand pelted her feet, bringing her out of her fantasy world and back to reality where Joshua was spraying sand around him as he turbulently dug his feet farther into the earth. "Payton Brave, are you gonna go out with me or not?"

There was a part of her that liked making him beg, so she refrained from offering a reply.

"I'm gonna keep on asking until you say yes, so you might as well accept now and save yourself the annoyance."

She took a deep breath, picked up some sand, and let it slowly run through her fingers as she tried to ignore the squeals and screams coming from the platform, and focus solely on the sound of the waves rolling to shore due to the extra activity out on the water. She watched the sand so intensely that it probably looked like she was trying to count each grain. Once her hand emptied, she picked up another fistful, raised it to eye level, and let the sand slowly fall to the ground. "It's like an hourglass."

Joshua's brow furrowed. "An hourglass?"

For a third time, Payton repeated the process. "Like it could turn back time," she muttered, now completely fixated on the stream of sand as it flowed through her fingers.

CHAPTER 3

August 12, 2016

4:00 p.m.

Payton, Starr, and Lindy were sprawled out on bright beach towels several yards away from the chaos on the swim platform. The sandy beach was too small, and smothered by the thick forest that surrounded it, but it was big enough for Payton and her friends to sunbathe on, and that's all that mattered. To them, anyway.

Dylan sat perched on a blanket a couple of feet away with Cole and Misty. They weren't close enough in proximity to be considered "with" the elite group, but not so far as to keep Dylan completely away from her sister. She wanted to stay close enough to keep an eye out, but far enough away to keep from being dragged into one of their daily melodramas.

The championship was in full swing, and the swim platform out in the middle of the water was so weighed down by competitors that the barrels under the floating deck could barely keep it from submerging.

The yearly event was three rounds of separate male and female competition: former CHS students versus more former students, followed by seniors versus juniors, followed by sophomores versus freshmen. Then, the final two survivors of each male and female round competed in one grand final battle to be crowned King of the Mountain.

Dylan sat at Cole's feet and watched him prepare to enter the water. He rolled his shoulders, stretched his neck by looking from side to side, and then swung his arms in large circles. To some, it might've looked like he was warming up his muscles. To Dylan, she knew he was buying time.

He squat down beside her and placed his mouth to her ear. "I don't want to do this."

"Then don't."

"But I'm a guy."

"I realize that."

"So it'll look bad if I don't."

She hated to see the anguish on his face, but realized he had a point. "True. Not taking part would pretty much be an affront to the entire male population of Cornwell. Especially since your daddy owns the local gentlemen's club."

He groaned.

"Unfortunately, Cole, you're fully expected to behave like a Neanderthal. Especially seeing as how the gentlemen's club is completely run down and anything but gentlemanly."

"Hey, at least it's clean." Perhaps he was a bit on defense since he was the one who cleaned it every morning. He stood and took a deep breath. "That all aside, nothing could look worse than not taking part in this thing when my girlfriend's all in."

"You'll do great. And very few people know we're dating again, so don't put *too* much pressure on yourself."

She smiled and playfully slapped him on the leg. As he gave her a shaky smile in response, she stood and started to rub a washcloth infused with baby oil all over the front of her body, then walked over to Payton and passed it over so she could wipe down her back and legs.

"Watch out for Joshua," Payton warned.

Apparently, Dylan wasn't the only one who noticed that the summer had done Joshua well. He'd grown a few inches taller and put on several pounds of muscle, which meant that pretty much every other girl in Cornwell would be happy to rest their head on his much-wider shoulders. She got the impression that even Payton was affected by the results of his growth spurt.

"He looks bigger this year." Dylan heard a bit of admiration in Payton's voice.

"Bigger doesn't mean faster."

"No, but it means harder to move. Harder to push aside."

"He's cocky. It'll be his downfall. Always is." She brushed off the imaginary obstacle by waiving one hand in the air, and then turned around to face her sister. "This is Joshua we're talking about, Pay. He's a problem stem to stern. Stay far away."

"Don't you worry about me. That boy doesn't affect me one bit." She ran the washcloth over Dylan's shoulders, and then tapped her on the nose, leaving a slick coating of oil on the tip. "Just make sure he doesn't affect you out on the platform."

Dylan turned back to watch Cole take out his hearing aids and place them in his tennis shoes for safekeeping. He'd come in second in the junior versus senior boys match. Quite a surprise for those who'd watched from the shoreline, and from his reaction after that round, even for Cole himself.

He raced across the sand, dove into the water, and swam out to the platform with an intensity that signaled he was either ready to take everyone on or he wanted to hurry up and get the whole thing over with. Knowing him as well as she did, Dylan assumed it was the latter.

"You got this, Dylan," Misty said with a large, confident grin. "They'll regret the day they messed with you."

"Thanks, girl." She turned to her sister one last time. "Wish me luck?"

"Go get 'em, Slugger." As Dylan walk toward the water, she heard Payton call out, "If you win, I get the gift card to the coffee shop."

Dylan waved over her shoulder, then dove into the lukewarm water, swam to the platform, and took her place in the center of the participants ready to go to battle.

She'd trained for this moment almost her entire life. Even as a sophomore the year before, she'd made it to the final round, but got manhandled by Kyle Merchant, a twenty-three-year-old graduate who returned to Cornwell for the weekend purely to be a part of the event.

Within moments of the whistle blow, Dylan turned to a senior girl who stood on the edge of the platform.

"Can you believe we made it this far?" Dylan asked with a girlish squeal.

"No. I never—" Dylan shoved her off the planks before she could say another word. In less than five seconds, she'd shown her dominance over the girl who quite honestly had no business being there in the first place, especially since she so easily fell for Dylan's girl-talk ploy.

Dylan knew that people on the outside of the platform got thrown off first, and as those doing the throwing were busy taking out the weakest links, she focused on simultaneously shoving them off. When someone did chance to get ahold of her, their hands slipped off her freshly slicked-up skin, and she used their confusion to get the upper hand.

Dylan cut her eyes to a male sophomore. In a quick swoop, her hard kick to the back of his knee caused it to buckle. Dylan used his brief weak and unsteady moment to elbow him off the platform.

"I'm unimpressed." Starr's blasé attitude didn't surprise Payton. She'd seen her eyes roll behind her stylish sunglasses almost twenty times since the moment they walked onto the beach. "And your sister's acting like an idiot out there. What sixteen-year-old girl still plays King of the Mountain?"

"All of 'em." Lindy didn't even look in Starr's direction. She remained perfectly situated on her beach towel, as if Starr wasn't worth receiving her full attention. At least not at the moment.

Payton glanced over her shoulder and snickered at their horrible, yet completely expected, attitudes.

"How do you figure?" Starr asked.

"Whether in the water or not, we're always fightin' our way to the top. We have nothing better to do."

Payton looked back out at the struggle on the platform as another girl collapsed into the water, quickly followed by Joshua, who fell victim to a quick, unexpected shove from Dylan. "Look at her out there. She's the only girl left."

Joshua broke through the water's surface. "Dylan, you're too sly for your own good. It's gonna come back to bite ya."

"Not today," she yelled back.

If Joshua was trying to distract her sister, it failed miserably:

without missing a step, Dylan shoved a sophomore between the rails of the ladder, and into another year of oblivion.

Joshua turned and swam toward the shore. As he approached, he rose out of the water with air bubbles flowing alongside him as if they were groupies chasing him the rest of the way in.

"Payton, why aren't you out there with us?" he shouted.

"Me? No way. Dylan's the truly brave one."

"Naw. I think you've got some fight in ya."

"Not that sort, I can assure you." She couldn't help but be proud of her sister, and maybe a little jealous. All eyes were on her, and she was kickin' butt and taking names. "Besides, Mama'd let me have it if I took part."

Payton joined Joshua at the water's edge as Brody crawled onto the shoreline and collapsed at their feet. She heard him panting, looked down and kept watch over his large, heaving chest until he finally caught his breath.

He rolled onto his stomach and laid his face on the sand. "I'm too outta shape for this mess."

The Celtic angel tattoo on the back of his calf glistened under the thin sheet of water that covered the lower half of his body. With just one look, anyone would be reminded that he was once a local high school football hero and two-time King of the Mountain champion, but while his frame was still large, a few years out of high school meant he was also a little softer. Especially around the middle. "Dylan's got a low center of gravity or somethin'. It's unreal."

"Right," Joshua chuckled. "It was her low center of gravity."

Finally revived, Brody rolled back over, perched onto his elbows, and looked out at the water. "Looks like Cole might take this championship."

Payton looked back out at the platform as Cole gripped Dylan by the shoulders, started to push her aside, but quickly pulled her to him and wrapped his arms around her.

A simple kiss of young love, but it looked sweet enough that the majority of the girls watching from their place on the beach were likely jealous.

"They're dating again?" Brody asked.

"For over a year. They just kept it on the down low."

As they watched Dylan and Cole continue to frolic on the swim platform, Brody said, "That doesn't seem very 'down low' to me. But hey, whatever floats your boat."

"Or your platform," Josh quipped.

Brody turned his attention to Joshua. "Did you see Payton's new Bug?"

Payton peeked over at Joshua and realized his eyes were fully focused on the platform, and most likely Dylan. "Her car?" he asked, his fixation unchanged.

"Yeah. She looks good, doesn't she?"

"Yeah, dude. It's red. Very, very red."

"I totally revamped her. She was rotting away, and now she shines like a lollipop soaked in spit."

Payton chuckled. "Interesting visual."

"You still like her, though, don't you, Payton?"

She looked down at him and offered a smile. "I love her. So much."

He proudly grinned back, and then turned to spy on Dylan and Cole for several moments before he quietly and stealthily crept back into the water.

After Brody had disappeared under the water and out of Payton's sight, she watched Dylan and Cole latch on to each

47

other's arms and start a playful tug-of-war. Obviously, neither would go down without a real fight, but within a few seconds Cole had the upper hand. He'd tipped Dylan off balance, and her overcorrection caused her to roll onto the edge of her foot.

Brody suddenly erupted out from under the water, catching everyone by surprise, then gripped Dylan's leg and pulled her off the platform. Cole appeared so caught off guard by her sudden takedown that he didn't seem to realize he was the last man standing until he looked over and saw spectators begin cheering on the beach.

"That didn't count!" Dylan's cry of foul started as soon as her head broke through the surface of the water. "Totally not fair, Brody." She shoved two hands worth of water in Brody's direction with a dramatic splash.

When Cole lowered his hand over the edge of a wooden plank, then grabbed Dylan's wrist and lifted her onto the platform, Payton's heart skipped a beat. It was a small gesture, but she wished her mama had been there to see it. Maybe seeing him be so caring toward Dylan would change her mind about him. Maybe if she witnessed what Payton just did, Mama'd give him a chance.

When Cole moved in for a second kiss, Dylan shoved him right off the side of the platform and claimed victory before he was even fully submerged.

Moments later, Cole popped out of the water and rested his arms on the platform, but didn't bother to climb back up. It was clearly Dylan's moment to shine.

CHAPTER 4

August 11, 2017

4:07 p.m.

Joshua touched Payton's elbow. "*Payton?* Are you okay?"

She heard Joshua's voice but was so focused on watching the grains of sand fall to the earth that she didn't bother to respond.

"Payton, I was talking and you—"

Her cell phone rang. At first, she considered not even answering it. All of her friends were at the cove, which meant that the only other person it could be was one of her parents. And if it was her mama, she wanted something.

She squeezed the last ounces of sand tightly into her fist and then dumped it out. "I guess I should get that. It could be news."

"But I—"

Sure, it could be news. News about her sister, or news about her case, but Payton doubted it. There hadn't been news for at least seven months.

She wiped the sand stuck to her hand off on the towel and then dug the phone out of her bag. As soon as she saw that it was her mama, she took a deep breath and dutifully answered. "Yes, ma'am?"

"Where are you?"

"The cove. It's the King of the Mountain Championships. I'm—"

"I'm going to need you to make a visit to the hospital."

"What? Why?"

"Misty delivered her baby." The phone went silent for several seconds. "Severely premature."

"Severely premature?"

"The baby didn't survive." The words were cold, almost no connection to emotion. It was her mama's new state of being: detached. "Anyway, I'm behind, and I have to get back to the clinic to see patients and finish working on some charts . . . I need someone to sit with her."

Payton choked on the words. Something about them made them hard to swallow.

"She's very alone." The phone was mostly silent again. All Payton could hear was her mama's breath and the beep of machines from the hospital's neonatal unit.

Payton placed the phone on mute and cleared her throat. "Misty McNeese had her baby."

Joshua's eyebrows hitched.

"It didn't survive."

"Really?" Joshua sounded almost as detached as her mama did. Only his detachment was probably more from a lack of caring. Her mama, on the other hand, was one who cared too much.

"Mama said she's all alone."

Joshua adjusted his sunglasses. "That's rough."

"Yeah."

"Payton? You there?"

Payton unmuted her phone. "Yes, ma'am."

"So I can count on you to sit with Misty for a bit, right?"

"I'm supposed to stay for the bonfire, I-—" She caught herself before she could deny her mama's request. "Yes, ma'am. I'll sit with her."

"Thanks." The line went dead.

Payton stared at her phone for several seconds, trying to will it to ring again and her mama to tell her not to worry about going, that she'd found someone else to make the hospital visit.

The call didn't come.

"So, about that date . . ."

Payton threw the phone into her bag with a heavy sigh and a fuddled mind. "I've got to go. There's something I need to do."

"But we weren't finished talking." His face turned red. "I—"

Payton left Joshua sitting on her towel, and walked to the well-worn foot path in the woods that led to the parking lot. But she passed Lady Bug.

The hospital wasn't far from the cove, and although Payton felt safer in her car than she did outside on the streets, she didn't worry something would happen to her. Under normal circumstances, if she wanted to go somewhere but not drive herself, just about anyone would've been willing to give her a ride. Joshua especially. She could've easily asked him to leave the bonfire and take her to the hospital. But this wasn't a normal circumstance.

And in reality, she rather enjoyed walking.

As soon as she walked through the double doors, the head nurse in the hospital's tiny obstetrics wing looked up from her computer. "Well, hey, Payton."

"Hey, June. How's everything going?"

"Great. Pretty calm around here. We've got a few new ones." Her bright smile slipped into a more concerned expression. "What about you? How you doin'?"

It could've been anyone asking that question. The tone in June's voice was familiar no matter the person who posed it; the inquiry held curiosity mixed with sympathy and a bit of anxiety.

"I'm good, thanks."

A lie. Payton's answer was always a lie, and she wasn't ever sure if anyone bought it, but they sure pretended they did. It kept them at surface level, which is where they seemed more comfortable. Payton came to understand that her grief made others uncomfortable, and it was best if she just kept it to herself.

"Your mama left a few minutes ago."

"That's okay. I um . . ." Payton glanced up and down the quiet hallway. At this point, she knew most girls would head to the nursery window, where they could oooh and aww over the latest arrivals. "Is Misty McNeese still here?"

June's face fell. Utter defeat filled each and every line on her face. "She is."

"I-I suppose I'm here to see her."

June's face lit up. "I bet she'd appreciate the company. Room 125."

A bit disappointed that June hadn't turned her away, Payton gave one last polite smile before she hesitantly turned to head down the hallway.

Payton and Misty hadn't spoken in over ten months, so she wasn't completely sure what she'd walk into when she entered the room. Payton knew there was a chance Misty would want nothing to do with her. She might send her away, or yell at her for showing up out of the blue, but she slowly opened the door to room 125 and stuck her head inside anyway. "Misty?"

Misty looked up. Her eyes, wide and glassy. "Payton? What are you doing here?"

"Thought I'd come check on you. Is that okay?"

Misty nodded, which caused the tears forming in her eyes to fall down her face.

The thumping in Payton's chest died down a bit as she slowly pushed past the door and walked to Misty's bedside.

"I can't believe you came," Misty wailed.

Payton gingerly sat down next to her. "To be honest, my mama asked me to come. But on my walk over here, I remembered how you sat with me after Dylan disappeared."

Misty looked over at her. Eyes still wide and filled to the brim with tears.

"While everyone else searched or got their fifteen seconds of fame by talking to the press, you sat in the closet with me. You didn't say any of the stupid stuff that everyone seemed to say. You didn't try to convince me that everything would be okay, and you didn't try to make sense of any of it." Payton took Misty's hand in hers. "You just sat there and held my hand, and since there's nothing I can say to make any of this better for you, I figured I'd return the favor."

Misty placed her phone in Payton's free hand. "He was beautiful," she said. Her voice, brittle and hoarse.

Payton gazed down at the photo of Misty's son. The umbilical cord was still attached to his tiny body.

"Yes," Payton offered. "He was amazing."

In response, Misty's cries briefly calmed and her face went blank. She stared off into who knows where.

Payton knew that unknown place well.

CHAPTER 5

August 17, 2016

10:37 a.m.

Payton placed her palms on the cool table in front of her, stretched out her fingers, and pushed into the hard metal. Maybe if she pressed hard enough, not only would she stop the shaking, but some sort of portal would open up to swallow her and she could escape reality.

The tiny room was packed full of bodies, but she'd never felt more alone. The air-conditioner blew at full strength, forcing the air out of an air duct above her head. The cold air made the skin on her arms erupt with goose bumps.

"Payton?"

With no hope of the alternate universe appearing, she relaxed her fingers and nodded.

"Are you up for this?"

She couldn't say no. Too much time had already slipped by, and there could be no more waiting. It was the first time in four days she'd felt coherent enough to think and speak to officers. The shock had finally worn off. "I . . . I don't know if I'm ready, sir, but I'd rather do it now so it's over with."

Sheriff Jackson pulled up a metal chair and sat down across from her. His powerful stare made the interrogation room feel even smaller than it did just a few seconds before. Payton noticed the sweat rings under his armpits and appreciated that it probably meant he'd been out in the heat searching for her sister, but it upset her to know that the search still came up empty.

"Can you tell me what happened on Saturday?" There was an edge of anxiety in his tone and a hitch in his breath.

"No." It was an honest response. She had no memory of what took place in the bathroom. All she knew was it hadn't been much bigger than the room she now sat in.

With her thoughts spinning, she fully took in the space. Several tanned faces stood out against the gray walls. She recognized each one.

Her eyes landed on Daddy, who was seated next to her. "Go ahead," he urged, squeezing her hand and bringing her back to the moment.

"Dylan went to the bus station with Nana . . . and I met them there." Payton felt her skin go clammy and her chest tighten. "That's all I know."

"That's all you know, or that's all you remember?"

"It's all I know."

"How do you know?"

"Everyone told me."

"But you don't actually remember going?"

She shook her head but concentrated on maintaining eye contact even though the sound of the sheriff drumming his fingers on the metal table practically begged for her attention.

He stared back at her, his eyes so focused and still that they almost didn't look real. "Do you remember that morning? Leaving the house? Heading to the bus station?"

Again, she could only shake her head.

"Do you remember going to the restroom?" The creases around his eyes tightened with each word.

"No."

"Think hard for me. Were you and Dylan ever in the bathroom at the same time?"

She placed her thumb on the inside of her wrist and noted the thumps of her heartbeat. It was beating so fast she didn't bother to try to count. She fought to stay in the moment and not pass out as the pressure in her chest mounted to the point she worried she was having a heart attack.

"I-I . . . I don't remember."

"Let me try to help you remember, because this is important. You were seen coming from the bathroom off the alley—and your sister was last seen heading in that direction. But why that bathroom, Payton?" The sheriff scooted his chair forward and leaned across the table. His glare, somehow more intense. "There was a bathroom just a few feet away from where your grandmother was waiting. Why did you go to the bathroom located outside?"

Payton shook her head. "I don't know."

"Was that your idea or Dylan's? To use the staff bathroom outside, off the alley?"

"Dylan's."

He glanced at the officer next to him, then focused right back on Payton. "It was Dylan's idea to use the bathroom out back?"

Payton noted the digital recorder on the table. "I don't know."

"You don't know if it was Dylan's idea to go out back?"

She shook her head again, which only increased her dizziness. "The inside bathroom was always full. Nobody from out of town knows about that other bathroom."

"Right. So, you decided to use that bathroom to avoid the line?"

"I don't know if that's why we did it. I just know that's the case."

"You know that's the case—"

"In general. They wouldn't know about that bathroom."

"Who's they?"

"The people from the bus."

"Okay." Sheriff Jackson sat back, took a deep breath, and rubbed his eyes with the palms of his hands.

The entire moment and the weight of the topic of conversation had her so wound up and confused, she hardly knew her own name, let alone the details of what happened in the nasty old bus station bathroom. Or why she and her sister were there in the first place.

"What's your last memory, Payton?" The sudden boom of his voice made her jolt back into her seat. His voice reverberated off the walls.

Payton closed her eyes and pictured herself walking through dense, dark clouds, and forced herself into each one, shoving them out of the way and trying to find just a speck of light. A fragment of a memory hidden deep inside.

"The cove. The last thing I remember is the cove."

"That morning?" Now his voice sounded hopeful. "You went to the cove that morning?"

"The day before." She opened her eyes in time to witness a scowl appear on his face before it quickly faded.

"Your only memory is of the day before?"

She nodded slowly, having obviously failed this test.

"What happened at the cove, Payton?"

Memories of the day raced through her mind like she was

watching a video on Netflix while scrolling the time bar at the bottom of the screen, in hopes she would find a scene interesting enough to stop and watch. But unlike when she used that technique to view an entire season of a show in a day, her mental storyline had no image worth clicking.

"Same thing that happens every year. The championship, the bonfire. Nothing different."

"And you don't recall anything between the cove and right now?"

"Um . . . Misty. She sat with me a bit. And my parents, I heard them talking to me. But . . ."

"But you don't remember anything that happened that morning?"

She shook her head.

"This is completely normal," Mama blurted, catching Payton by surprise. She hadn't even realized the woman was in the room. "She's been traumatized. We all have. Give her some time to process."

"After forty-eight hours, leads go cold. We're now double that—"

"Our daughter is missing and you have us stuck in here when we should be out there looking for Dylan. I need to be looking for Dylan."

"I understand that, Laurie, but I need to ascertain whether Payton knows if Dylan even wants to be found."

Payton's body seemed to seize. Her vision turned blurry.

"You think she left on her own accord?" Defiance hung in Mama's voice. "You think my child ran off?"

"I think it's a possibility. You know Dylan, she's a ball-buster. Always testing her boundaries. She—"

"My daughter did not *run off*," Daddy added. "She wouldn't do that. And Payton wouldn't be so frightened right now if Dylan just up and walked away. Something happened in that bathroom."

"What?" the sheriff demanded, his voice raised. The normally gentle man seemed to teeter on the edge of hostile. "What happened in the bathroom?"

She felt her mama stand and grip her shoulders. "Let's go. I'm getting you out of here."

Sheriff Jackson rose to his feet, shoving the chair backward with a violent scrape as he went. "Laurie, I wouldn't advise—"

"Rex. Payton said she doesn't remember. She isn't a liar, and she has nothing to hide. You know that."

"She—"

"You've known them since the day they were born. You know my girls."

Mama once told her that the sheriff grew up as a kid from the wrong side of the cove, just like she had. They'd been best friends all the way through high school, and he was one of the few people who stood by her when she became a young, single mother. Payton even suspected Rex Jackson knew the name of her birth father.

"What about my birth father?" The words fell out of her mouth before she could contain them. "Did you question him?"

The sheriff blinked in surprise, and swallowed hard. "We're questioning everyone that could possibly be connected."

"Including my birth father?"

The sheriff's shoulders slumped. "David, take her home for the night. Let her get some rest. Bring her back tomorrow to—"

"I'll bring her back when she has something to share. In the meantime, go look for my daughter."

Daddy stood and pulled on Payton's hand, causing her to rise out of her seat. "We'll be in touch." He walked her toward the door.

"David." The sheriff's booming voice cut through the room and stopped them in their tracks. "I'm going to need to see you and Laurie first thing in the morning. We've got more questions."

"You're turning your focus to us?" he asked.

"You know that we have to look at every possible—"

"Then speak to our attorney."

CHAPTER 6

August 12, 2017

7:00 a.m.

Payton partially woke up to the sensation of warmth on her forearm. She labored a bit before she could fully open her eyes, and once she did, looked up to find Kasi peering down at her with a small smile. Her thin, blonde hair hung limp, past her shoulders.

"How is she?" Kasi whispered.

Both girls looked over at Misty. She was laying on her side in the fetal position, holding a small teddy bear. Payton felt her heart hitch.

"She didn't get much rest. She cried most of the night, and the nurses kept coming in and out to check her vitals."

"When will she get to go home?"

"They said later today." Payton stared at the teddy bear for several long seconds. "Do you know why her parents aren't here?"

"They kicked her out when they found out she was pregnant."

Payton's heart hitched again.

"She's living with a cousin, I think."

The revelation made Payton sick to her stomach. Seventeen and completely alone. It was unfair, and made the weight she carried on her thin shoulders feel heavier. At least when her own mama became a teen mom, she had the support of Nana. She wasn't left to struggle all on her own.

"What about you?" Kasi leaned against the windowsill and placed her full attention on Payton. "You look exhausted."

"I haven't been getting much sleep lately," Payton admitted.

"Why?"

Payton was taken aback by the question. It was only one word, but she was shocked that someone cared enough to ask. "Nightmares."

"About . . ."

"Dylan. She's showing up in our room."

"What's she doing once she gets there?"

"She just sits and tells me it's almost time."

"Almost time? Hmm." Kasi folded her arms across her chest and her eyes narrowed. "Well, it is the week of the anniversary she went missing. Maybe she's talking about that. Maybe she's just trying to prepare you. Emotionally."

Payton gave the thought a few moments to roll around in her head. "Maybe."

"It's going to be an emotional week, and now this." She looked back at Misty, her eyes heavy.

The girls sat in silence for several seconds before Kasi stood up and walked to Misty's bed. "I'll stay with her and make sure she gets home. Why don't you go get some sleep?"

As good as sleep sounded, Payton wasn't convinced it was what she truly needed, but also didn't know what would help.

She reluctantly removed the blanket from her lap, stood, and handed it to Kasi. "I guess I'll pass you the torch." She walked to the doorway, and then turned back. "Thanks, Kasi."

"It's what friends are for. Right?"

Payton felt herself smile; it was one of the few times in recent memory she hadn't forced herself to do so. "I suppose it is." She turned to walk out of the room.

"Hey, Payton—"

Payton spun back around. "Yeah?"

"I don't mean to add more to your plate, but I figured I should give you a heads up."

An immediate ping ached in her chest. "'Bout what?"

"I was filling in at the coffee shop last night, and Starr and Lindy were there. Anyway, word's out that you came to see Misty and Starr's not happy about it."

Payton rested her head against the door and groaned. "Of course she isn't."

"You're way too nice for her. Why are you two friends, anyway?"

Payton felt her shoulders drop as she lifted her head, and looked back at Kasi. "Honestly, I've been asking myself that a lot lately." She turned back around, walked out of the room, and practically ran right into her mama.

"Payton?" Mama's normally wrinkle-free forehead was scrunched up in shock. "What are you doing here?"

"You asked me to come."

"I didn't ask you to stay the night."

Payton looked down at her feet and chewed on her lip for a moment. "I don't know. I felt like she needed me, or something."

Mama placed the tip of her finger under Payton's chin and gently lifted her face to hers. "That was nice of you." Her mama's perfectly smooth skin returned, and her eyes were softer. "She meant a lot to Dylan. I know your sister would appreciate the gesture."

They shared a moment. Just a tender look between them. Mama's eyes shimmered a little.

"It was nice of you to stay," Mama whispered, then quickly stiffened her back and straightened her physician's coat. "Do you feel all right? You look horrible." She placed the back of her hand to Payton's forehead. "You feel a little warm."

"I just had a blanket on me, that's all."

"Okay, well . . . go home and get some rest." She walked into Misty's room, and then stuck her head back around the doorframe. "Text your daddy and let him know where you are."

"Yes, ma'am."

Mama disappeared back into Misty's room, which freed Payton to start the stroll back home. Once she turned onto Main, she started a text to her daddy: I was at the hospital with Misty. Heading home now. She pushed the Send button.

Okay, he replied. See you soon.

Payton tucked the phone into her back pocket and rounded the corner. She'd been so busy texting that she didn't realize she was in front of the bus station.

It was about the same time in the morning that she and her sister arrived at the station a little less than a year before. The bus to Atlanta sat parked in the lot, and people stood on the pavement stretching or walked inside to grab some snacks . . . or use the restroom.

Payton closed her eyes and tried to unlock the space in her brain where those bus station bathroom memories were hidden.

She imagined herself walk into the bathroom situated at the backside of the bus station, just off the alley. She remembered the smell of urine and diesel fuel assault her nose as she entered. She soon recalled that the heat was intense.

She pushed her foggy memory deeper. Pictured herself squatting on the toilet seat.

"Dylan!"

The bottom of her shoes slipped on the seat, almost causing her to fall over.

"Dylan!"

The overhead light turned off.

A bus honked.

Payton opened her eyes, blinked several times, and looked up and down the street, trying to remind herself where she was. The bright sunlight momentarily made her believe she'd entered the heavens, but the vision was short lived. Another bus honk brought her back to her dark reality.

She turned her attention back to the bus stations and looked beyond the passing cars to watch the Atlanta bus pull out of the parking lot just as the Charleston bus pulled in. They were like clockwork. The only thing that was certain on the day Dylan went missing was that two buses came and went that morning. As far as anyone knew, Dylan could've been on either one of them.

But she wasn't. And somehow, deep in her gut, Payton knew it.

She started to watch each person milling around the station, and made a mental note of each one she recognized.

Fred Perkins. Russ Northside. Gloria Jennings . . .

She recognized fewer than a dozen people. Everyone else was simply making a stop in the small town.

Once the bus fumes disappeared and the air cleared, Payton stood and walked the rest of the way home in a mental haze. With each step the pressure in her chest mounted and the invisible weight on her shoulders increased.

"Hey, Dylan."

A chill ran up Payton's spine. Her stomach churned. Something in her brain dislodged. Her fingers shivered. She looked up and down the street, and searched again for the memory as if it were playing hide and seek.

"Dylan?" Payton shook her head. Turned toward the voice, toward her porch. "You okay?" Nana asked.

"No."

Nana sat up taller. Her eyes narrowed.

"I meant, no, I'm not Dylan. It's me. It's Payton." Payton closed her eyes and took a deep, calming breath. "And I'm just fine." She opened her eyes, shoved her trembling fingers into her pockets, walked across the yard, and forced a large smile on her face as she climbed the patio steps.

Situated at the front entrance of the funeral home, the large covered patio beckoned visitors to the home offices and gathering parlor, which sat on the first floor and extended into what in most homes would be a large garage. The family lived on the two floors above and Payton had the top floor, the attic bedroom, to herself.

While the property was the largest home in the city and seemed enormous from the outside, the inside felt cramped and smothering.

Payton sat down in the rocking chair next to Nana and Pugsley, who sat at Nana's feet.

"I'm sorry. I'm always confusing you two. You look so much alike." She sighed. "Just getting home?"

"Yes, ma'am."

"From where?"

"The hospital. A girl from my school had her baby." She

allowed her smile to evaporate. "He didn't survive, though. Never even cried."

"Sad that it died never having something to cry about."

"How's that sad?" Payton asked. "I wish I didn't have things to cry about."

"If you don't ever get a chance to cry, you don't realize how wonderful it is when you finally get to laugh." Nana uncrossed her leg, set it on the ground, and used it to push off so her chair would start rocking again.

The sound of an approaching vehicle brought Nana to her feet. "It's the bus!"

"No, ma'am. Just a visitor."

Nana sat back and thrust her arms into a fold across her chest. "Dang blasted."

Moments later Joshua's silver Lexus pulled into the parking lot, and he climbed out with a large smile plastered on his face.

"Who is it?" Nana asked.

"Joshua Toobin."

"You mean the Rhett to Dylan's Scarlett?"

"That's the one." Payton stood, walked to the top step, and wrapped her arms around one of the large white pillars that supported the second-story balcony. Pugsley followed and then, seemingly worn out from his two-foot walk, sat down next to her feet with a snort.

Joshua bent at the waist, leaned to his left, and peered over at the elderly woman in her rocking chair. "Hi, Nana. How are you?"

"Why are ya screamin'? You don't have to scream at me. I may be old and crazy, but I ain't deaf."

"Nana, be nice," Payton urged, as she repeatedly slapped her flip-flop against the bottom of her foot.

"I'm too old to be worryin' 'bout hurtin' people's feelin's. Especially Rhett's."

He cringed and slowly straightened. "Yes, ma'am. Sorry, ma'am." He set his eyes on Pugsley. "I swear that thing looks more like a pig than a dog. It's the fattest pug I've ever seen."

"He's a kleptomaniac," Payton said. "He steals food from the pantry while we're gone."

Joshua didn't seem surprised to hear the Braves owned a dog with a pilfering problem. Maybe he figured it fit well within the unusual family norm.

"What are you doing here on a Saturday?"

"Even though you left me sitting at the cove like an idiot yesterday, I thought I'd give you another chance."

She couldn't tell if he was being serious or sarcastic, so she erred on the side of serious and started to explain. "I had a rough night and—"

"I'm going for a drive. Wanna join?"

"Um." Payton worked to recover and adjust to the change of topic. "I don't know." She glanced over at Nana, who shook her head. "It might be nice to get away for a bit," Payton whispered.

"We can head out on our ride once the bus gets here."

"I'm not sure it's coming today, Nana." Payton noticed Nana tighten the grip on her pocketbook, and then looked back at Joshua.

He cocked his head and grinned. "Come on. You know you want to."

"No, ya don't," Nana whispered.

"Where to?" Payton asked.

"Some hiking trails, maybe a fro-yo. Whatever you want." His smirk made her insides flutter against her will.

The urge to say yes and her reaction to say no warred while Joshua and Nana watched and waited for her answer. "Let's go," she finally answered.

Nana sat back in her chair with a groan.

Joshua ignored her. "Payton Brave wants to take off and leave the world behind, huh?"

"I guess I do." She turned to Nana. "Not a word of this to Mama."

Nana's eyes bore into Payton as she pursed her lips in defiance.

"Nana, please. I just want to get away for a bit."

She sat back up, steadied the pocketbook on top of her knees, and glowered at the street. "Fine."

"So you won't say a word?"

"A word of what?"

"Thank you." Payton kissed her nana on the cheek and raced down the steps as Joshua opened the car door and swept his arm toward the seat.

Once Payton was situated inside the vehicle, Joshua closed the door, looked up at Nana, and waved. "Bye, Nana."

Payton snickered as she looked through the window and saw Nana scowl back at him as he walked around the car.

Once he was situated on his side, Joshua slowly drove through the streets of Cornwell. Payton knew good and well that every person who saw the car would know who was in it, and word would travel fast that they were together—and she was pretty sure Joshua knew it too. That's why he was driving so slow; but as soon as they reached the outskirts of town and passed the Gentleman's Club, she felt him look over as if soaking in the sight of her. "You ready?"

She looked back at him with a grin. "Absolutely."

Joshua pressed his foot to the floor, and they peeled out of town. Payton gripped him by the arm and squealed all the way. They may not have been going far, but they were traveling farther than she'd been in over a year, and much farther than her mama would be comfortable with, which made it even better.

Her breath held in her chest each time the car slipped around a turn. A frightening thrill gripped her. A momentary escape that felt necessary and justified.

He eventually parked in a small lot near a lookout point of Stonebridge Valley State Park, an hour outside of town. "Wanna go look around?"

"Sure." She opened her car door, climbed out, and headed straight for the overlook, furthering her race into freedom. To Payton, the air smelled fresher and the atmosphere felt less smothering than it was back in Cornwell. She could take in a breath and expand her lungs fully. She almost felt alien. "I haven't been here since we were kids," she said over her shoulder.

Joshua walked up behind her and slipped his arms around her waist. "I hike out here all the time."

The tensing of her body and curl in her toes against the foam of her flip-flops caught her off guard. She hadn't expected to have such a negative response to his touch, and apparently neither had he.

"Something wrong?" he asked.

She willed a smile onto her face and looked over her shoulder. "Just a chill." When she saw his eyebrow hitch, she added, "From the breeze."

"You get cold in August?" he laughed, pulling her closer. "No doubt you're one of a kind."

Payton took a deep, relaxing breath, surveyed the lush green hills and valleys, and tried to silently command her body and mind to be in the moment.

Joshua's arms dropped, but in the flash of a moment she felt his hand slip into hers, followed by a tug of her arm when he pulled her toward a path that wound through the brush. The ominous trail felt stifling, too narrow, and her lungs, suddenly constricted again, seemed unable to take in air fast enough. Her heart raced. Like a reflex, her hand squeezed his.

"What's wrong?"

She stared at the trail for a moment longer, then took a deep breath, loosened her grip, and nodded. "Nothing, I'm good."

It wasn't the truth, of course. Her gut begged her not to go. It screamed at her. But Payton never truly knew whether her fears were valid, something strange brought on by her sister's unknown circumstances, or simply passed down from a mama drowning in anxiety.

The battle was constant. It raged in her head during every conversation. Every interaction. People needed her to act normal. Be normal.

So in times like this, when she wasn't sure what to do and the fear and anxiety flooded in, she did what she thought *they* would want her to do. What would make *them* feel like things were back to normal—even though they weren't and quite possibly never would be again.

For a few hours, she acted like all was fine and let Joshua walk her up and down the ridges of the valley, as she genuinely tried to enjoy the scenery. He attempted to kiss her several times, but with each pursuit she dodged him. A duck here, or a fake foot slip there.

"Let's go a little farther," he suggested.

Payton cautiously peeked down the route shrouded in thick brush. This time, she couldn't ignore her trepidation. "Not for me, Josh."

Again, she felt him grip her hand and yank on her arm. "Come on. Just a bit farther."

Payton jerked her hand out of his. "I said no!" Her reaction shocked her. But it was proof her instincts still worked, and this time she wasn't going to ignore them. She jammed her hands into her back pockets so that he couldn't grab them again. "You go. I'll meet you back at the car."

Joshua's jaw tightened. His fists momentary clinched. "Fine. I'll be back in a few minutes." He tossed her the car keys, cleared his throat, and smiled.

The smile was forced and Payton knew it. She'd done it herself, and witnessed her Mama do it enough times in life to recognize the same tensed lips. If the smile were sincere, the corner of his eyes would've creased. As it was, they were smooth as porcelain.

"I'm gonna walk down to the creek bed. See if all this rain we've been having has filled it up."

"Knock yourself out." There was still an edge in her tone, causing her voice to sound borrowed from someone else.

Payton defiantly stood on the trail and watched until Joshua disappeared around the bend, then turned to head back the direction they'd come. The path was well worn, but the heavy layer of tree foliage hanging over the dirt passageway made it feel almost tunnel-like. Much darker than even a few minutes before, or at least it seemed so.

She slowly walked through, unable to even remember the

days before she hesitated at every unknown. It now felt like she'd been born this way.

She'd only taken a few steps into the passage when a brunette in her late teens jogged past her, almost knocking Payton off the trail and into the brush. "A bit overzealous?" she yelled over her shoulder, again surprising herself, but she quickly justified it by reminding herself that she was on edge by being out of her element.

The girl, with earbuds jammed into her ears, apparently didn't hear. Her toned legs propelled her down the dirt path, and her ponytail swung violently as she left Payton in her wake.

Payton turned and continued her journey back to the car, and by the time she approached the crest of the hill, she was panting and out of breath.

She walked to the car and steadied her hands enough to unlock the door, then climbed into the backseat and laid down in an effort to sneak in a bit of shuteye before Joshua returned from his hike. Due to her lack of sleep the night before, she felt herself drift off within a matter of moments. Then, suddenly, she heard the driver's side door swing open.

"Sorry."

Payton opened her eyes and gazed up at Joshua, who was nearly out of breath. His hair was disheveled on his head.

"That took longer than I thought it would. I got a little preoccupied," he admitted. "I usually don't go that deep," he added with a devilish smirk. As pompous and forceful as he could be at times, she couldn't deny the boy was a charmer.

He started to climb into the backseat, but Payton beat him to the punch and slid between the two front seats and took her place on the passenger side. As soon as she was settled, she slid her seatbelt across her body and locked it into place. "We better get back before my mama has a fit."

"I don't want to deal with that." He slipped into the driver's seat. "We'd better be going anyway. Looks like the gods are about to unleash."

She leaned forward in her seat and looked out the front windshield at the angry, gray sky. Clouds mounted into thick, heavy bundles that hung perilously close.

Within moments, large pellets of rain battered the windshield. Once the gear was in drive, he floored it, throwing Payton back against her seat with a jolt.

She tightly gripped the bar above the passenger side window. "Josh, it's wet. Slow down."

"I'm good." She stared at his foot on the pedal and waited to see him release the pressure, but he didn't. "If I drive fast enough, I don't even need windshield wipers. The rain just runs off."

Payton clenched onto her seat with her left hand and closed her eyes. She wanted to scream at him, beg him to pull over and let her out of the car, but she didn't. She'd reverted to ignoring her gut, and the thought of her vacillation made her stomach queasy.

She stayed quiet, frozen in place as she tried to summon the return of the girl who'd stood firm less than an hour before. He watched the road ahead of them for a few moments, then suddenly stared at her. "See?" he said with a wink.

She wrapped her fingers around the handle and momentarily contemplated opening the door, reasoning it might be the only thing that would make Joshua stop the car, and then removed her hand from the handle, placed it on the dashboard, and looked over at him. "See what?"

74

"I was right. We're good together." She felt his hand slither into hers just before he lifted it to his lips, and kissed it. "I told you we would be."

More and more uncomfortable by the second, she held her breath for a brief moment, then slipped her hand out of his and pretended to wipe sleep from one eye before placing the hand back in her lap.

As soon as they entered cell phone coverage, their phones blew up with text messages. She'd been right; news traveled fast and everyone wanted the scoop. Payton scrolled through her phone and rolled her eyes at all the messages begging for an update.

Where are you?

Heard you were at the hospital.

So, you're with Joshua?

Having fun yet?

What are you two up to?

Don't do anything I wouldn't do.

Heard you skipped town.

When are you heading back?

"Who is it and what are they saying?"

She scrolled some more and tried not to think about the rain or the slick tires or the winding roads that now felt menacing. "Starr wants to know what we're doing. I'm sure she hopes we're up to no good."

"She knows me too well," he laughed. "I guess we're official."

Payton forced another smile and couldn't help but wonder if there had been a real moment between them the entire day. How long have I been faking my life? Or at least faking the joy of it? How long have my interactions been so counterfeit?

"Will you drop me off at the cove?" The words spilled out of her mouth. The cove was closer to their present location than her house, which meant this ride would end sooner. "I left my car there yesterday."

"You don't want me to take you home?"

"No. The cove will be fine. You're actually doing me a huge favor."

"Okay. Sure." He made a quick left down Jefferson and passed the dirt road that led to Brody's shop, and then they passed the Bagel Barn, Val's Flower Shop, and an old, vacant Chevron building. "I'll pick you up later tonight. I'm sure I can find us something to do."

"Um . . . let me make sure I'm not grounded for life first."

"I can talk to your mama if that'll help. Ask her permission. Parents like me, remember?"

"Trust me, talks with my mama about that sort of thing don't go over very well."

Minutes later, he pulled up next to Lady Bug. As soon as he put the car in park, he turned toward Payton and leaned in her direction. She placed her hand on the door handle, pulled the lever, and was out of the car before he could even realize he'd been rejected. Again.

"Okay. I'll see you in a—"

She pushed the door with more force than she'd intended. As he drove away, she turned and, feeling compelled, walked down the trail and stepped onto the beach.

She stood in the sand, and a little bit chilled by the breeze blowing off the water, wrapped her arms across her stomach.

The cove wasn't very far from downtown, but the distance was enough that most people her age went there to "get away." The small, sandy beach was the go-to destination for New Year's celebrations, end-of-school-year parties, Fourth of July firecrackers, bonfires, make-out sessions, and just about anything else a person could think of.

Dylan, you sure did love it out here. She looked out at the platform and smiled. Briefly remembering Dylan fighting for her King of the Mountain life and loving every second of it.

Her phone pinged in her back pocket, immediately causing her smile to dissipate.

If she'd had her choice, she'd stay there with her feet covered in sand and remind herself of the happier times, but she didn't have a choice. And rarely ever did.

Payton pulled the phone from her pocket, saw it was a text from Mama, and rushed back up the trail into the parking lot.

As she walked to her car, she saw several scratches across the paint. She'd noticed one a few days before and thought nothing of it, but these scratches were newer. At least they seemed newer. She knelt down and ran her fingers over the deep key marks.

A brush rustled over her left shoulder, at first causing her to cower slightly into the wheel well before she gathered the courage to stand and stare deep into the overgrown greenery to look for whatever it is that had caused the disruption.

"Hello?" She moved her focus to the short path she'd just walked back on. Suddenly, the trail and the cove felt like the last place she wanted to be. Especially alone.

"Hello?" she repeated.

There was no response. The only sound, a ripple of the waves nearby.

Still unsettled, she quickly jumped inside Lady Bug, locked the car door, and then looked out her rain-soaked windows and into the surrounding dark woods.

CHAPTER 7

July 30, 2016
8:30 a.m.

"Payton and Dylan Brave! Breakfast is ready!"

Dylan stuck her head out of the closet just as Payton jumped into her gold sandals and grabbed her Kate Spade purse. "Tell her I'll be right down."

"No, ma'am. No way. I'm not going to deliver your bad news."

"Bad news?" Dylan hopped around as she pulled on a pair of skinny jeans with one hand and ran a brush through her long brown hair with the other. "I'm running a few minutes late."

"Exactly. Bad news."

Dylan zipped up the jeans, then threw on a vintage tank top, but stopped cold when she noticed her sister's scowl.

"She's not going to let you wear that shirt and you know it."

Dylan inspected the ribbed fabric. "What? Why?"

"Too tight."

Dylan gripped the shirt between her fingers and pulled. "Nope. It's got some give. I'm good." She grabbed a pair of gray Converse from a pile of shoes on the floor and plunged her feet inside. "Besides, she'll be so hopped up on birthday festivities, what I'm wearing will be the last thing on her mind."

"Famous last words. Let's go. She'll be upset if we don't come down toge—"

"Girls! We'll be late for our breakfast reservation at the club!"

The girls shared a look and simultaneously rolled their eyes.

"Two more years." Dylan grabbed a pile of clothes off the end of the bed and threw them to the floor, and then grabbed her unearthed purse. "Two more years and we'll be off to college, and won't have to listen to—"

"Girls!"

"That." She followed her sister out of the bedroom. "Thank the Lord we won't have to listen to that."

"You're really going away for school?" Payton asked.

"You really aren't?"

"I'd never even considered it an option."

Dylan snickered. "And they call me the crazy one."

She followed Payton down the steps to meet their parents and Nana, who stood on the second-floor landing wearing bright smiles and holding balloons. "Happy birthday!"

"Lordy, I can't believe you're sixteen," Nana said. "Practically full-grown."

Daddy held a birthday cake in his arms. Sixteen candles perched on top were nearly burned down to the quick. "If you'd taken any longer, I would've had to go find sixteen new candles and start this thing all over again."

Dylan moved past Payton, kissed her daddy on the cheek and gave his shoulders a tight hug, almost causing him to tip the cake off its brilliantly polished silver platter. "You're the best, Daddy."

She kept her arms wrapped around her daddy and watched Payton take the balloons from Mama and kiss her on the cheek. "Thank you, Mama."

"Sixteen." Mama sighed. "You two are officially as old as I was when I had you." Dylan could almost hear the relief in her voice. Relief that both girls made it to sixteen without actually becoming mothers themselves. Now, if she could just get them past graduation, Dylan hoped Mama would finally relax and enjoy motherhood a little. "It just doesn't seem possible."

Dylan couldn't stop her eyes from rolling at the comment. "And here she goes. Somehow making our birthday all about her." It was half spoken under her breath, but loud enough for Daddy and Nana to hear.

Nana tsked.

"Be nice," Daddy warned.

Dylan walked to the side table and picked up a thick stack of envelopes: birthday cards from friends and family. "Granddaddy and Grandmama Brave. Bet we each got a hundred bucks," she said as she tossed it to the side. "Uncle Arthur. Probably five bucks. Auntie June—"

"A Walmart gift card," Payton answered.

"You think?" Dylan slipped her finger under the edge of the envelope and slid it along the thin paper, tearing it open. She pulled the card out and two Walmart gift cards fell to the floor. "You nailed it."

"Take 'em," Payton laughed. "They're all yours."

"Cool." Dylan picked them up and stuck them in her back pocket. Unlike her sister, who had an image to keep up, she didn't have anything against shopping at Walmart. She could get three or four T-shirts for what her sister spent on one at the latest and greatest store at the mall in the city.

Dylan continued through the stack of cards, tossing them into piles until she'd worked her way through the entire stack.

"Nope. Nothing this year." She looked over her shoulder at Payton. They shared a disappointed glance. "I guess he maxed out with the necklaces a few years back." She gripped the angel pendent between her fingers and silently made her birthday wish. To meet him one day.

Between the two of them, Dylan yearned to meet their birth father more than Payton did. Not that she didn't love Daddy, because she did. She loved him more than she could imagine loving anyone in the world, but her heart ached for a man she'd never laid eyes on.

"You'd think he'd care or at least try harder, seeing as how we came from his loins," she added, in an attempt to shove the ache in her heart out of her chest.

"Enough of that talk," Mama said with a shoo of her hand.

"His loss," Nana added.

"Mama, you said when we were old enough, you'd give us more information—"

"Eighteen. I said when you're eighteen." She disappeared into the kitchen, officially ending the conversation.

A loud, odd honk pierced the awkward silence of the house, bringing their mama right back out of the kitchen in a flash. "I wonder what that could be?"

"Gee. I wonder," Dylan muttered.

"It's here!" Payton tore down the steps. The others struggled to discard their birthday paraphernalia and follow behind. Dylan took the rear, since she had zero interest in what just pulled into the driveway.

By the time she got to the door, her sister was squealing like a three-year-old hyped up on birthday cake and ice cream, and running through the yard with equal pep and vigor.

Brody climbed out of the car and tossed Payton the car keys. "She's all yours."

Part of Dylan could understand her twin's excitement: Payton picked out her car long before she was even old enough to drive. She'd seen a red, vintage convertible Volkswagen Beetle during a trip to the beach, and mentioned to their parents that her dream would be to have one of her own someday. Daddy—being Daddy—decided to find one for her sixteenth birthday. Dylan was home, putting out flower arrangements for a funeral, when Daddy showed her the match he'd found online. Soon after, it shipped to Brody's body shop to be updated and repainted the red Payton asked for.

The rest of the family made their way over to the Bug, and once again Dylan followed behind and watched everyone's excitement but couldn't muster up excitement of her own.

"She's beautiful, Brody," Mama exclaimed as they approached. "Just beautiful."

He gave her a polite nod and grin. "Thanks."

Daddy slapped him on the shoulder and lightly squeezed his neck. "You did a fine job, son."

"Thank you, sir. I gotta say that I'm pretty proud of her. Even got the right tires. See that? And the hubcaps are bowl-shaped."

"I see." Dylan watched the only males of the group squat down and salivate over the tires, while Payton ran the tips of her fingers across the shiny red surface, over to the silver door handle, and then climbed inside. From Dylan's vantage point, it looked like Payton nearly absorbed into the tan leather interior.

"It's completely swoon-worthy!" Payton purred, a large, lopsided grin on her face. "I'm so in love I can't stand myself."

"You're finally catching up with the rest of us, who can't

stand you already," Dylan quipped. The verbal thought earned her an expected ice stare from Mama.

"She's from sixty-two," Brody announced. "Four cylinders, four-speed manual transmission. I had to find a new pure white canvas top, though the leather seats, they're original. They were a mess but I cleaned 'em up real good. I don't think anyone could've done it better. Heck, I even patched up a few tears. You'll hardly notice 'em."

Dylan kept her distance, but circled the car, giving it the once over before she walked away from the car show and made her way to the tree swing just a few feet away.

"I used a mattress stitch. The same one cosmetic surgeons use to reduce scarring." Brody took a quick breath and continued. "The engine, clutch, transmission, they're all solid. Original to the vehicle, so I had to do some major overhauling, but it was worth it."

Dylan sneered as she dropped onto the wooden swing seat. "You don't think the red is a little much?"

Brody looked over at her with his mouth ajar. "It's candy apple red."

"No, it's arrest-me red. Sheriff Jackson's gonna spot Payton from a mile away if she drives that thing around town."

"That's exactly right," Payton sang.

"It's what she asked for," Brody added. "It's even got the fluted European-style headlight lenses. They're amazing. And the bumper bars, I polished them to the point where you can see your reflection."

"We sure know Payton loves to see her reflection." Dylan hitched her eyebrows and shrugged. "But at least it's not pink. Like her pants."

Payton glanced over her shoulder and shot her sister a

smirk. "Don't you for one minute think I didn't consider bubble-gum pink."

"Oh, I know you did."

". . . the engine is a 1192cc, eight-to-one compression . . ." Brody continued, even though everyone had tuned him out more than a minute before. "Stainless steel valves, dual springs, solid rocker shafts . . ."

"I always wanted one of these," Mama said, almost in a daze. Dylan watched her from afar as she allowed her eyes to slowly take in each and every centimeter of shiny red and crisp white detail. She could almost see her imagining herself a wild and free sixteen-year-old driving through town without a care in the world. "If only."

Their daddy finally stood and looked over his shoulder at Dylan. "I feel bad not giving you a car too," he said.

She kicked the dirt ground below her, causing the swing to sway. "A car isn't what I want."

He pulled out a folded manila envelope from his back pocket as he walked toward her. "You know it took me almost the entire year to get your mama to even consider your request."

Dylan jumped out of the swing but contained her excitement enough not to hop around like her sister had. "She said yes?"

He handed her the envelope. Dylan gripped the corner, tore it open within seconds, and pulled out a stack of pamphlets. Daddy chuckled. "Look out, Europe, here she comes."

She pulled the stack to her chest in a hug. "I can't believe it."

"You sure that's what you wanted? You've gotta wait a full year to—"

She jumped into Daddy's arms and hugged him tight. "It's exactly what I wanted."

While Payton begged and begged for the beautiful piece of transportation that she, Mama, Nana, and Brody were ogling, all Dylan wanted was a getaway. A summer abroad was her opportunity to escape Mama's clutches and tour Europe, as well as make some friends that weren't from Cornwell and didn't even know she had a sister, especially not a perfect one. It was her first chance at freedom in sixteen years, and the only one she'd have before college finally took her away for at least four years.

Over Daddy's shoulder, Dylan watched Brody stand and walk to them. "I gotta admit, I was a little disappointed that I didn't get to work on a car for you too."

"Why's that?" she asked.

"There's no telling what you would've picked. Probably a hot rod or something."

Dylan shrugged. "Hadn't thought about it." It was the truth. Unlike her sister, Dylan hadn't even considered asking for a car for her birthday. She spent most of her time with either Cole or Payton, and both would have vehicles, so her transportation needs were all but taken care of. Or she could walk, which she actually enjoyed.

She held up the pamphlets and waved them in the slight Mississippi breeze. "I'm going to Europe next summer."

"Wow." Even Brody seemed impressed. He'd never been outside the state, let alone on a plane to another country. "That's cool. Not as cool as a remodeled car, but cool. When do you leave?"

"Early June, a little over a year from now." She took a long, satisfying breath and looked over at him with what she was sure was a sparkle in her eye. "Imagine that, Brody. In a year, I'll be outta here."

Dylan looked back toward the driveway and saw Payton flip herself so she was nestled on her knees, facing the tree swing and running her angel necklace across the chain. "Your trip is going to be awesome, but in the meantime, I'll be driving around in this beautiful car. There won't be a doubt in anyone's mind who's heading their way when Lady Bug and I are coming down the street. You watch—I'll be the envy of every girl this side of the Mississippi."

Dylan rolled her eyes, turned and walked back toward the house.

"Okay, except maybe you!"

CHAPTER 8

August 12, 2017
3:50 p.m.

Payton sat between an aged brick wall and an old, rusted washing machine in the gravel alley behind the Suds 4 Duds—and a bit away from a mass of black smoke that rose into the air in torrential amounts. Her heart raced and her fingers tingled, her toes in a tight curl inside her flip-flops.

Excitement. Craziness. Chaos. It all unfolded on the other side of the building, although she didn't necessarily understand how she got in her particular predicament.

Anyone who saw the cloud from afar would assume that something much more substantial than her little red convertible was up in smoke. That is, of course, if there were anyone left in town who were actually at a distance. As it was, it appeared that every living soul stood on the sidewalk to watch as fire consumed the car's metal body. Even the small city bus pulled off to the side of the road. Every occupant's face was glued to the windows in awe and wonderment.

It was a spectacle. Other than the disappearance of Dylan a little more than a year before, this was the biggest thing to happen in Cornwell since Opal Wonders ran into the fire hydrant over on Cypress Street back in 1992, and the entire town lost water service for two days. But according to Nana whenever she told the story, that wasn't even the most newsworthy part. What really raised everyone's eyebrows was the fact Ms. Wonders was wearing nothing but a dress slip, and when she climbed out from behind the wheel, the water flowing out of the hydrant soaked the thin material and gave all those watching from the sidewalk quite a show.

While she wasn't wearing a slip dress, Payton could certainly understand how it felt to be the center of attention at the worst of times.

The ragtag volunteer fire department had presumably decided not to waste any water on Payton's vehicle. The three men—who happened to be the town veterinarian, the adult entertainment club owner, and newspaper editor—did nothing more than keep people at a safe distance.

In fact, she looked around the corner and saw Harold England pull a notepad out of his shirt pocket and jot down some notes, showing he was much more interested in getting the story than fighting the fire. After all, this story was front-page news—in a four-page newspaper. Two of which were devoted to sports.

Just as Payton originally intended, everyone in town knew it was her when she drove around. The car became her identity; Payton Brave and her cute, bright-red bug. Now, that part of herself was gone.

Payton heard footsteps approach from behind her. She turned and spotted Brody walking in her direction. His motor oil-stained overalls and red T-shirt covered his husky build, and his moppy hair partially covered his eyes. He was in his own world, looking at his phone with a huge smile on his face as he moved down the alley.

He looked up, and startled at seeing her sitting there. She hid her face behind her hands and peered at him through her split fingers. "Pretend you don't see me, Brody."

He shoved his phone in his pocket. "Pretend? I can't. I'm not good at acting."

"It's best if you leave now, or you're going to witness a murder right here in the alley."

His mouth dropped open and he slowly eyed the area. "Murder?"

Payton lowered her hands to the ground and peeked around the corner at her burning car, then tucked back behind the wall. "Yep. I'm dead."

Brody walked to the corner of the building and looked toward the street. "What did you do to Lady Bug?"

"Nothing."

"You burned her up. Why would you go and do a thing like that?"

"I didn't. She . . . She just caught on fire."

"Cars maintained like yours don't just catch fire, Payton." He scratched his head and started pacing. His heavy work boots struck the pavement with a thud each time he set a foot down. "I worked hard on that thing. She was beautiful. Some of my best work."

"Maybe you can fix her."

His attention skipped from Payton to Lady Bug until he finally groaned and shook his head in what appeared to be utter disgust. "There's gonna be nothin' left to fix. Look at her!"

Payton sighed. "Yeah, I know. She's a goner."

"Payton?"

Cole's daddy, Carl—the owner of County Road Gentlemen's

Club—walked toward her with a smile. No matter the circumstance, he always had a smile on his face. Payton always figured it was due to his occupation.

"Payton, your daddy's on his way."

"I'm dead."

"Say what?" he asked.

"My daddy's going to kill me. I'll be the next person on his slab."

"Quit sayin' that," Brody grumbled.

"Aw, now, he's not gonna kill ya. You didn't do nothin' wrong."

"Carl, my car's in the middle of the street with fire pouring out of it. Isn't that the very definition of wrong?"

"Well, it's wrong, sure; but you didn't cause it."

"Trust me, someone's about to be planning *my* funeral."

"I don't think you should talk like that, given the circumstances. It kinda loses its hilarity, saying you're dead and all."

"I suppose . . . if you say so."

"I say so."

Brody stopped pacing and stared down at her. She could almost feel the weight of his disappointment. "What do you think your mama's gonna do? I mean, everyone in town is watching this."

Payton sighed. "She'll be horrified at all the negative attention."

Carl turned and watched the fire. Payton did the same, and then eyed the crowd. A lot of people took pictures and video with their cell phones, which only solidified Payton's shame. Others chatted or stood with their eyes wide and their mouths hanging open.

A loud explosion startled Payton and drew her attention back to the blaze.

"It was just a tire," Carl explained.

"Aw, crap," Brody groaned. "Your daddy's here."

Payton watched Brody head back down the alley the way he'd come.

"Wimp! Consider yourself uninvited to dinner!"

"This is one I don't mind missin'," he yelled over his shoulder as he disappeared down the street.

Payton turned and clasped onto the fireman's leg, and gave him her most pleading look. "Please don't go anywhere."

"Pay—"

"Please."

"All right. I'll stay right here."

"Payton!" Daddy ran up, his face practically ghost white. He knelt down in front of her, placed his hands on either side of her face, and did a quick inspection. "Are you okay?"

"I'm fine. I managed to escape before the fire got too intense."

"Well, thank God for that." He stood, rested his hands on his hips, and stared at what was left of the car.

"David," Carl said with a small nod in greeting.

"Hey, Carl." Daddy shook Carl's hand and turned his attention back to his daughter. "What happened?"

"Daddy, I can explain . . . Well, okay, I can't."

Another explosion rang through the air.

"That was a tire," Carl said quickly, before Daddy could be alarmed.

"Why aren't you guys trying to put the fire out?" her daddy asked.

"By the time we got here, there was nothin' we could do. There was no salvaging it."

"So we just let it burn?"

"Yep. We've gotta let it burn itself out."

"Okay . . . well . . ." He watched the flames for several more seconds, and then looked down at his daughter. She could sense the pure, unadulterated pity in his eyes. "Let's go, Payton. No sense in making you sit here and watch it perish."

Drained from all the drama and attention, she slowly stood and picked up her iPhone and purse, and then spotted the distant parking lot and groaned. "Aw, Daddy. Did you have to bring the hearse? It's so embarrassing."

"I thought you were burning to death in a car. I didn't stop to think which one of the vehicles would embarrass you the least. I jumped in the one that was closest to the exit."

She dropped her head in shame and utter humiliation, and then followed behind him as they made their way through the alley so she could avoid having to endure more gawking glares. "There's not a body in the back, is there?" she asked. "I don't think I can handle three deaths in less than twenty-four hours."

"Three?"

"Misty's baby, Lady Bug, and whoever's in the back of that thing."

"There's nobody in the back."

"Thank God for small favors."

He opened the car door and waited for her to climb all the way inside. "Sit tight for a minute. I'm going to talk to Harold." Just before he shut the door, he lowered his face to hers. "And you're sure you don't know what happened?"

She had a momentary flash. A raging fire. The heat from the flames felt like it was burning the large grin off her face, and the key chain she held tightly in her hand warmed in the heat, the metal keys woven between her fingers becoming almost unbearably hot.

Payton looked up at her daddy and smiled lightly. "No, sir. I'm sorry." She gulped. "I have no idea what happened."

4:20 p.m.

"Hey, Dylan!"

Payton looked over at her daddy with her perfectly practiced puppy dog eyes. "Please. I'm too worn out to correct her again."

Daddy wrapped his arm around Payton and squeezed her tight. "She's a bit confused, that's all."

"A bit?"

"Okay. A lot." He kissed her on the temple. "No, Nana," Daddy soothed with a look back to his mother-in-law. "This is Payton. Remember? Payton?"

Nana grimaced. "Cotton-pickin' . . ."

Daddy and Payton walked up the porch steps and joined her on the patio.

"It's all right." He took her hand in his.

"Well, what on earth happened to her? You ran outta here like the house was on fire or somethin'."

"The house wasn't on fire, but her car was."

Nana's eyes widened. "Well, I'll be."

"Maggie walked into the embalming room and told me that someone called and said Lady Bug was on fire, and then hung up. I was scared outta my mind." He squeezed Payton close again, like he was double-checking that she was actually still

94

standing there. "They didn't say where she was or if Payton was in the car."

"Sorry," Payton muttered.

"I drove down Main until I got past the tree line and then saw the smoke plume coming from the center of town. Led me straight to her."

Nana nodded, as if she was all-knowing. "Like the three wise men followed the North Star."

"Something like that." Daddy kissed Nana on the top of the head and finally let go of his daughter. "Of course everyone in town got there before I did. They just stood there and stared at me as I ran around looking for her. I was frantic."

"Of course you were, you're a good daddy. Good daddies worry."

He smiled down at her. "I suppose they do."

Payton watched Daddy walk inside and leave her and Nana to deal with Joshua, who'd just pulled into the parking lot with a screech loud enough to cause Nana to stop rocking, sit forward in her chair, and crane her neck to try to get a good glimpse of the possible bus.

Joshua jumped out and walked to the bottom of the porch steps. "You're alive?"

"Looks like I'm standing here, so . . ."

"How?"

"My dad drove me home. I—"

"No. I mean, how did you get out of the car?"

Payton struggled to understand what he meant by the odd question.

"I heard there was an explosion," he added.

"Well, then, you heard an exaggeration."

95

"You scared people to death."

"How's that?"

"Maggie called Lindy's mama screaming that your car was on fire and you weren't answering phone calls. So, her mama drove by and saw your car on fire, but you were nowhere to be found. Everyone assumed the worst."

"They always do."

"Lordy, I know that's true," Nana said.

He pulled his cell phone out of his pocket and started typing. "The whole friggin' school is in an uproar. They thought another Brave girl . . . Anyway, my phone was blowing up with questions."

In Payton's experience, lightning-speed group text messages helped destroy someone; but in this particular instance, it was nice to hear it'd be used to announce that her family hadn't lost another girl after all.

"Sorry you were bothered." She realized her palm ached, and when she glanced down saw her car keys were grasped tightly in her hand. She loosened her grip, raised her hand, and inspected the key teeth marks in her skin.

"You aren't hurt?"

"No." A flash of red caught her eye. She raised the keys and closely inspected them, noticing small chips of red paint stuck in the grooves of several keys.

"Not even a little?"

She didn't respond. She stared at the paint chips, and what seemed like a memory filled her mind: of glancing around the school parking lot, then scraping the edge of her keys across the side of Lady Bug until she'd left a deep, metallic crevice in the otherwise perfect paint job.

"Payton?" Joshua nearly scolded.

She came back to the moment and looked up at him. "Nope. Not a scratch or a burn. I'm completely unharmed."

He slid the phone back into his pocket and left his hand inside. He smiled, but she noticed it disappear moments later when Cole pulled his old truck into the parking lot. He glared over at Joshua for a brief moment before climbing out of the cab.

"Guess I better go," Joshua said. "See you at school in the morning."

Joshua turned and stared at Payton as Cole approached. She wasn't sure, due to the slight distance, but she thought she saw his jaw harden and the corner of his eyes tighten before he climbed into his car and peeled away.

Although Cole hadn't actually done anything to cause Joshua to dislike him, like with so many others in town, it was well known that Joshua's daddy wouldn't let him hang out with the likes of a strip club owner's son. But Dylan choosing Cole over Joshua seemed to compound his hatred for Cole.

"All these cars and not one bloomin' bus anywhere." Payton glanced over her shoulder at Nana, who was now sitting up straight and staring after Joshua's car. "What kinda bus station is this?"

Cole walked up the steps and knelt down in front of Nana. Just as he did every time he came to the house, he handed her a flower and kissed her on the cheek. "How are you doing, Nana?"

"I'm good, Coleman."

"Still waiting?" he asked.

"Patient as Noah waitin' on the snails."

"I know that's true." He gave her a gentle pat on the knee before standing, Payton's quizzical eyes on him the entire time.

"My mom asked me to come get the vases that we left for the Suitor funeral last week."

"Did you hear about Lady Bug?"

"Not much. But I saw the smoke."

It made sense that he wouldn't stay up to date on the latest local gossip, especially seeing as how he and his daddy were so often the topic of it. Carl never marrying Cole's mama, plus owning the local strip club seemed to give everyone the opinion that they could make up just about any old story about his family and spread it as truth. Cole once told Dylan that he'd learned to ignore it all and go on with his life. And if he couldn't ignore it, he turned his hearing aids off so he couldn't hear it.

"What happened to her?"

Payton rested her forehead against the edge of the open front door. "I don't even have the energy to explain. Give me a few minutes. I'll get your mama's stuff."

Without saying a word, Cole picked up Pugsley and sat in the seat next to Nana. Payton watched Pugsley make himself comfortable and then walked inside, leaving the trio to wait for the illusive bus.

A few minutes later, she walked out the front door with the box of vases in her arms. Nana's chair sat empty, but Cole was still in his chair holding Pugsley. The dog looked right at home. Of course, Pugsley'd known Cole longer than he'd known the Braves; Cole gave the pug puppy to Dylan two years earlier. Payton still remembered when he'd carried Pugsley up the front porch with a big red bow tied around his neck. Dylan ran onto the patio in a fit of squeals, but the puppy infuriated Mama to the point of conniption fits.

"Where's Nana?" she asked.

"Bus station closed."

"Oh, of course." She dropped into the seat Nana'd left vacant, took a deep breath, and slowly let it out. "She's gone." She looked over at him, curious as to what his response would be.

Cole looked up at her, and his eyebrows were low and practically touching beneath his heavily creased forehead.

"Lady Bug," she added. "Burnt to the ground. There's nothing left of her but the metal frame."

He nodded but didn't provide her with any real reply.

"Please talk to me. I don't like quiet."

"Why? What's wrong with a little quiet?"

"It makes my mind wander."

His expression softened. "Where does it end up?"

Payton hesitated, turned, and absently scanned the quiet, tree-lined street. "With Dylan."

When she turned back to him, she noticed he was surveying her face.

Uncomfortable with the sputter it caused in her chest, she quickly looked away.

Cole placed Pugsley back on the ground, stood, and picked up the box of vases. "Sorry for your loss."

"Loss of which? Dylan or my car?" she asked.

He glanced at the ground, then back to her. "Both."

CHAPTER 9

August 12, 2016
5:30 p.m.

Dylan twisted her big toe deeper into the sand. She was surrounded by the upper echelon and wanted to be almost anywhere else, or better yet, wanted them to be anywhere else.

"You sure you don't want to hang out with us at the bonfire?" Starr asked.

"Doubly sure, but thanks for the offer."

Cole and Misty stood in the back of Cole's truck and looked down at Dylan while Payton adjusted the large crown resting on Dylan's head. Usually Payton was the one being crowned, but she still knew exactly how to pin a crown on someone else. Even an oversized one. Probably because Payton, Mama, and Nana loved to watch beauty pageants together, and Dylan and Daddy loved to find just about anything else to occupy their time while they did.

"Ouch!" Dylan winced at a bobby pin practically stabbing into her skull.

"Sorry. Hold your head steady."

"It is steady. You need to be more careful."

She felt Payton's hands grip her head and force it to center over her shoulders. "Quit your gritch'n."

"Who has bobby pins with them at the beach? Where'd they come from, anyway?"

"My ponytail. Now shush."

Another pin scraped the surface of Dylan's scalp but eventually rested in a clump of hair.

"There. Perfect," Payton announced.

Lindy crossed her arms over her chest and glared over at them. "You just won the King of the Mountain Championship. I think it's required that you be at the bonfire."

Dylan glanced up at Cole and Misty, and then cut her eyes back to Lindy. "And who would require that?"

"Us," Starr spat.

"Oh. Got it. Thanks for the warning, but I think we've got plans of our own."

Lindy looked into the truck bed and eyed Cole. "I'm sure you do."

Payton put her hands on her sister's shoulders, and placed her face next to Dylan's. "Let the queen be. All right? There'll be plenty of people at the bonfire. After all, it leaves more s'mores for us."

"Always the peacemaker," Dylan muttered.

Payton walked around Dylan and moved toward the fire. "See you at home, later."

Misty watched the royal court walk away then jumped out of the truck bed. "I'm outta here."

"Why?" Dylan asked.

"I'm pretty sure you two would prefer to be alone . . ."

Dylan arched her left eyebrow, knowing full well there was more to the story. "And . . ."

"Joshua asked if I might wanna hang out."

Dylan and Cole exchanged a quick, knowing glance as Misty grabbed her towel and beach bag. "Have fun, you two."

"You too," Dylan said. "But not too much fun—it's Joshua Toobin, after all."

Misty walked away, seemingly ignoring the warning, and left Dylan and Cole on their own for the first time all day.

Dylan hopped up onto the tailgate, wiped the sand off her feet, and readjusted her crown. "Love my sister for trying, but my crown's still a little off."

"Well, you're a little off, so it fits." Cole arranged the cushions he'd borrowed from his mama's seventies-style couch.

One early morning when Dylan and his mama, Val, drug Cole garage sale shopping, his mama bought the sofa for fifteen dollars. A tropical storm had just passed through and flooded the seller's house. They were even lucky enough to find matching pillows a few houses later, and there were plenty of them to cover the couch—or, as often happened, fill Cole's truck bed so he and Dylan could lay out under the stars and pretend that the rest of the world didn't exist outside the truck bed walls.

She playfully threw her sweatshirt at him, but he caught the sleeve while most of the shirt was still in her hand, pulled her to him, and kissed her quickly before he fell back into the pillows.

"Maybe I am a little off, but I still beat you out on that platform, so . . ."

"Very true." He extended his long legs out in front of him in the shape of a V. "You're the Queen of the Mountain. That's quite an accomplishment. You impress me."

Dylan inched along the truck bed, crawled into Cole's lap, and arranged herself so she sat with her back against his chest and her head resting just beneath his collarbone. "You know, we should probably be at the bonfire celebrating with Payton and the others."

"Since when do you do what Payton and the others are doing?"

"Since never."

"Exactly."

Dylan reached into her bag, pulled out her now-worn legal-sized manila envelope, and removed the stack of brochures. "Here's an idea. We can plan our trip."

Cole kissed her on the temple and wrapped his arms around her, as she opened the first brochure. "The Louvre. I can't say I'm excited about that one," he admitted.

"I've heard you could spend weeks in there and still not see the same thing twice."

"Weeks, huh?"

"Weeks."

Maybe it was all the Disney princess movies her mama forced her to watch, or a love of any place other than Cornwell, but Dylan had admittedly started fantasizing about Europe, castles, and strolling ancient streets to a near obsessive point. And while Cole wasn't really much for travel, or airplanes, he'd agreed to go on the trip since it meant a lot to her. He'd even worked extra hours at his mama's store and cleaned his daddy's club every morning to raise the money to go.

She knew that for Cole, it would be the trip of a lifetime. But for her, it would be the first trip of many.

"Payton's so sick of me talking about our trip, she claimed this morning she'd puke the next time I brought it up."

"I'm sure she'd follow through on the threat. As long as she could do it like a lady." He laughed.

"We'll be off exploring the world, and she'll be here . . ." She eyed the bonfire and the "royals" performing their annual duties. "Doing the same things she always does."

She nestled deeper into his chest, as if she could hide away there and escape the world. "We leave in less than nine months. Think about that. Nine months from now, our lives will be completely different."

"It's weird to think about, but honestly I'm shocked that your mom even agreed to let you go. Especially since I'm going too."

Dylan closed the first brochure, shoved it back into the envelope, and opened the next. The Palace of Versailles.

"Dylan . . ." There was an accusatory tone in his voice. "You told her, right?"

"You know Marie Antoinette? The queen that got her head chopped off? Although I can't remember why . . ."

"Dylan."

She shoved the other brochures into the envelope, sat up, and turned around as he burrowed his face in his hands. "You promised," he moaned.

"I'm gonna tell her."

He lowered his hands and gazed over at her. Usually the pout on her face was enough to distract him, or make him go easy on her, but it wasn't working this time. "You were supposed to tell her before they bought the tickets so they'd know the whole story before they said yes."

"But if I told her you were going, they never would've said yes at all. You know that."

"They could've surprised you."

"No. They couldn't." She sat crossed-legged and tried her hardest to make sad eyes that were even half as effective as Pugsley's.

"She can't even deal with us dating right under her nose. There's no way she'd allow it."

Dylan studied the woods surrounding them. "You know what they say, 'Cornwell has eyes.' And I'm convinced those eyes are my mama's."

"Do you think she'll ever realize we're actually pretty good together and stop trying to break us up all the time?"

"Pretty good? We're great."

Cole took a deep breath and blew it out in a gush of wind. "It's exhausting. No matter what I do . . . it's not enough."

"It will be." Dylan looked up at him and felt a rush of adoration flow through her. "You're smart. Kind. Trust me, Cole. She'll see it all one day."

"But she'll never accept me if she finds out you're lying to her. She'll blame me."

"I'm not lying. I'm withholding information."

He looked over at her. His face was deadpan. "Look cute all you want, but I'm not dropping this."

When they first started dating, Cole always gave in. He'd let her win any argument, and she suspected it was because it was easier than trying to convince her that she might be wrong. Eventually, however, he'd decided to stand his ground and play hardball. Or at least play as hard as she did.

His face turned stern. "If you don't tell her, I will."

"Cole!"

"No way am I going to let you go another day without her knowing. So . . . you tell her or I will."

Dylan straightened her body and stiffened her face. It was meant as defiance, but Cole wasn't fazed by it.

"The longer you wait, the worse it's going to be. Fess up."

"The last time I tried to talk to Mama about us, she talked me into breaking up with you and going out with Joshua."

He groaned.

"How'd that work out? Huh?"

"We found our way back together, so I say it worked out pretty well. And no matter what she's done, she deserves the truth."

Dylan felt the fight leave her body. "Fine. I'll tell her tomorrow before we leave for Charleston. At least that way she'll have a few days to calm down before she sees me again. If they take my tickets away, I'll just get another job or two and pay for it myself."

Daddy paid both girls minimum wage to help him at the funeral home, but Dylan spent a lot more hours working there than Payton did, and she knew she had enough customer service or office work experience to get a job at any small business. As the only mortician in town, Daddy had the corner on the funeral business, which meant almost anyone who was anyone had been to her house and seen her hard at work or helping with a funeral.

She ran her hand over the manila envelope. "I'll be on that trip no matter what. We'll make it work. Right?"

"For you?" He grinned over at her. "Absolutely."

Dylan smiled back at him. She still got butterflies when he looked at her—a look of complete devotion and acceptance. He knew her better than anyone, and he loved her anyway. "You're really dreamy," she said, only half teasing.

He laughed. "No way. You're not buttering me up."

She playfully crawled toward him. "What do you mean, buttering you up?"

Cole leaned back and playfully pushed her away. "You know

exactly what I mean. Your games won't work. I'll still tell her if you don't."

She collapsed into his arms with a sigh. "I'll tell her in the morning. Promise."

"Thank you." He slightly lowered his face to hers, letting their lips meet for a brief moment.

"Cole, this time next year, we'll just be back from an awesome adventure. We'll be sophisticated, cultured world travelers. We won't be afraid of anything, and will be ready to get out of Cornwell forever."

"That sounds perfect."

CHAPTER 10

August 13, 2017

6:00 p.m.

Payton reached across the desk to hold Misty's hand, unsure what else she could do. They'd sat facing each other for over thirty minutes, a funeral brochure between them, but Misty hadn't stopped crying enough to speak.

Payton didn't know what to say. This wasn't a normal circumstance, like speaking with the family of an elderly person who'd lived a full life, or of a sick person who'd been warned death was approaching. Instead, it was facing the end of several futures. Mama told Payton that the Gibbs and Misty came to an adoption decision almost immediately after she found out she was pregnant; they'd paid all her medical bills and went to her doctor's appointments, but they weren't in the hospital room when the baby was born. They quickly realized it couldn't survive, and they didn't feel it was their responsibility to arrange and pay for a funeral.

They'd agreed to adopt a baby, not a body.

Payton tried not to judge the Gibbs for deserting Misty in her time of need. Their dream just died and they weren't thinking properly. There were a lot of people who lost their minds or weren't able to think clearly after their loved one departed. Sadly, it was common. Nobody knew that better than the Braves.

But again, Misty's situation was different. Since her parents kicked her out of the house and the Gibbs walked away, Misty was left to not only arrange, but pay for the funeral of a child she never intended to keep but still loved.

"I, um . . . I asked Cole to come over. He should be here any minute. I know you two are friends and I thought you could use the additional support."

Misty nodded as she wiped her nose with a balled-up tissue.

Payton waited for just the right time to speak again. That moment when Misty's chest stopped heaving and her eyes cleared. When the tears became more of a puddle than a downpour.

"What about the father?" she asked. "Do you think he or his family might be willing to help?"

"No way."

"Are you certain?"

Misty glanced down at the floor and shifted in her chair. "We dated off and on for eight months. Or at least *he* thought we did. I never went out with anyone else. We were only *together-together* once. My first and only time, and I got knocked up. I swear my life is like the perfect example of what not to do."

Payton couldn't come up with a good response, so she said nothing.

"He dumped me for good the next day," she continued. "In April, when I figured out I was pregnant, I tried to tell him but he didn't want anything to do with it. He told me it was my problem and that if he had his way, I'd get an abortion. 'Course, he wasn't willing to help pay for it or anything. Not that I would've done it if he had. I swear, I wanted to rip his head off and spit down his throat."

"Does he know the baby was born?"

Misty raised her head. "Didn't you tell him?"

"Me tell him? Tell who?"

"Joshua."

Payton's breath caught in her throat as her mouth clamped shut. If she hadn't already been sitting, she would've fallen to the floor in shock, awe, and a hefty amount of distress. "J-J-Joshua? Joshua Toobin?"

Misty nodded, a grimace on her face.

"Joshua Toobin's the father?"

"Didn't he tell you?"

"Why would he tell *me*?"

"Aren't you two together now?"

"Together? No. Not even close. I mean, he tried—but I—"

"He told me he finally realized we were meant for each other . . ." Misty's grimace intensified to a near cringe. "And that he thought he was falling in love. I was stupid enough to believe him." The puddle of tears again became a downpour.

Payton pushed the chair back, peeked under the desk, and momentarily contemplated hiding underneath. As she listened to Misty repeat some of the same phrases Joshua tossed her way during their hike, she felt physically ill; it was puke-worthy.

"I'm sure it's different with you." Misty's face brightened a bit, and her eyes widened. "Maybe he's learned his lesson."

"A tiger doesn't usually change his spots."

"Don't you mean stripes?"

"Those either." Payton's mind raced, and her anger and embarrassment intensified by the second. For a moment, she wished she'd followed him down that trail and pushed him right over an embankment.

A car honked outside. Payton stiffened, and she swore she actually saw red.

"What's the matter?" Misty asked. "Who is it?"

"The tiger." Payton stood, and worked to erase the increasingly appealing vision of pushing him over the valley edge. "I'm gonna give him a chance to redeem himself. See if he'll help with this burial."

"You think he might?"

There was hope in Misty's voice and a light in her eyes that made Payton feel bad for even offering the suggestion. "I doubt it, but it's worth a shot." Payton picked the cell phone up off the desk and shuffled it around in her hand. "Misty, why don't you go hang out in the family room. Make yourself at home." She walked toward the door, and glanced over her shoulder. "And be sure not to set your food on the coffee table. Pugsley'll have it and be gone before you even notice. He's fat but he's fast."

Payton stormed out of the house, past Nana and off the porch.

Joshua leaned against his car. A large grin was on his face, and he held a small bouquet of flowers in his hand. "Ready to go?"

"Nope." She stopped a few steps away from his car and hung her thumbs on her back pockets. Anger surged through her body so forcefully that she had to concentrate on keeping her feet to the ground so she wouldn't surge across the yard and wrap her hands around his beautifully tanned, but pretentious, throat.

"You look upset."

"Ya think?"

Sarcasm. Payton wasn't necessarily known for it, but she couldn't help herself. It felt appropriate and sounded natural.

With impeccable timing, Cole pulled up beside Joshua's car. He got out and walked inside with only a nod to the pair.

Once Cole was inside the house, Joshua turned his attention back to Payton. "What's the problem?"

"Did you get Misty pregnant?"

The smile melted off his face; his usually puffed-out chest caved.

"Did you?" Payton demanded.

He shook his head. "It was a mistake. The whole thing was a mistake."

"You and I were together at the cove when Mama told me the baby was born. You didn't say anything."

"What was the point? What does that have to do with us?"

"You don't think I'd want to know that before I decided whether or not to go out with you? You didn't think you should tell me?"

"I don't know, Payton. Do you go around telling everyone every mistake you've ever made? Advertise your screw-ups?"

"I never get the chance. Usually somebody else advertises them for me."

"Look." He leaned toward her and slid his hand down her arm in an attempt to grasp her hand. "The past is the past."

She jerked her arm out of reach and took a step back. "The past is the past?"

"You're only seeing things from her side. We weren't working; there was no chemistry."

"And it was only after you slept with her that you figured that out?" It came out at a higher volume than she'd intended.

"I didn't make her do anything she didn't want to do. And I didn't lie to her."

"Well, don't you deserve a humanitarian award."

He scowled at her and then angled his head around her, at the house. "What's she doing here, anyway?"

"Planning the baby's funeral."

Joshua didn't respond. His face was completely blank. Zero emotion.

"I'm sitting in there planning the funeral of *your* baby!" Her voice was now so intense and thundering that the entire town probably heard her.

"Quiet down," he hissed.

"Don't you tell me to quiet down!"

He lowered his eyes. The pitiful flowers hung limp at his side, and when she noted that they were obviously purchased from a convenience store instead of Val's, she got even angrier.

"Misty can't afford a burial. Are you going to help her?"

Joshua looked back up at Payton with gritted teeth. "When she told me she was pregnant, I told her I didn't want anything to do with it. I told her to have an abortion, and if she didn't I wouldn't be helping her out later. She didn't have it. I'm off the hook."

"Off the hook?"

"She's the one who decided to keep it."

The rage that built up in Payton scared even her, and her screams must have gotten Cole's attention, because within seconds she saw him appear on the porch and sit down in the chair next to Nana.

Payton swallowed hard, glanced back out at the street, and realized people had stopped to watch the second Payton Brave show in under twenty-four hours.

Joshua placed his head next to hers and spoke in a hostile

whisper. "If she would've just done what I told her, she wouldn't be in this mess. All she ended up with was a dead baby anyway."

Payton's elbow made contact with Joshua's nose before she even contemplated ways to attack.

He threw his hands over his nose and screamed out in pain. "What the— You crazy— You—you broke my nose!"

Payton raised her chin and closed in again so there were only a few inches between them. "Good!"

Joshua's eyes watered. He held his hands under his nose to catch the drips, but not before a gush of blood ran down his chin, drained onto the ground, and splattered all over his shoes.

"Now, are you gonna do something to help Misty or not?"

"Hell no!" He looked down at his newly crimson shoes and leaned farther forward so the injury drained onto the dirt.

Noticing his body weight was off balance, Payton hauled off and kneed him in the stomach with as much power as she could muster.

He groaned and fell to the ground in a clump.

Out of nowhere, Cole appeared, pulled her away and wrapped his arms around her, controlling her flailing arms.

"She's whippin' Rhett," Nana screamed, with more joy than Mama would appreciate.

Payton turned to the porch and found her parents and Misty standing next to Nana in shock. "Payton Belle Brave," her mama screamed, as she descended the porch steps and took flight across the yard. "What are you doing? Stop it right this instant!"

"Settle down," Daddy shouted as he closed in on the chaos. "Everyone just simmer down."

Mama was wide-eyed. "Payton, what has gotten in to you?"

"You're crazy!" Joshua yelled. "Just as crazy as the rest of your family!"

Cole released Payton but lurched forward to place himself between the brawler and her victim.

"I'd rather be crazy than a scuzz bucket!" Payton threw her fist toward Joshua's temple, but Cole caught her hand before it made contact.

"Payton Brave! Not another word," her mama screeched.

Cole eventually let go of Payton's fist, and she was free to pace back and forth across the yard like a caged animal looking for an escape.

"People die, Mama."

Her mama stumbled backward, as if Payton had punched her.

"Teenage girls get stolen out of bus station bathrooms. Boys use girls and then throw them away."

Mama's eyes suddenly filled with tears.

"Payton, please stop," Cole urged. "You're about to say something you're going to regret."

"There's more bad in this world than there is good, and no matter how hard you try to make me, I'm not going to walk around acting like there isn't."

Payton couldn't stop the flood of thoughts that raced through her mind and poured out of her mouth. "I'm tired of trying to be perfect. I'm tired of trying to act like my sister isn't dead or being tortured by some monster every day. And most of all, I'm tired of you. I'm tired of you running away from our house of mourning and misery and leaving me to deal with all of it on my own. We don't get to just check out and pretend that none of this is happening!"

Mama stiffened her back and straightened her shirt by giving it a tug on the bottom hem. "I won't be talked to like this."

She turned and walked away, causing Payton to fly into hysterics. "Don't walk away from me! That's all you ever do—walk away!"

Cole grabbed Payton's arm, spun her around, picked her up, threw her over his shoulder and marched toward the house. She screamed all the way inside, and even after the door closed behind them, she screamed like a banshee.

"Calm yourself down or I'm going to have to do something drastic," Cole ordered.

A year of pent-up anger had finally boiled to the surface. A year of being silent. A year of trying to do and say everything right, and she could think of no reason to stop screaming.

Cole stomped up the stairs, into the bathroom, where he turned on the shower and tossed her in, fully clothed.

When the cold water hit her, she shrieked and flailed around. "Turn it off!"

"Not until you settle down!" Cole shouted.

She thrashed around a minute more before her legs gave out, forcing her to slide down the wall and land in a heap.

"I'm not crying because I'm sad. I'm crying because I'm ticked off . . . and my elbow hurts."

"Do what you need to do," he answered.

"I will." She lifted her face to the water, let it wash over her, and convinced herself that the shower hid her cries.

Cole walked out the door, leaving the cool water to wash the heat of Payton's anger down the drain. After a few minutes, he came to turn off the water, handed her a baggie full of ice, put the lid down on the toilet, sat and turned to face her.

"Are you going to be okay?"

She shook her head and placed the ice on her elbow. "I don't know." Payton rubbed her face with her free hand and glanced down at her palm. It was smeared with black mascara. "I can't pretend anymore."

"Pretend what?"

"That everything's okay. Or will be." She felt her chest tremble, brimming with more cries. "I don't think it will, Cole. I don't think things will ever be okay again."

"They'll be different. And maybe sometimes they'll feel okay, and other times they won't. None of that's going to change based on whether or not you're pretending. All you're doing is causing yourself more grief."

"I can't be that anymore. It's exhausting," she admitted.

"I know." His voice was gentle. Soothing. A part of her understood why her sister could sit and talk to him for hours.

Misty poked her head in the bathroom. "Payton, the police are here. They want you downstairs."

Cole slapped his hands on his face and groaned before he stood and looked down at Payton. "Go change your clothes." He then turned to Misty. "Go downstairs, and tell them we'll be down in a minute."

By the time Payton and Cole walked out the front door a few minutes later, there was quite a scene outside the funeral home. Two cop cars were parked in front, a throng of people were being held back by a few police officers, and Sheriff Jackson, Joshua's dad, and the mayor all stood in a clump by Joshua and his car. Nana hadn't moved from her chair, and Payton noticed Misty was sitting on the front step feeding Pugsley Pringles.

"Ms. Payton Brave?" the sheriff barked as he walked toward

her. "Joshua said you inflicted bodily harm. I've got to take you down to the station."

"If I'd known I'd be arrested, I would have done more damage."

"Not helping." Cole hid the warning behind a cough.

"I mean, yes, sir." Accepting her fate, Payton held her hands out to the sheriff.

"I'm not gonna cuff you." He lightly gripped Payton by the arm and led her to the front seat of the cop car. After guiding her in, he shut the door behind her, and then walked back to the porch to interview the witnesses.

Payton slunk down in her seat until she could barely see out the window. She focused on the instrument panel in front of her.

The view was too familiar.

CHAPTER 11

August 13, 2016

8:25 a.m.

Payton sat sideways in the front seat of the patrol car with her legs draped out of the doorway. She vaguely was aware that the cotton fabric of her maxi dress had pulled up above her knees, but she didn't feel strong enough to stand up and adjust it.

"Just stay right here, Payton. Try to relax. I'll be back to get you in a minute." Sheriff Jackson gently squeezed her shoulder and then walked over to Nana and Lester, a bus station employee. As they spoke, the sheriff took notes in a small notebook and occasionally glanced up at them over the top of his sunglasses.

She couldn't remember how she got there. Her eyes darted to the movements and sounds surrounding her, but nothing clicked. Her fingers trembled in her lap. Something was wrong. Like a part of her was missing.

Sheriff Jackson raised a walkie-talkie to his lips, and Payton heard his words over the scanner in the car. "Dispatch, this is two-eight-five. Do you copy?"

"Two-eight-five, this is dispatch. Go ahead."

She inspected her white-tipped fingers and rubbed them on her legs to try to get some feeling back.

Sheriff Jackson walked a few steps away and turned his back to Nana. "Code two. Cornwell Bus Station. I've got a ten fifty-seven."

"Ten-four." Static blared for several seconds before a voice returned over the radio. "Any units available for a ten fifty-seven at Cornwell Bus Station?"

She rubbed her legs even harder. None of it made sense.

"Two-five-three, responding. ETA three minutes."

"Two-six-eight, responding. ETA six minutes."

"Ten-four." Static. Silence. "Two-eight-five?"

"Go ahead," the sheriff prompted.

"Description please."

"White female. Aged sixteen. Brown hair." He looked down at his notepad. "Wearing blue jeans, a red T-shirt with a peace sign emblem, and black Converse sneakers."

Payton's hands went completely still. Her ears perked. Her chest ached. Payton squeezed her eyes shut, clenched her fists, and held her breath, counting the seconds just like she and Dylan often would between bolts of lightning. The more seconds that passed, the safer it became, and the closer the storm was to being over.

"Name . . ." Jackson continued.

Payton's body stiffened. Not enough seconds had passed. She wasn't safe.

". . . Dylan LaurieAnn Brave."

CHAPTER 12

August 13, 2017

7:12 p.m.

Payton sat alone in a small holding cell in the back of the jailhouse. The sheriff wanted to keep her away from the drunkards in cell one. Based on the catcalls they'd made as she walked by, there was a chance she'd still overhear some things her parents wouldn't appreciate but her classmates would enjoy hearing about later.

She was trying to tune some of those comments out when Officer Harris slid the door open, walked in, and placed her book bag next to her on the bench. "Your mama wants you working on your homework. Said you might as well make some use of your incarceration."

Payton rolled her eyes at her mama's passive aggressive scolding. "Thanks, Ian."

"Once they press charges we'll get you fingerprinted and such."

"Wonderful," she quipped.

Ian was several years older than Payton. He was often given eleven fifty-two—code for funeral detail to the burial site. Whenever he was on duty, she brought him a cup of coffee he could sip on while he sat in his patrol car waiting for the funeral service to end.

"I left you one piece of contraband," he whispered.

"Contraband?"

"You know? Things you're not allowed to have." He loudly smacked his gum, then took it out and stuck it under the bench.

Payton recoiled. "I left you a pen, all right," he said. "You're not supposed to have pens in here."

"Why? What am I going to do with a pen?"

He looked down at her and raised his eyebrows.

"Oh." She took a deep breath and let it out in a quick burst of air, causing a strand of hair to soar. "How about a hairband. Did you leave me one of those?"

"Nope. Contra—"

"Contraband. Got it, but I'm not sure what I could accomplish with three inches of elastic."

"You'd be surprised."

Payton chuckled. "Trust me, I'm not going to hurt myself any more than I already have."

"Good to know."

"At least, I don't think so," she muttered.

He rocked back on his heels and folded his arms across his chest. "I'll be keeping a close eye on you."

"Knock yourself out."

He walked out of the cell and slammed the door behind him with a loud clang that hurt her ears and rattled the bars.

"It stinks in here!" she yelled, as he disappeared down the hall.

"I know."

She looked down at her backpack, then reached in and pulled out the first book her fingers touched.

The Complete Tales and Poems of Edgar Allen Poe.

It was the one piece of homework she actually enjoyed

doing every night. Payton felt an odd connection to Poe. He was slightly unhinged and had a bend toward the morbid. Since she was surrounded by death and literally had a cemetery as her backyard, his writings made sense. Over the last few weeks, she'd almost found them comforting.

Payton pulled out the single piece of contraband, and with the tip carved *Payton* on the already heavily distressed bench. She stared at her etching. The longer she focused, the faster and harder her heart beat.

She counted the seconds and waited for the storm within her to subside, but when she realized that the rage was only intensifying, she violently scratched through the name, marring it beyond recognition.

She slammed the pen down, and looked up at the gray ceiling. Somehow, even the surface several feet above her had been violated by previous cell guests. Graffiti and scratches marred the already peeling gray paint, and she wondered if she'd be shocked if she knew which of her fellow townspeople spent time sitting in the same dingy cage.

One thing was for sure: the townspeople would be shocked to know that Payton Belle Brave now had.

She focused back on the book and turned to page three hundred and four, found the place she'd left off.

> Presently, I heard a loud groan, and I knew it was the groan
> of mortal terror. It was not a groan of pain or of grief—oh no!
> It was the low stifled sound that arises from the bottom of
> the soul when overcharged with awe. I knew the sound well.

The words felt familiar. A similar sensation often visited her when she slept, and drifted around her in moments of silence.

She closed the book, which was now shaking in her hands, threw it to the dingy floor, and picked up the pen.

Poe. She chiseled the name into a part of the wood with no words around it. Then she carved it again and added a second name. *Brave.*

"Hey."

She lifted her head and was astonished by who she saw standing on the opposite side of the metal bars.

"Cole? Why are you here? Did you get arrested too?"

"No." She noticed him shuffle his feet a bit. "I figured Dylan would want me here."

She gulped, stunned by his bluntness. The topic of Dylan was never the elephant in the room when it came to Cole, and Payton appreciated it.

"She'd want me to make sure you were all right." He watched Ian unlock the door and slide it open, and then walked inside the small cell as Ian walked away, leaving the door wide open.

"You seemed pretty distraught back in the bathroom. Are you okay?"

"No." She felt the back of her throat tighten. A sign that tears were about to come, and no matter how hard she tried to swallow down the lump in her throat, the tears broke through anyway. "I feel like I'm losing my mind."

He walked farther into the cell and sat down next to her on the bench.

"Like . . . I can't think. I can't remember . . ."

"Payton, I—"

"Poe." She raised her eyes to meet his. "Call me Poe."

He stared back at her, and she felt like he was trying to look through the tears in her eyes and somehow understand what

124

was going on in her head. "Okay, Poe. I would think the way you're feeling is totally normal. Tomorrow's the anniversary of her going missing. We all still have a million questions—"

"But I should know the answers. I should remember. Something, anything. And I don't." Since she couldn't control the tears, she let them fall. "I feel more alone than I've ever felt, and now I'm stuck in here, and—"

"The sheriff told me you're free to go. They didn't press charges."

"What?" She wiped the tears from her eyes with the back of her hand. "Why not?"

"My dad reminded Joshua's dad that the gentleman's club has a lot of crime, and all that crime forces him to have cameras in the club. Mrs. Toobin probably wouldn't like finding out that her husband spends so much of his office time *not* sitting in his office."

She gasped. Not that she was shocked by Mr. Toobin's behavior, but that Carl would be so willing to make it known. "He blackmailed Mr. Toobin?"

"We call it more of a friendly reminder. He couldn't let you suffer for trying to help a friend. Truth is, Joshua deserved worse than you gave him."

"I thought Joshua would—I don't know—remember he's a human being and want to help. It's like he has no heart."

"He doesn't." Cole shook his head. He bent down and grabbed the book lying on the floor. "You know, I think other people moved on after last year and they forget that in some ways, we're still stuck back there. We're still hoping Dylan will come home."

CHAPTER 13

August 16, 2016
6:00 p.m.

"*. . . anything's possible, Laurie, but we* need to talk to Payton before we can really put together any sort of theory."

Sheriff Jackson, Mama, and Daddy looked into the closet. Their faces clouded with worry, matching the dreary weather that had painted the usually sunny town and her bedroom a shade of gray.

Payton didn't move or respond to their stares. Everything felt like nothing more than a strange play happening around her, one where most of the action occurred off stage. And she really didn't care what it was about.

Mama and Daddy looked back at the sheriff.

"Go on," Daddy encouraged.

"The Atlanta bus made two stops before we caught up with it and checked to see if Dylan was aboard. She wasn't, but as far as we know, she could've just as easily jumped off the bus at the first stop and taken off to just about anywhere."

"But she wouldn't," Nana said from her spot in Payton's desk chair. "She wouldn't have gotten on a bus without me."

"Had Dylan been acting strange at all?" the sheriff asked. "You know, not like herself?"

"She seemed to be gone a lot more. She was spending quite a bit of time with Cole. Acted distant. David and I noticed she was acting more peculiar. And she was spending a lot of time at the library doing homework, but her grades never really seemed to improve."

"And she wanted out of here."

"Brody!" Mama scolded.

He appeared almost out of nowhere. "Well, she did. She asked for that trip for her birthday."

The sheriff rubbed his eyes and then hung his thumbs on his holster belt. "We need Payton to talk to us. To tell us what she saw. Or what she knows."

They all turned to look at her, and again, Payton didn't respond. She couldn't.

Through slightly blurry vision, she saw the sheriff place a hand on each of her parents' shoulders. "I'll leave you be. Maybe some family time will draw her out."

Daddy and the sheriff walked in opposite directions, but both were suddenly out of sight. "Call me as soon as she comes to."

She listened to his footsteps move across the floor and down the two flights of stairs. The thunder of his heavy feet on the wood floors almost got lost amidst the crunch of the bedsprings—presumably from her daddy taking a seat on the edge of the bed, just like he did every time he came upstairs to chat with the girls.

"It's been three days," Mama whispered as she looked back into the closet. "She's hardly eaten."

"Neither has Nana." Brody peered around Mama. "She's been on that patio almost every second since you brought them home."

127

Payton heard bedsprings crunch again, then saw the top of Daddy's head appear at the edge of the closet. "The doctor told us to let her be. He said she'd come around when she was ready."

"But, David, three days. And you heard the sheriff, he needs to know what she saw."

"Why is she so messed up?"

Mama snapped at him again. "Brody!"

"No, I just mean . . . she's in shock or something. Do you think she saw what happened and it messed with her head? Post-traumatic stress disorder, or something? I've read a lot about that. It can really mess you up."

"I don't know." Soon, Daddy knelt down in front of her. "Payton. Sweetie, can you talk to me?" When she didn't respond, he placed a hand gently on her arm. "Payton?"

After a moment, she looked up, made eye contact with her daddy, and felt a vague awareness wash over her—the first thing she'd actually felt in days.

"That's my girl," he said with a large smile. "Are you hungry? Maybe you could come down and eat something with us."

She summoned the energy for three quick blinks. Her daddy rubbed her arm, as if hoping it would do something. Ignite something in her. Stir her to awareness. She surprised herself by being able to nod, but was only able to bob her head back up enough to see Brody walk up behind Daddy.

"Hey, Payton," Brody said, gently. "Welcome back to us."

She took a slow breath, but didn't move to look directly at him. She concentrated on opening her mouth and managed a "Thank you" through dry, cracked lips. Her voice sounded scratchy to her ears. "I'm thirsty."

"I'll get you some water." Brody darted out of her vision, and she heard rapid footsteps down the stairs and below her.

"Here . . ." Daddy took her by the hand and gently pulled her to her feet. "We've got some tomato soup. Your favorite."

"My favorite . . ." She let him lead her out of the closet. "What happened? Why was I in the closet?"

Daddy and Mama shared an anxious glance. Soon after, heavy steps pounded back up the stairs.

"Payton, you . . . you don't remember?" Mama asked, just as Brody reentered the room.

He handed her the glass of water and then stepped out of the way.

"Remember? Um . . ." She racked her brain, trying to conjure up memories. Her body felt heavy and weak.

"Payton, you were at the bus station," Brody whispered, as if he were helping her cheat on an oral exam.

"Do you remember anything at all?" Mama asked.

Payton searched the room, hoping something there would help remind her of the answer they wanted. The right response.

And she wished she hadn't found it.

"You remember!" Daddy's relief was obvious.

Payton shook her head again. "Code ten fifty-seven. The radio." She looked back to her parents. "Dylan's gone."

CHAPTER 14

August 16, 2017

5:40 a.m.

"... *One thousand four. One thousand* five. One thousand six . . ." A large clap of lightning sliced through the dark night and caused the window to tremble.

Poe clutched Dylan's hands as they huddled in the back corner of the closet among the dresses they'd tried to hide from their mama, hoping she'd forget they ever had them.

She focused on the dark outline of Dylan's face and they started counting again. "One thousand one . . . one thousand two . . . one thousand three . . . one thousand four . . ." Another electric bolt erupted outside the window, briefly illuminating the sky.

"The storm is coming," Poe warned. Her voice shook like the glass panes of the window. "It's getting closer and closer."

Dylan stood from the floor and motioned for Poe to get on her feet.

"No," Poe protested.

"You have to. Come on." Dylan led Poe through the bedroom, into the bathroom, and to the back window just as another explosion of light hit the night sky and pierced the darkness.

"Look at it. Don't be scared."

The girls stood together and watched the storm loom. "You can't pretend the storm isn't here. You have to look at it. Poe, you have to stare it down until it goes away."

Another boom rattled against the panes.

Poe sat up in bed with a jolt at the sound of lightning outside her window.

The dream tore through her mind. Like her nightmares often did, it continued to churn up visions. Her heart physically ached.

Stare it down.

She followed the footsteps she and Dylan took in the dream and peered out the porthole window that faced the centuries-old graveyard just a few steps from the Brave's back porch. Fourteen years of living in the house meant she'd been on the cemetery grounds hundreds of times. But she'd never actually stopped to look at the headstones the way Dylan did. Never appreciated their beauty, or the stories they told even though Dylan was an expert on them. Her sister had spent hours in the historical society looking up the history of the people buried on the property. And afterward, she'd often dream up stories about those lives. Payton usually drowned her out when she rattled them off.

Once her makeup was applied and she was dressed for the day, she picked up a wide-tooth comb and ran it through her damp, long locks, then sectioned off her hair. As she absently began making braids, she peered back down at the headstones covered in dirt and moss. Two hundred years of existence had left them beautifully flawed.

As she tied an elastic band around the last braid, she spotted two small headstones, side by side. The granite reflected a thin layer of moonlight that snuck through the trees as it made its decent below the horizon.

With the storm newly passed, she slipped on a pair of knee-high rain boots, then quietly walked down the steps, out the back door, and into the muddy cemetery, arriving at two small, cracked headstones partially buried in the soil. She was drawn to the fact that they looked somewhat brighter than the others around them, as if the storm had cleared off the moss and dirt. When Poe came in for closer inspection, she noticed another interesting detail: they were identical in every way but the names.

Olive and Nettie. She vaguely remembered hearing Dylan mention the names.

Poe brushed away the remaining soil and moss that caked the bottom of the headstone, revealing the same dates.

May 20, 1843–April 2, 1845.

She took a deep, sharp breath. "Twins. Born together. Died together."

She wondered what type of tragedy would take two babies' lives simultaneously. Whatever it was, it was certainly heartbreaking. Knowing how close twins are, she thought it might be easier for them to go together than for one to be left on their own.

"Trust me, I know from experience that almost nothing feels worse than being the one left behind."

Poe studied the engraved angels that hovered above each name. She knew from listening to Dylan that they were common on old gravestones as symbols of protection, rebirth, and wisdom; but while most angels depicted weeping, the angels on Olive and Nettie's headstones soared, and she found it almost beautiful.

Tragically beautiful.

Poe laid back on the soil, her hands cushioning the back of

her head, and immediately felt as if she were melting into the earth. Burying herself among the others. Her clothes seeped in the moisture from the ground, but she didn't care.

She closed her eyes and listened to the wind as it blew through the trees, then allowed herself to drift away.

Mist surrounded her. She was inside her bright red Bug, driving onto a muddy road. After several feet, the tires spun, and the car struggled to move forward. She pressed the gas, but it only resulted in chocolate-covered earth shooting against the sides of the vehicle.

Unable to move and nobody to help her. She was stuck and completely alone.

"Payton Brave!"

Poe's eyes flew open.

"Breakfast is ready!"

She sat up like a shot, and realized leaves and grass covered her hair. Once she'd picked most of it off, she smelled the sleeve of her shirt. The scent of saltwater air, dirt from the ground, and a hint of the Sargassum seaweed that had recently washed up on the shores left a perfume that had seeped into every fiber of her clothing.

"Payton! Quit lollygaggin'!"

Again, Poe took in her surroundings. "Mama, I'm comin'!"

The back door flew open. Her mama stuck her head outside. "What are you doin' out here?"

"Not sure," she answered, more to herself.

"Get in here so you can get on to school!"

Mama slammed the door shut, but left Pugsley sitting on the back porch staring out at Poe.

His bark brought her fully back to the moment.

133

"You're just as bossy as Mama." She made the short walk through the cemetery, swung open the door, and floated inside with a gust of wind. The door slammed behind her. The violent closing caused several of the crosses that covered the back wall of the house to shift out of alignment. Her mother meticulously hung each and every cross, making sure they were perfect. Previously, Payton would've quickly straightened each and every one back, but things had changed, and Poe wouldn't be adjusting anything, let alone crooked crosses.

As Poe pulled off her muddy boots, she heard Mama muttering away in the kitchen and going about her usual morning routine. "I swear that girl could start an argument in an empty house."

"I take after you."

"Watch it, young lady."

She walked into the kitchen, where Pugsley immediately started sniffing around for any crumbs or small gifts of food that might have been thrown to the ground. He sounded like a snorting pig mixed with a Hoover vacuum cleaner.

Mama's eyes narrowed, and she glared over at her. "What were you doin' in the cemetery at the crack of dawn?"

"Talking to Olive and Nettie."

"Olive and Nettie?"

"Twin girls from a couple of centuries ago."

"Don't talk to dead people, or people'll think you're crazy."

"Maybe I am."

"Payton." Mama's eyebrows drew together and her eyes narrowed. "Go change clothes. You're muddy. And hurry up, or you'll be late."

"It's Poe." She was surprised she'd talked back to her mama

134

so freely. So effortlessly. But it felt good. Very good. "I want you to call me Poe from now on."

"Poe? I won't do such a thing. Your name is—"

"Poe." She stood her ground and kept her head held high. "My name is Poe."

"Get your clothes changed!"

Her courageousness fleeting, Poe ran upstairs before she pushed her luck and ended up grounded. Once upstairs, she walked straight to her closet. But when she flipped on the light switch, the closet stayed dark.

Following her daddy's example from a few days before, she reached up and tightened the bulb back.

The light flashed on.

She instinctively reached for clothing from her side of the closet, but quickly stopped herself. She turned, sorted through Dylan's clothes, and then eyed hers again.

After a few moments of thought, she selected one of Dylan's vintage concert T-shirts and a pair of her own jeans. As she pulled her dirty top off, she caught a sliver of her reflection in the mirror and noticed that she had mascara smeared under her eyes. She took a step closer to the dresser and was about to inspect the makeup further, but instead focused on the photos that covered the mirror.

Two years' worth of photos. Formals. Sporting events. Parties. All with people she now realized never knew the real her, and she probably didn't truly know back.

She peeled away a photo of her and Starr at the King of the Mountain bonfire from the year before. She peeled away a photograph of her and Lindy at Zoe's sweet sixteen party. She peeled away a photo of the in-crowd cheering in the front row at a football game.

Picture by picture, she removed them until she could see herself clearly. No longer hidden by the other personalities and their expectations.

With further inspection of her reflection, she reached into her makeup bag, grabbed a makeup-removing cloth from a packet, and began to wipe her face. With each swipe, she removed more of Payton, and allowed more of Poe to shine through. No more foundation to hide the freckles. No more blush to make her appear more lively than she actually was. No more eye shadow, or brow liner. And no more mascara.

She looked back, completely barefaced and feeling pounds lighter.

"Payton Brave! You're gonna be late!"

"My name is Poe!"

Poe threw on Dylan's T-shirt, the pair of jeans, and a pair of Converse and charged back down the stairs.

Poe's outfit caught Mama's eye as soon as she reentered the kitchen.

"What on earth are you wearing?"

"Clothes."

"What's with the attitude? This isn't like you at all."

"Maybe it's totally like me."

Mama applied mustard to the bread with gusto. "Please stop. I hate to start the day in an argument."

Poe pulled the elastic bands out of her hair and ran her fingers through the now-dried braids, allowing her hair to hang down her back in newly formed waves. She tossed the elastic bands into her purse, and then turned to watch her mama make her sandwich. "What's with baloney?"

"You've never taken issue with baloney before."

"Well, I'm taking issue with it now. Do we have any pimento cheese?" Mama's hands dropped to the counter as her eyes passed with a heavy scowl. In response, Poe opened the chip drawer, grabbed a bag of Cheetos, and threw it into the brown lunch bag.

"She'll take the baloney sandwich and she'll love every bite of it," Daddy's voice sounded as he walked into the kitchen. He picked the newspaper up from the counter and looked over at Poe from the corner of his eye. "Won't you?"

She dramatically threw her head onto the counter. "I suppose I will."

"She wants us to call her Poe," Mama spat. "Can you believe it? What kind of name is that?"

"Poe?"

Poe nodded.

"Please deal with her. Okay? I'll see you later on tonight." Mama raced past her and down the hall. Daddy took a seat at the kitchen table as the front door slammed shut.

"Poe." It came out of his mouth slowly, as if he was trying it out for size.

"Who've you got down there with you this morning?" she asked before he could start the inquisition Mama asked for.

"Bettie Thomas."

"The librarian?" She spun on the stool and ran the angel pendant around her neck, back and forth on its chain. Like Dylan, she hadn't taken off the necklace since their biological father had them delivered on their fourteenth birthday, wrapped in Disney Princess wrapping paper.

Her daddy poured a cup of coffee, dipped his spoon in the sugar bowl, and scooped up a full heap. "That's the one. Her family will be in to finish making arrangements this afternoon."

"But didn't she prearrange sometime last year?"

Daddy dumped the sugar in his coffee and looked up at her, his face practically contorted. "Uh . . . yes. Now that you mention it, I think she was here after she was diagnosed last year. I can't believe you remember that."

"I remember Dylan talking about it. Mrs. Thomas wanted to pick her own coffin 'cause she was afraid her children would choose something gaudy." Poe hopped off the stool and walked to the office. She pulled the paperwork out of the metal file cabinet and glanced over it as her daddy walked into the room carrying his coffee. "Yep. The file says she chose the Lady Rose with steel gauges. It's simple and elegant," she said. "Nothing gaudy about it at all."

Daddy took the file out of her hands and studied it. "I'll try to get it ordered after I finish her up downstairs."

She took the folder back. "I'll order it this morning during study hall, if you want."

"You will?"

"It's what Dylan would want—for me to help you out. So, open casket or closed?"

"Open. She looks good."

"Then you should tell the family to choose an outfit that'll stand out against the white lining of the casket." She closed the file and stuffed it into her backpack next to her sacked lunch.

"You sure are in a take-charge sort of mood today."

"Actually, I think I'm in a take-charge sort of phase. I fully expect it to last a while."

"Well, alrighty then." Daddy beamed over at her. "Poe."

"Thank you."

"I appreciate your help with this."

"Sure. I'm guessing they'll schedule the service for some time Friday or Saturday afternoon."

"I bet so."

"I saw she wanted multicolored flowers, but you should try to talk them into pink. And maybe a standing spray—"

"Don't worry about it right now. Go. Take my truck and get on to school. I'll see you this afternoon. We can talk about all of this then."

"Maybe we can have the family bring her favorite book—"

"Go!"

A newly energized Poe rushed out the front door and hopped down the stairs. "Bye, Nana!"

She looked over her shoulder and watched Nana sit up in her rocking chair and wave wildly. "Soar, Payton Belle Brave! Soar!"

As soon as the truck's ignition turned, Poe changed the radio station from her daddy's preferred country to the oldies channel that played music from the eighties twenty-four hours a day, seven days a week. The tunes kept her in an excellent mood during her drive to school. It was only after she parked that things went south.

With every step, she recognized a new pair of eyes was watching her. Even the fresh air outside somehow felt smothering.

"Hey, slugger!"

Poe winced.

"Watch out, everyone, Payton's on the move."

She didn't know who made the comments, but it didn't matter. Everyone knew about the altercation from the day before, and there was no way they'd let it lie.

"Payton!"

Joshua's voice rumbled across the parking lot. She picked up the pace and practically sprinted toward the school entrance.

"I know you heard me. Hold up a minute."

Poe took several steps more, then abruptly came to a halt. She tapped her foot and waited for him to arrive, but didn't bother to turn and watch him move her direction. He wasn't worth her energy.

He walked up next to her, and took a deep breath. A grin was on his face, even behind the bandage that covered his nose.

"Payton, I know we both said some things yesterday that we regret—"

"I regret nothing."

"But people think we'd be good together—"

"Well, most people are crazy, so . . ."

"I think we just need to forgive each other and move on."

"We hung out for a day before I found out you're a child-abandoning pig. Trust me, Joshua, you're a nobody, and certainly no one I want to 'move on' with."

Joshua's jaw tightened. His face reddened. "You're making a mistake."

"I doubt that." She continued her walk toward the entrance. "Just act like I don't even exist. Shouldn't be too difficult; you're an expert at it."

She might as well have been on a float covered in tissue paper flowers the way people stared at her when she entered the school hallway. While it was obvious that everyone knew every sordid detail about the day before, they apparently wanted to hear the news firsthand.

After being asked the same questions on a near-constant

140

loop, Poe was so fed up with the inquisition that she stood in the middle of the hallway and spoke to everyone at one time. "Please spread the word, as I know y'all can. Yes, Joshua and I hung out. It was nothing earth-shattering, and it ended before it truly started. Now leave me be, 'cause I don't wanna talk about it." She sucked in some air and walked on.

"What about your car?" someone asked.

She stopped mid-stride. "My car caught on fire. No, I wasn't hurt. No, I'm not grounded, and, yes, I'm getting a new car."

She took a step. Stopped. "And I'm not answering to Payton anymore. Either call me Poe or call me nothing at all."

Frustrated with life under a microscope, she spun on her heels, marched to the office, threw open the door, and walked in.

The receptionist barely looked up from her desk. "Yes, Ms. Brave?"

Poe leaned on the counter, to the point she felt her feet lift off the floor. "I'd like a name change form, please."

"A name change form?"

"Yeah. You know, so all the teachers know that I changed my name."

The receptionist slowly spun around in her chair and looked over at Poe with dead eyes. "First off, there is no such thing as a name change form. Second, if you legally changed your name, your parents need to come in and fill out some official paperwork. Everything has to be official. If it wasn't, everyone and their dog would be in here changing their names every other week. I'd be up to my eyeballs in name change forms."

"So you *do* have name change forms, then?"

"Get to class, Payton."

"It's Poe." She turned toward the door. "If you'd let me fill out a form, you'd know that."

She swept out of the office, walked back down the hall, pulled the file for Mrs. Thomas's funeral out of her book bag, and thrust it at Cole, who was standing at his locker. "We've got flowers to order. Mrs. Thomas died. The funeral's probably gonna be on Friday or Saturday."

After several seconds, he peered through his blond bangs and removed the black set of earphones from his ears.

She leaned against Dylan's locker. Out of the side of her eye, Poe realized she had placed her head against Dylan's photo, so their profiles were side by side. She shook the thought from her head and focused on the folder. "Cancer," she whispered.

He opened the file and flipped through the pages. Seeing as how he and Dylan worked on so many funerals together, he'd probably seen more funeral files than Payton had.

Payton helped out a lot at the funeral home all the way through middle school, but once her social life took off, she devoted less time to the family business and more on climbing the social ladder. But funeral planning was in her blood, and since she'd jumped back in, it was like she'd never left at all.

"Did you hear me?"

He didn't respond to her question.

"Cole, did you forget to wear your hearing aids or are you ignoring me?"

"They're in."

"So you're ignoring me then?"

"Not necessarily."

"Pink flowers with a few white ones here and there." His cloudy-gray eyes scanned the file as she gathered her thick hair onto the back of her neck and kept right on talking. "Open casket. So, a standing swag."

He finally looked at her out of the corners of his eyes, and she noticed he momentary focused on her T-shirt, then her brown eyes. "I'm trying to read her file and you're busy yapping away. Just give me a sec. Not all communication has to be done with words."

"I like words."

"I noticed." He turned his focus back to the file, and flipped a page as she pulled a marker out of her bag. "Is that all you want, a swag?"

"No. I can get you the rest of the order after Daddy meets with the family."

She felt his eyes on her again as she marked through the nameplate on her locker and wrote her new name over the top.

"Poe." He handed the file back to her. "Interesting choice."

"You wouldn't understand."

He slammed his locker shut and started to walk off. "I understand a lot more than you think."

1:30 p.m.

Poe exited Spanish class and left a room full of angry classmates behind. For the first time since the start of the school year, as she took the test, she put her head down, focused on the questions, and kept the answers to herself. It was liberating.

While the people left behind in the classroom held a quiet, yet menacing revolt, the discussions in the hallway were almost deafening. Everyone was riled up, and the air in the musty, metal-lined hall was electric.

As Poe approached her locker, her phone alerted her to a Twitter notification.

@SavageJosh2016: Beware! Crazy slut on the loose. @PaytonBeBrave

Accompanying the post was a photoshopped picture of Payton's face attached to someone wearing a straitjacket and standing in a padded cell.

She glanced up and down the hallway, watched everyone type on their phones, and tried to ignore the incessant pings on her phone from each mention.

At the start of the school day, everyone was afraid she'd died inside a fiery car. Now, based on their tweets, they practically wished she had.

Poe reread Josh's tweet, and then focused her attention on the aged flyer still attached to Dylan's locker. Their stories somehow encapsulated just a few feet apart: One on paper; the other spread through the social media world. One an urgent plea; the other, nothing more than propaganda. Unfortunately, everyone was more interested in the propaganda.

Cole walked up to his locker, reached over, and snatched the phone out of her hand.

"Ignore it," Cole urged.

Kasi walked up behind him. "How could Joshua do something so cruel at a time like this?"

"He thinks that, under the circumstances, I'm weak." Poe started to work on her combination. "What could've happened to cause all of this?"

Poe's phone chimed again. Kasi grabbed it out of Cole's hand and read the tweets out loud.

> **@SavageJosh2016:** So @PaytonBeBrave Was I not supposed to tell about the "fun" we had on our trip?
>
> **@SavageJosh2016:** @PaytonBeBrave Pick a fight so your parents wouldn't find out that their perfect princess is far from perfect?
>
> **@SavageJosh2016:** @PaytonBeBrave Don't you hate it when a perfect plan backfires?

"Only an idiot with a limited vocabulary uses the word *perfect* three times in two tweets," Poe muttered, and shook her head. "None of those tweets are true, by the way."

Kasi softly stroked her arm. "Not everyone believes him."

"Enough do." Out of habit, Poe started to force herself to smile, but stopped and turned her full attention back to her locker.

Poe dug through her locker until they'd walked away and she could be left in peace.

"What's going on with you?"

What little peace she'd gathered fled when she looked over at Starr, who now stood next to her violently tapping a foot on the ground, her hands thrust on her hips.

"What do you mean?" Poe asked.

"I mean, you're acting like a crazy person all of a sudden." Starr looked around the hallway and then leaned closer. "You almost ruined Joshua's reputation."

"*I* almost ruined *his* reputation? Are you kidding me?"

"You need to set the record straight so we can all move on and get back to normal."

145

"I don't need to do anything. Especially not get back to normal. Whatever that means." Poe turned to face her supposed best friend. "Starr, you know me better than that. You're gonna believe Joshua Toobin and whatever he says over me? A person you've known for years?"

"Correction. I knew you. You changed overnight. I don't know who you are anymore."

"I'm still me."

"Really? So the real you is a liar and violent?" Starr rolled her eyes. "And is it true you're planning a funeral for Misty's baby?"

"Well, my daddy does own the only funeral home in town. But yeah, I'm personally helping her plan her baby's funeral. She needs some support right now and—"

"The girl's in her current situation because of her choices. You go throw her some kind of pity party and it makes it seem like what she did is okay."

Poe felt rage sprout from her toes. She threw her hands into her pockets so she wouldn't be tempted to hit her former friend. "How dare you," she whispered.

Starr crossed her arms across her chest and set her jaw. "How dare me?"

"You have no right to judge her for anything."

"Look, if you want to hang out with the Mistys of this world, you go right on ahead. But if you do, don't expect to spend any time with me."

"It sounds like things will work for both of us then."

Starr darted her eyes to Poe's locker and released a sharp laugh. "I should've seen this coming when you asked people to start calling you by that ridiculous name."

"Really, *Mary*? What should I have expected when you changed yours to Starr?"

Poe kicked her locker shut and stormed into the Calculus room.

She felt everyone's stares but tried not to show an ounce of bother as she slipped into her seat.

Her phone chimed again. A text from Brody. So, you and Josh, huh? Didn't know you had it in ya!;)

"Payton," Mr. McDonald barked. "To the board."

She groaned. More from the text than getting called on. "I didn't get my homework done," she admitted.

"Then work the problem on the board. Number three."

"But—"

"Since when do I allow buts?" he asked.

Poe's jaw tightened and she swallowed hard. After grabbing her book, she slid out of the desk chair with a moan, tossed her phone on the desk, and glanced back at Cole. The sympathetic look on his face made her fingers tingle.

After making it to the board, she took the top off the dry erase marker and looked down at her book. It was nothing more than gibberish. She wrote the requested equation on the board and then stood back and stared at it while Mr. McDonald's other victims feverishly worked their equations on either side of her.

Poe took a guess, wrote the answer on the board, and turned to go back to her seat.

"Wrong," Mr. McDonald snapped. "Try again."

She turned back around, erased the answer with the side of her hand, and gave it another go. This time, she tried whatever theorems she could think of for several minutes before she finished and turned to face him.

"No."

She turned around and again wiped away the answer.

What felt like hours later, Mr. McDonald walked over to her. "Take a seat." He turned to the others. "Now, for the rest of you . . ." She tuned the rest out as she walked back to her desk, focused on holding back tears.

Humiliation and rejection; two emotions Poe hadn't felt in over a year—at least not as Payton. Apparently, they'd rushed in like a flood, along with the name change and new attitude.

She tried to concentrate on the teaching, but out of the corner of her eye she saw people looking at her. Some, like Spencer and Zoe, appeared amused. Others, those she hardly knew, sympathetic.

When the bell finally rang, she grabbed her backpack and tried to beat the others out of the room.

"Ms. Brave?"

She stopped at the door, looked at Mr. McDonald, smiled, and hoped it would help her cause. "Yes, sir?"

"You have a zero on that homework assignment."

Since she couldn't find any words to say that wouldn't get her in more trouble, she simply nodded.

"But, given your family's circumstances . . . I'll give you the opportunity to get it done and turned in late. Get it to me when you can."

"Yes, sir." She rushed out of the room before he could change his mind.

She wanted to hide, disappear even, but knew she wouldn't find refuge inside the building.

So she slid out the back entrance, wove through the deep brush, and slowly made her way through the foliage to the cove.

It wasn't the fastest way, but it kept her out of sight of anyone who might want to haul her back to school and subject her to more misery.

When her shoes finally hit the sand, Poe slipped off her Converse and left them behind as she walked to the center of the empty beach, relieved to have escaped the confines of Cornwell High and its suddenly vicious students.

She took in a deep breath of fresh air, sat, and stared out at the platform. How would it feel to be someone who'd never been invited to lounge in the sun on its aged wooden planks? She was surprised it had never crossed her mind before. She decided the sting of rejection might be more like a harpoon through the heart. At least based on how she felt now.

Poe laid back onto the sand and closed her eyes, hoping to escape to some happy place in her mind as she allowed herself to fall asleep.

The cell phone vibrated.

She opened her eyes and looked around to reacquaint herself with her location.

The phone vibrated again. She cleared her throat and answered. "Yeah?"

"Where are you?" Cole screamed.

Unsure herself, Poe sat up and jumped to her feet. "Why?"

"Your mother is having a heart attack. A literal friggin' heart attack. She thinks you've been taken by someone."

She scanned the waterline, reacquainted herself with her location, and realized the sun had nearly disappeared below the horizon. "Crap!" She sprinted toward the woods.

"You've been gone all afternoon—"

"I zoned out. Wasn't thinking."

"Where are you?"

"The cove."

"I figured."

"I'll walk back to the school and get the truck. Take the short way."

"No. Stay put. I'm on my way."

The phone went dead. "Cole?" She pulled the phone away from her ear and checked the home screen. It was dark. He'd hung up.

She came to a halt at the tree line and started to search around for her shoes. She kicked the brush from side to side and ran her hands along the tall grass, but didn't see her shoes anywhere.

By the time she'd searched the grounds for several minutes, Cole appeared from the path that led to the parking lot. His feet pounded against the sand as he walked in her direction. "What's gotten into you?"

She backed up until her heels touched the water. "Nothing."

"Nothing?"

"Honest, Cole."

"Look, I get it. You and your parents are suddenly on the outs, but this . . . Taking off and not letting them know you're safe is just plain cruel. They don't deserve it."

"I know."

"Walking through the woods all by yourself? You keep doing crap like this and you're going to get yourself killed."

"I'm already dead!" she screamed. "Or might as well be."

"Enough!" he yelled. "Enough!"

She blinked in shock, unable to respond.

"Cry, scream, change who you are. Do what you've got to

150

do to grieve. But don't hurt your family any more than they've already been hurt. Don't cause them more worry."

"I wasn't thinking."

"Your sister wasn't thinking either. That's why she's gone."

His brutal honesty felt like a kick to the gut. She shook her head and tried to push his words out of her mind. "We don't know that. Thanks to me, we don't know anything."

He stopped and inspected the woods around them. His hands thrust into his hair. For the first time, she noticed his face was pale, most likely from worry. "You can't just go walking off alone like that." He ran his fingers through his hair several times and then shoved his hands in his pockets.

She turned and looked past the swim platform. The water sparkled in the orange light cast by the setting sun. "I wasn't thinking . . ." She repeated the statement but knew that she meant it as much about that morning at the bus station as she did the hours that slipped away today.

She turned back to him, recognized tension in his neck.

"My shoes disappeared."

His head spun around. His wide eyes focused on hers. "What?"

"I took them off so they wouldn't get sand in them, but they're gone."

"Where did you leave them?"

She lifted her hand and pointed to her left.

Cole pulled his hands out of his pockets and walked to the line where the sand and dirt converged and started to pace up and down the hedges. "How far in?"

"On the edge."

He walked the perimeter for a second time. His march

151

intense and hurried. When the search came up empty, he turned back to her.

"Get in the truck." His quick pace behind her forced her to almost run up the beach, over the small path, and into the parking lot. They only parted when he walked toward the driver's side and she ran and climbed into the passenger seat. He got in, slammed the door, threw the truck into drive, and peeled out.

Poe laid her head back on the headrest and closed her eyes as tears ran down her face.

He let out a groan. "I'm sorry I yelled at you. You just . . . You worried me . . . Everyone."

"I know." She took a deep breath and let it out slowly as she tried to mentally prepare herself for the uproar that she was about to encounter at home. "Why were you looking for me?"

"Your mom started calling around when you didn't come home from school."

"She called you?"

"No. She called my mom to see if you were at the store ordering flowers for the Thomas funeral. My mom called me and told me that your parents were starting to panic. I figured you were here."

He reached over and briefly took her hand in his. "Don't worry about it." Cole placed his hand back on the steering wheel and gripped it so tightly that his fingers turned white and matched the color of his face just a few minutes before.

"What about Daddy's truck? I left it at school."

"You can get it tomorrow. I need to get you home."

Poe scrolled through the text messages from her mama. There were more than three dozen, all in caps. Several exclamation

152

points followed each request for Poe to text back and let her know she was okay. Cole was right, her mama was frantic.

Cole turned the truck onto the Braves' road and stopped a few houses away.

Poe looked up from her phone and groaned. The two cop cars parked in front of the funeral home made her stomach queasy. "They called the cops. I'm in so much trouble."

Cole pulled the truck into a spot in the side alley and looked over at Poe with raised brows. She closed her eyes and she breathed slowly in through her nose and out through tense lips.

"Ready?" he said softly.

Poe didn't respond. They sat in complete silence.

The lecture awaiting her wasn't what had her feeling anxious. The tone behind it—the pain, the grief, the fear—that would be excruciating.

"Let me know when you're ready," Cole urged.

She opened her eyes. "One more sec."

"Okay." He glanced out the window, then turned back to her. "It might be best just to get it over with."

"Fine." Poe threw her car door open and jumped out before she could change her mind. Cole was already waiting for her on his side of the truck as she came around the front, and once she was at his side, he followed behind as she walked toward her punishment.

When they turned the corner, Poe spotted her parents, Nana, Brody, and several police officers on the patio. They all turned and watched Poe and Cole walk to the bottom step.

"Sheriff, I'm sorry you came out for all of this. It's all my fault." Poe felt her face flush. All of the attention caused her to feel even more shame for being so careless. "And Mama, I had a really rough day at school, went for a walk . . ." She lowered her eyes and stared down at her bare feet. ". . . I lost track of the time."

Her anxiety skyrocketed when Sheriff Jackson broke through the crowd. She watched his shiny black shoes as he walked down to the second step. "We didn't come for that. We came to let your family know that another girl's gone missing."

As Poe lifted her eyes to the sheriff, she felt the blood drain from her face. The cool sensation of the skin on her cheeks was the polar opposite of the temperature of her fingers once Cole slipped his hand into hers.

She didn't know why he took her hand—if it was to offer her silent support, or because, maybe, he was the one that needed some comforting. But no matter what compelled him to do it, it was exactly what she needed.

"From Cornwell?" he asked.

"No. Lincoln."

Poe couldn't form words. Her mouth and throat were dry. Her mind blank.

"That's close by," Cole said.

"Yeah." The sheriff made eye contact with Poe. "'Bout the same age as you. Same hair color. Similar features. No sign of violence."

"You don't think she ran off?" Poe asked.

He shook his head.

"But you still think Dylan ran off?"

The sheriff started to speak, but pinched his lips together and shook his head.

Poe's legs turned to Jell-O. Her vision went spotty. She looked over at Cole and silently pled for him to take over the questions.

154

"You're thinking someone took them?" Cole asked, as if he somehow read her mind.

"We think so, yes."

"So he's close by," Cole said.

"Possibly."

Poe let herself drop slowly to the ground. She was instantly in a black tunnel, only seeing what was directly in front of her; she felt like everything around her was either closing in or falling away completely.

She kept a grip on Cole's hand. Partly because she couldn't move enough to let go, and partly for fear that if she did let go, she'd fall backward and pass out completely.

The sheriff sat down on the ground in front of her. She took long, deep breaths and tried to prepare herself for more news. "Payton, I'm not gonna sit here and lie. I'm worried about you. This is now the third girl who's gone missing."

"Th-third?"

"When Melissa disappeared, it reopened another disappearance case. One that happened about six months ago. Everyone assumed she was a runaway."

"Melissa, she's the girl from Lincoln?"

He nodded.

"And this other girl, the one from before, they don't think she's a runaway anymore?"

"No."

"Why do you think these girls are tied to Dylan's disappearance?" Cole asked.

"Melissa disappeared on Saturday. Just a few days before—"

"The one-year anniversary," Poe muttered.

"Yeah. There are some other leads we're following. Patterns.

One, it appears they were all taken from a public restroom. Melissa was last seen in a stall over at the state park. They found her car keys and student ID on the ground. The other girl was likely taken from a gas station bathroom. We have her on video pumping gas, then walking toward the bathroom, but the camera didn't have a view of that side of the building. She never came back."

Keeping hold of Poe's hand, Cole sat down. "Is Poe in danger?" He looked over at her and smiled softly before addressing the sheriff again. "That's what Payton wants to be called now."

The sheriff raised his brows briefly. "Uh . . . okay. We don't know. There's a possibility the girls were lured to these bathrooms. Maybe by someone they met on the Internet who'd then arranged a meet-up."

"But you checked our computers after Dylan went missing. You said yourself there was no sign of her visiting chat rooms."

"We found out Melissa and Kennedy—the other girl—used library computers to hide their chat room activity. There's no way to trace who's doing what on those things. And since Dylan frequented the library—"

"Dylan never went to the library," Poe reputed. "She wouldn't be caught dead in there."

"Yes, she did," Mama corrected. "She went all the time."

Poe shook her head adamantly. "No. No way. Especially not to talk to random strangers on the Internet."

"She specifically told me she went to the library to do her homework. It was quiet. She could think better."

"She was probably lying . . . "

Mama's eyes darted to Cole, and when they landed they were nothing but slits.

"So that you wouldn't know she was with me." He turned his attention to Sheriff Jackson. Probably too ashamed to make eye contact with Mama any longer. "If I'd known all this time that you thought she'd been going to the library, I would've told you."

"It only takes a few times, Cole. And . . . well, there are a lot of possibilities. We have to consider all options at this point," the sheriff added.

"Is Poe in danger?" Cole repeated, this time more emphatically.

"I don't think this guy would come back here and risk being caught. Realistically, it's too dangerous to come after the sister of a girl you've already taken."

"Poe's shoes went missing," Cole announced.

"What do you mean?" Brody asked.

She swallowed. "I walked to the cove. Took my shoes off at the edge of the sand, but a few hours later when I went back to put them on, they were gone. Cole couldn't find them either."

The sheriff's back straightened, the veins in his neck protruded. "But you didn't see anyone?"

"I was sort of out of it."

He glanced over his shoulder at one of the officers. "Have a unit meet you at the cove. Look for her shoes." He paused. His brow furrowed for a moment. "Or signs that someone else was there."

The younger officer immediately left the patio, climbed into his car, and took off.

"He'll take a look. We'll figure it out."

Poe wasn't convinced. She didn't believe they'd figure anything out and didn't bother to act like she did.

The sheriff must have sensed her doubt, because he leaned toward her and looked over at her with a more gentle expression.

"I don't want you to lose sleep or be afraid to go anywhere. I just want you to be cautious. Try not to go anywhere unusual. Especially not alone."

Poe held his gaze. "Do you think these girls are dead?"

He grimaced. "I'm going to be honest, painful as it might be. I think it would be unlikely for someone to abduct several girls and be able to keep them all alive."

She took her eyes off the sheriff, looked up at her mama and watched her body tremble. Her daddy looked like he'd been hit in the face with a fence post. Brody was motionless and silent. She wasn't coherent when her parents experienced hearing the news that Dylan was missing. She'd missed the shock and distress. Now, seeing their faces as they received the update was agonizing.

"Unlikely." She turned her attention back to the sheriff. "Unlikely, but not impossible."

Sherriff Jackson smiled, but his grief-filled eyes revealed his true opinion. "Not likely. But not impossible."

She nodded as if she believed in the idea that her sister might still be alive. But there, between the two of them, and with just a simple look, part of her finally accepted that her sister would never walk up the porch steps.

Poe pulled her hand away from Cole's. "I'd like to be alone."

Without another word, she walked to the cemetery and sat below an old moss-covered tree. Pugsley trotted behind almost immediately, but while her parents talked to the officers on the front porch, she noticed Cole made his way around back as well. She decided not to let on she knew he was there, keeping an eye on her from a chair on the back patio.

CHAPTER 15

August 19, 2017

7:30 a.m.

The latest news from sheriff Jackson about the change in Dylan's case and the two additional missing girls spread through town and gave Poe a good excuse to miss school for a few days, work on Misty's son's funeral, and try to forget the image of herself in a padded cell.

The new revelations also meant that Mama and Daddy's hovering increased exponentially. At her parents' insistence, she spent the next three nights sleeping in Nana's room so she wouldn't be left alone. They were some of the worst nights of sleep Poe ever endured. The futon in Nana's bedroom wasn't even a little bit comfortable, so even her bones ached, and the two fans that blew on her all night made the room feel closer to the Arctic Circle than the Gulf of Mexico.

In the few minutes Poe did eventually sleep, fear seeped into her bones. It surged through her veins and made her heart beat rapidly. It settled into her lungs and complicated her breathing. Then it hovered in her mind and brought on a whole new set of nightmares.

In the worst vision, she entered the dark gas station bathroom and slipped on the slick floor. Once she flipped the lights on, she realized she was standing in a pool of blood, and with each passing moment, the puddle grew in size until it covered Poe's shoes and every inch of the bus station bathroom floor.

Her imagination tortured her throughout the night, and she was relieved when she woke up and the image began to fade from her mind.

A weary and sleep-deprived Poe sat at the kitchen counter and chewed on a plain bagel smothered in strawberry cream cheese. Under normal circumstances, Mama wouldn't let her eat such a large, heaping scoop of cream cheese, so she must've been too preoccupied with her grief to argue.

Every once in a while she'd spin herself ever so slightly so she could peer over at her parents and Nana, who ate breakfast at the kitchen table.

She could tell by the silence between them that they were anxious. Usually her mama would be chattering away about her patients, or the latest gossip she heard at Women's Club, while her daddy tried to swallow down his dry whole-wheat toast and act like he enjoyed both the gossip and the meal.

Today, before each bite, he stared at the bread for a good, long while. Poe counted ten seconds before he slowly brought it to his mouth and took his latest small nibble. She didn't know what he was thinking about, but if it were anything like what she was thinking about, along with each bite he was trying to digest a new truth.

Dylan more than likely wasn't coming home.

But sitting there at breakfast, it was time for the family to push through the fear and move forward. The death of Mrs. Thomas and Misty's baby meant that, for the Braves, life needed to continue.

The show had to go on.

Poe watched her daddy take his final bite of toast and then glance at his watch. "Whelp." He stood and threw his cloth napkin on the table, then took a deep breath. "Best get busy. Mrs. Thomas's family will be here in a few hours." She watched him disappear from the kitchen, and listened to his footsteps move down the stairs, onto the first story and into the viewing room to prepare Mrs. Thomas for her fellow townspeople to come pay their respects.

Most of the town made an appearance at the viewing the night before, but Poe was convinced they'd come more to see the Brave family than to pay their respects to the Thomases.

Not much different than news about an approaching hurricane, Poe'd always thought the attention given to the Braves walked a fine line. On one hand, she truly believed there was genuine concern for Dylan and the mental health of the Braves (Nana, especially); but on the other, she was convinced people watched the storm approach and secretly wished for enough destruction to keep the drama high but the causality count low. They were attracted by the theatrics, but repelled by the damage left in its wake.

Being in the eye of this particular storm, Poe didn't understand how anyone could get elation out of possible devastation coming over the horizon and landing on your front porch.

During the viewing the night before, Poe laid on the second-floor landing and carefully watched each person as they walked through the front door. Part of the reason she didn't walk to the ground level to join the visitation was to avoid their empty words, but she'd mainly chosen the spot so she could watch each person through the protection of the stair railing. If Dylan's abductor was close by, why wouldn't he take advantage of the open property and simply walk right in? He could easily feign grief over the loss of a beloved librarian, walk inside, and survey the house and possible entry points into the living-area floors without anyone so much as raising an eyebrow—or even simply get a glimpse of Poe. Chances were, he'd done that very thing at one of the funerals before Dylan disappeared.

The monster could've walked among them in their own home. The girls had always been vulnerable, and no one gave it a second thought. Nobody realized they'd needed to.

But now, Poe was on guard. And so was the sheriff. From her vantage point on the second story, all she could see were Sheriff Jackson's shiny black shoes, but it was enough to know that he was standing guard on the front porch. He pivoted from time to time, or came briefly in full view when he descended one step to assist elderly women onto the porch, but he stood watch as every single visitor arrived.

"Are you a family friend?" she'd hear him occasionally ask. "Were you two close?" Along with several follow-ups, as needed, that she sensed were his way of finding out if anyone was there who shouldn't be.

Once the viewing ended, he'd stepped inside the entryway, spotted Poe above, and offered an encouraging nod.

His nod helped more than any words could've. He was on her side, when so many others were still on the fence or altogether adversarial.

As she shook herself back into the present, and took in the rush of preparations for the baby's funeral, Poe saw Cole walk past the front window with his arms full of flowers. "There's a patrol car out front. Is that good or bad news?"

162

Poe removed a few of the vases from his arms to lighten the load. "Both. Good that he's here to keep watch. Bad that they feel like we need someone to be on the lookout."

"How's the Thomas funeral going?"

"Daddy texted a few minutes ago and said the First Baptist Church is packed out. We asked people to bring brand-new books in lieu of flowers so we could donate them to local school libraries. Daddy said they got so many books, they've covered the front sanctuary steps. They should be back soon."

"That's great. I'm—"

"Enough about that." She set the vases down on a cabinet, removed the rest of the flowers from Cole's arms and set them down, and then pulled him into the kitchen.

"What's up?" he asked, turning up his hearing aids.

Poe looked into the hallway to make sure nobody was eavesdropping, then reached into her backpack, pulled out several sheets of paper, and laid them on the counter in front of him.

"What are these?"

"I made copies of Mrs. Thomas's visitation guest book before her family took it home with them last night."

"Okay . . ."

"I counted two hundred and twenty-seven people come through last night, but only two hundred and seventeen signed in."

"That's probably not uncommon. Sometimes my mom signs for me when we go to weddings and funerals and stuff."

"I included families in my count." She pulled out a piece of paper covered with two hundred and twenty-seven strokes of a pen. "A slash per person, and families are circled. I'm telling you, Cole. Ten people didn't sign in."

He stared back at her, the corners of his eyes tight. "I'm not following."

She walked to the doorway and checked again, then walked back to him. "A possible murderer is roaming around and my house just sat open for more than two hours. Anyone and their dog could've been here."

"You heard Sheriff Jackson. They don't think he'd come back. It's too risky—"

"Then why are cops parked outside the house keeping a watch out?"

Cole shut his mouth. His eyes narrowed.

"And my shoes?"

He shook his head. "No. Poe, I told you. That could've been anyone."

Exasperated, she rubbed her temples, tied her hair into a loose ponytail at the nape of her neck, and then gripped his hand and pulled him out the back door, down the porch steps, and deep into the cemetery. "I don't know. Maybe I'm crazy, I—" She felt her throat tighten and her airway constrict.

"You're not crazy."

"I can't remember anything, but . . . but . . . I know there's something in there." She inhaled deeply and slowly, trying to stop the shaking of her hands and reduce the tension in her neck.

Cole pulled her to him and wrapped his arms around her. "It's okay. We'll figure it out."

"If she's alive, she's wondering why we haven't found her. I was there. She knows I was there. She knows I would've seen—"

He pulled away and cupped her face in his hands so she was forced to focus on him. "Poe—"

A soft call of "Payton . . ." traveled on the breeze, as if it was barely there.

"She might be alive, Cole."

"Payton!" The voice was now strained, and pointed, slicing right through her thoughts.

Poe jumped away from Cole and turned toward the house. The way Mama stood on the porch, staring out at them with her arms tightly folded across her chest and a scowl on her face, made Poe want to cower behind a headstone. "Payton, we have visitors and you're . . ." Her eyes traveled between them. "You're whatever it is you're doing in the middle of a cemetery."

Cole took a step her direction. "I was just trying to—"

"I know what you were trying to do."

He shoved his hands in his jeans pockets and clinched his jaw. Her eyes cut to Poe. "Misty's here. She's looking for you."

Poe took another long, calming breath and then marched toward the house, leaving Cole to stand in the cemetery alone.

"What was that?" Mama asked, as Poe stepped in from outside.

"He's here to support Misty."

"Then why is he outside with you instead of with her?" Her voice held an accusation. She'd heard it any time Mama asked Dylan questions about Cole.

"Mama, he misses Dylan and I miss Dylan. He's just being nice, that's all."

"He—"

"Mama. He lost Dylan too. Now, leave it be." Poe pushed past her mother, walked into the kitchen, swept her file off the kitchen island, and stormed out of the room on a search for Misty.

1:00 p.m.

Poe expected a very small group for Baby McNeese's funeral: just Misty, Cole, Brody, and her. So, she did a double take when Carl pulled into the driveway with a car full of people.

Poe watched carefully as, one by one, the occupants climbed out. Cole's mama wore a simple navy skirt and silky blouse with flats. The three girls from the club who followed behind each wore blue jeans and a nice shirt. At a glance, no one would ever guess their occupation. Poe found it comforting that there wasn't a pretentious one in the bunch.

Moments later, she was even more shocked when Sheriff Jackson pulled up close to the curb and climbed out along with Officer Harris and two other officers. All were dressed in uniform.

Poe stepped inside for a brief moment to make sure things were still running smoothly and found Misty standing at the back of the service room, welcoming each person as they arrived. She wasn't sure if Misty knew anybody, but the way she hugged each one, you'd never guess they were strangers. They looked like long-lost friends reuniting after years apart.

Poe checked her watch. It was only a few minutes until one and Cole was nowhere to be seen. She looked over at Carl. "Where's Cole? He was here."

Carl shrugged. "Why? What do ya need?"

"Misty would want him here." They were the words that left her mouth, but they weren't entirely true. She wanted him there too.

"We'll get started in just a moment," Daddy announced. "Please join us in the service room."

The collecting guests moved past Poe and made their way into the small chapel to take their seats in front of a tiny coffin that sat on a stand, surrounded by floral arrangements donated by Val.

Poe felt like it was a small but respectable arrangement, but felt pity for Misty, who sat alone in the first row.

After several long minutes, Cole finally walked back through the front door.

Poe rushed to him and gripped him by the arm. "There you are! Where did you go? I—"

Cole looked over his shoulder as a couple in their late forties made their way into the chapel.

Before Poe could question Cole again, a voice came from behind her. "Ms. Brave." The minister from the First Presbyterian Church reached out his hand to greet her. "It's been a while."

She stared at his open palm, hesitated, but eventually slipped her hand in his and shook it. "I guess it has."

"You think you'll be coming back for a visit anytime soon?"

"Not sure." She pulled her hand away and hid it behind her back.

He smiled and placed his newly free hand on her shoulder. "Well, just know that you're always welcome."

Poe let him take a few steps before she followed him into the back of the room. She stepped in just in time to see the quiet couple walk up to Misty, drop onto the pew on either side of her, and embrace her through sobs.

Poe clutched on to Cole's arm and drug him into the office.

"Are those her parents?"

"Yes."

"They haven't talked to her since they found out she was pregnant. How did you get them here?"

He shrugged. "I just went and gave them the news."

"And?"

"And told them that she needed them." He pulled an envelope from his back pocket and handed it to her. "Here."

"What's this?"

"My dad and mom, some of the club waitresses, and some of the guys down at the police station all chipped in to cover Misty's funeral expenses."

"*You* arranged this?" Tears filled her eyes as she took the envelope from his hand. "Thank you, Cole."

"Not everyone is bad, Poe. Try to remember that."

CHAPTER 16

August 20, 2017

9:00 a.m.

She was one of a kind, at least in Cornwell, anyway.

Not only would no one have anything like her, no one would want anything like her, and that appealed to Poe as much as anything else about the glorious heap of junk that sat on four wheels in front of her.

Poe and the car salesman walked the length of the old recreational vehicle.

"What year is it?" she asked.

"Well, ma'am. It's a seventy-two."

"Nineteen seventy-two? Wow. My mama wasn't born yet."

"And see here . . ." He swept his hand along the long maroon stripe down the side. "It ends in the signature *W*. All Winnebagoes have 'em. No matter the model. This one here's a Brave."

The purple-hued paint had faded over the years, but she could still make out the model name, stamped in block letters. The name sent a thrilling chill up her spine.

"Brave. It's perfect."

"She's only eighteen feet long. A little longer than your average station wagon."

"Station wagon? What's that?"

He blinked in surprise. "Never mind. Don't matter. Just know that she's short, so she'll be easy to maneuver."

"I bet the engine's in horrible shape."

"No, ma'am. This thing's got a fully restored Dodge engine with an automatic transmission. It'll purr like a kitten."

Poe looked it over. Bit her lip. "She's the tackiest thing I've ever seen."

The salesman winced. "Well, I—"

"It's perfect."

He rubbed his chin and kicked a tire. "Now, of course I've gotta tell you that there's no return policy. Once you drive it off the lot, she's all yours."

Poe stepped inside and took it all in. No doubt it needed a little work. The golden mustard-yellow vinyl tile flooring, small apple-green oven and three-burner stove, and toilet and small shower stall needed some serious scrubbing; but the orange-leather driver and passenger seats were still in good condition, and the upholstered dinette seats were still firm and comfortable.

"Very retro," she muttered.

All in all, the Brave was a little worse for wear and more than likely wouldn't be accepted by anyone in town, but neither was Poe. Not anymore, anyway. They were perfect for each other.

"I'll take it."

After throwing down two thousand eight hundred dollars, Poe drove her Winnebago Brave off the lot and into the street. It took a bit of time to get going, but the speedometer eventually made it to thirty-five and it was smooth sailing the rest of the way home. It was only when she pulled "Winnie" into the driveway that the pair hit rough waters. While it might have only been eighteen feet long, it was still a little bit difficult to park in her usual parking spot. And when she applied the brake, it howled so loud that it brought her daddy onto the front porch.

"What is that thing?" Daddy asked after she climbed out.

"It's my new car," she said, proudly holding her head high.

"Your new car?" The only part of his face that wasn't beet red were the purple veins that bulged in the center of his forehead. "You can't be serious."

Poe slightly rotated her body as if she were modeling a new skirt. "Oh, but I am. I love her."

"You love her?" he groaned.

"I do, Daddy. It was love at first sight."

"It's a tin can on wheels!"

"You don't think she's cute?"

"Cute? Pay— Poe, it's the ugliest thing I've ever seen."

"So ugly she's cute? Sort of like Pugsley? So ugly you can't help but think she's adorable."

"Nothing like that. It's just plain ugly, and it can't be environmentally sensitive. I'm sure it's a gas guzzler."

"Daddy, I drive like five miles a day. That sucker has a twenty-five-gallon gas tank. It'll probably go a month or more between fill ups. Besides, you said I could pick whatever I wanted."

"I didn't think you'd pick *that*!"

Out of the corner of her eye, she watched Mama walk onto the front porch and stand next to Nana. While Nana didn't look the least bit surprised by Poe's selection, Mama appeared horrified. Her mouth hung open, and her eyes were wide and practically popping out of her head. Aside from some of her heavier crying fits, this was the most unattractive Poe'd ever seen her.

"Don't you dare tell me that you bought that thing," Mama finally managed to say. "Don't you say it."

"Okay, I won't."

"Did you? Did you buy it?"

"Yes, ma'am, I did."

"I told you not to say it!" Mama stormed off the patio and across the yard. "I am not gonna have my daughter driving around in a glorified bedroom on wheels. You'll have every boy in town thinking you're easy."

"Glorified bedroom? Mama, trust me, those couches are so nasty right now, I have no intention of sleeping on them."

"Who said anything about sleepin'?"

"And the hideaway bed over the driver's seat? There's only like a foot of space between the bed and the ceiling. There isn't room for anything else to happen. I don't think it would be humanly possible. Unless maybe you—"

"Not another word!" Poe jumped out of the way as Mama closed in on the vehicle, threw the small door open and stomped inside. "For the love of Pete! This is horrendous."

"Don't worry, I'll fix her up. She just needs a little cleaning, that's all."

"A little?"

Poe poked her head inside and watched her mama pace along the length of the floor, but was sure to keep a safe distance. Mama wrinkled her nose as she inspected the interior. "And what's that smell?"

"It's a little musty. She needs a chance to air out."

"Is that the bus?" Nana yelled from the patio.

Poe glanced over her shoulder. "No, ma'am. It's a Winnebago."

Nana shook her head and sulked. "I was hoping it was the bus."

Poe turned her attention to her daddy. They briefly made eye contact but she quickly looked away. Lately, she didn't like looking him in the eye. For every second he managed to hold her gaze, it felt like he was figuring her out. And she surely didn't want him to figure her out before she got a chance to.

"Payton Belle Brave . . ."

Poe knew she was about to get her butt handed to her. "Yes, ma'am?" she asked, hesitantly sticking her head back inside the door.

"I don't believe I need to tell you that I'm disgusted by this piece of junk."

"No, ma'am. I think I figured that much out on my own."

"I'm disappointed in you for taking advantage of us. We work hard for our money. We trusted you enough to let you go pick out the car on your own, and this is the thanks we get . . ."

Again, Poe jumped out of her mama's way when she bounded out of the RV and started to pace around the yard. Poe stepped inside and sat down at the dinette, where she could still see Mama's fury through the doorway or the window that sat above the table.

"After everything we've been through," Mama ranted. "You're gonna put us through this? It's like you've lost all common sense or . . ." She turned to face Poe, threw her hands on her hips, and glared at her daughter through the doorway. "Well?"

"What do you want me to say?"

"What's going on with you? We can talk about this."

"I like it," Nana shouted.

Poe beamed. "Thank you, Nana!"

"I can't believe you've gone and done this."

"Look, she only cost me two thousand eight hundred dollars. You gave me ten. I plan on using some of the money to fix her up, but I'll give the rest back."

"That's right you will," Daddy barked. "After that, any money spent on this car—or whatever it is—comes from your pocket. I'm not paying for the upkeep on this trash heap."

"Fine."

Mama looked over at her husband with her mouth hung open and her eyes wide and wild.

"What else can I do?" he mouthed.

"Tell her to drive it back to the lot," Mama whispered.

"I can totally hear you," Poe announced.

Her parents looked back at her.

"And there's a no-return policy."

"Of course there is." Mama's eyes rolled as she turned around and walked back toward the house. "I don't even wanna think about what the ladies from the club are going to say about this."

"Do what you gotta do," Poe said. "Say what you've gotta say."

"That's it!" Her mama spun back around, causing Poe to recoil. "I'm sick and tired of your horrible and disrespectful attitude. You're grounded for a week, and every time you open your mouth and even a syllable of sarcasm comes out, I'm adding another week. Do you hear me?"

"Yep."

"You may not like me, but I'm your mother, and you will respect me. You're gonna drive that thing to school and right back home. That's it. That's your life for the next week. You got me?"

"Yes, ma'am." Aside from the part about Winnie, that's what she'd already been doing over the last few days. Her punishment wasn't much of a punishment at all.

After Mama stormed back inside, Poe slowly turned back to her daddy. He stood staring at the monstrous vehicle. His brow

174

was heavily creased, and she knew that his opinion hadn't weakened. He hated her new car. With a passion.

"You're scaring me, Poe," he finally muttered. "I feel like I don't know you anymore."

She stepped out of Winnie and took his hand in hers. "It's just a car, Daddy."

He looked over at her and finally smiled. He always gave in, eventually. "I don't want to argue. So . . . give me the tour."

"She's only eighteen feet, so it shouldn't take long." They stepped into Winnie and stood in between the two couches. "The sales guy said that she's a little longer than a station wagon, whatever that is. And she's got a fully restored Dodge engine. I thought you'd like that. Everything's in working condition."

He opened the refrigerator and laughed, then looked around with a wistful look. "This is kinda cool. I probably would've killed for something like this when I was your age."

"Really?"

"It's like having your own apartment."

"Exactly. Wanna take her for a spin?"

"Sure. I drive."

She tossed him the keys and they simultaneously climbed into the front seats, like two young children about to take off on some wild adventure.

He pulled the lever, putting the car in reverse, and then turned to her. "Just promise me you're gonna be a good girl. That's all I ask."

"I promise."

"And no matter how comfortable this thing is, you'll come inside for a visit every once in a while?"

"Of course." She took a moment to crank up the charm.

"Especially if you'll let me start working in the office again. I'm gonna need the money for gas."

Her daddy chuckled. "Of course. Especially after the two beautiful services you just pulled off. You were magnificent, and the families were appreciative."

"Thanks."

He slowly backed out of the driveway, put Winnie in drive, and got going. "You know, we need to put a microwave in here."

"A microwave?"

"We can get you one pretty cheap if you want one."

"That would be great."

Daddy slowly pressed the brakes. They screeched until the vehicle came to a complete stop. "Brakes need some work. Have Brody look at 'em as soon as you can."

"Yes, sir."

He looked both directions, and then slowly drove through the intersection. "She actually drives pretty smooth."

Poe settled into her chair and looked over at her daddy. "You think Mama'll ever forgive me for this?"

"Of course. Your mama's a good woman, Poe. Maybe one day we'll get our lives back and you two can get to know each other again."

"I hope so."

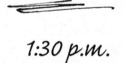

1:30 p.m.

Eventually, Daddy admitted that he'd accepted the fact that Winnie was going to be a part of their lives, but made sure to add that he didn't fully appreciate her, and he insisted that Poe park her in the alley beside the house.

"Poe," he hollered as he ran an extension cord from the house to the RV. "Now, you're more than welcome to use this to charge her up, but make sure she stays parked out of view from the funeral home parking lot. Or the driveway. Or the road."

She stood back and eyeballed the side alley from all directions. "Well, Daddy, that leaves me about twenty feet of space."

"Perfect." He strolled back inside and left Poe to stake her parking spot with two orange cones spray-painted black so they wouldn't look tacky.

Mama called that irony.

In the entire town, Poe knew there would only be one person who would appreciate Winnie's beauty the way she did.

As she sounded the foghorn-like horn while pulling onto Brody's property, she couldn't wait for him to lay his eyes on her new pride and joy. Sure, it wasn't like anything she'd ever loved before, but things had changed. She'd changed, and Winnie felt like the perfect addition to her new life.

Brody opened the large garage door and immediately laughed, just like she knew he would. Poe smiled and gave a proud thumbs up. He gave a thumbs up back, before he walked backward and guided her into the garage like he was directing a plane down the tarmac.

At a snail's pace, Poe managed to maneuver Winnie inside and stop just a few inches from a row of oil drums, plastic tubs, and metal shelves that separated the service bay from his tool station.

"I like her," he said with a smile, as she hopped out of the driver's side door. "I like her a lot."

"I knew you would. We're the only two that do."

"Only 'cause no one else has the great taste we do."

Poe kept an occasional eye on him while he meticulously inspected the RV, but she took a moment to look around his immaculate body shop.

"You've cleaned the shop up a lot since the last time I saw it."

"Yeah. My dad left it a mess. It took a while to get it all organized."

Every tool neatly hung in its own spot. Screws and small items were stored in plastic tubs, and there wasn't a speck of dirt on the floor.

She picked an automobile part up off his workbench and looked it over. "This looks sort of like a huge, mechanical heart pump. What is it?"

She felt him walk up behind her. "A carburetor." He reached around her and gently removed it from her hands and placed it back with such care that you'd think it was a priceless museum piece.

"What's it do?"

"It mixes the gasoline and air and makes sort of a combustible mixture . . . an energy, which is basically what runs your engine."

She reached for it again.

"Dispatch . . ."

The female voice caught her off guard, and made the hairs on her arms stand. She knew the voice. It was the same one that announced Dylan was missing.

"This is one-eight-one. Do you copy?"

She shook her head, dislodging the memory and forcing it to separate from what she was hearing in the present. "You listen to the police scanner?"

178

Brody pulled out his phone. "It's an app that lets you listen in to police and rescue scanners. I listen to it all the time. Don't you?"

"Uh, no."

"It helps me keep up with what's goin' on. If there's an accident or something, I can jump in the tow truck and head over. If I get there first, I get the business."

"Smart."

"Your daddy's helping me think bigger. He thinks if I focus, get more serious—"

"Dial back the partying . . ."

He nodded and rolled his eyes. "That too. Anyway, I can really make a go of the shop. You know, make something of myself. Maybe have some of the things you do."

She swept her hand in the direction of the RV. "Like this marvelous creature?"

He laughed. "Something like that. Yeah."

Brody scratched his head with his motor oil-stained fingers and turned back to Winnie. "I don't know, Poe. I thought you'd go for more of a sports car or something."

"I was in the mood for something new."

He raised an eyebrow.

"Metaphorically speaking."

"Oh. Okay. So, what did your parents say?"

She stared over at him. "Do you even have to ask?"

"I'd bet your mama is humiliated."

"She thinks the Women's Club council is going to give her a hard time."

"They will. And it'll be great."

They shared a laugh at her poor mama's expense.

"Does this thing have a name?"

"Winnie. Short for Winnebago."

"Perfect." He looked Winnie up and down. "Yep. I think she's got a lot of potential."

"I thought so too. A new paint job maybe? Do you think you could do that?"

"Sure." He walked around the RV with an inspecting eye. "Do you want the colors to go back to the original, or do you want to change them?"

Poe sat down on one of the oil drums that was laid on its side and rolled it back and forth under her legs. "I think I want it to stay the original colors. She's a classic. Why change her?"

"I'm with you. Especially if I can make her as good as new. If not better." He ran his fingers over the *W* and stripe that stretched the entire length of its side. "I'll do some research. Make sure I keep her true to her past."

"I knew you would."

He looked over at her and smirked. "Give me a tour of the inside."

She hopped off the oil drum, causing it to roll back a few inches, and bounded up the steps and inside.

He stepped inside behind her. "Classic yellow linoleum. Man, Poe, this thing is a beaut."

"Yep." She climbed in, peered over the driver's seat, and ran the angel pendant along the chain as he inspected the interior.

"Doesn't look like a whole lot of work is needed in here. Are you planning on changing any of this?"

"Nope. Just want to make sure everything is working. That's about it."

"Once I get the paint, it should only take me a few days to get it done."

"Good. This is the only vehicle I've got. I'd rather not have to drive one of the hearses around."

"I don't blame you for that." He glanced around the space again. "You've gotta real winner here, Payton, I mean, Poe." He opened the oven and looked inside. "Mind if I ask about the name change?"

"No, I don't mind." She rested her chin on the back of the driver's seat and thought about it for several seconds. "I didn't pick the name as much as it picked me."

He leaned against the stove, crossed his arms, and looked over at her, waiting.

"I don't know. I just . . . I think I needed a break from all the expectations. You know? Everyone knew exactly how Payton would act or what she would say, and Poe, she's a little more mysterious. Even to me. I don't know what I'll do or say because I just—"

"Do it. You don't second-guess anymore."

She was tickled that he got it so easily. "Exactly. I just do what comes naturally or feels right." She let her head fall back as she laughed at herself. "I don't know that I've ever done that before. It actually feels pretty amazing."

"I kinda get it. Everyone used to keep an eye on me when I played ball. I had to put on airs in case a recruiter was watching. But when things changed and ball ended, so did the attention."

"Were you relieved?"

Now he was the one laughing. "I don't know about that. I kinda liked all the attention. It was a little hard to go from hero to zero pretty much overnight."

"But you did it for the right reasons. To help your daddy."

"I guess." He rubbed the palms of his hands on his overalls,

181

cleared his throat, and took one more look around Winnie. "Anyway. She's great. Really great."

She realized she'd hit a sore spot, so she did what too many people weren't always willing to do with her. She didn't ask any more questions.

He leaned down and closely inspected the counter before he ran the tip of his finger over the surface. "She's scratched. When you bring her back, I'll buff that out."

"Sounds good." She turned around in her seat and started the engine. Then turned back to him.

"How much pressure do you have to use to scrape paint off a car?"

"Depends on what you use."

"Keys."

He rubbed his nose. "Um . . . I don't know. Why?"

"I came out of school one day and there was a key scratch in Lady Bug's door. Then, a few days later, I noticed a few more."

"How deep?"

"To the metal frame."

"Then it took some effort."

"Intentional effort?" she asked.

"Yeah. I don't think something like that would happen by accident. At least not twice."

She thought about his analysis for several seconds. "That's what I'm afraid of," she muttered. "Oh well. Lady Bug's gone now, so it doesn't make a difference."

"Okay, well . . . Need help backing this thing out of the garage?"

"I think I got it. That's why I didn't pull in all the way."

"All right." He took one last look around and then climbed

out. She waited until he approached her window. "Enjoy her, Poe. She's a one of a kind."

9:00 p.m.

Poe left Winnie parked in its spot between the two black safety cones, where it would be unnoticed by anyone who wasn't specifically on the lookout for it. She was close enough to the house for Mama not to fear that she was in any danger, but far enough away that she could get some privacy. And listen to hokey music extra loud if she felt so inclined.

Her newfound freedom left her feeling more energized and less weighed down. Like a burden was lifted and she was out from under the constant attention from her family and scrutiny of the people from town. And if she felt the pressure start to mount, she could escape inside Winnie's walls and hide away until she'd bottled up enough fortitude to face the outside world again.

But at the moment, she wasn't as much hiding away as she was decorating. And dancing. She taped photographs to Winnie's bathroom stall and sang at the top of her lungs while she simultaneously shook her hips and bobbed her head. If she'd been blessed with more space, she could've done the choreography to the dance numbers. She knew them that well.

"My dad probably has an opening at the bar if you're interested."

She nearly hit her head on a cabinet upon hearing Cole's voice. Once her heart slowed slightly, she tucked her head between her shoulders and turned to face him with an embarrassed cringe. "I'll give it some thought."

He chuckled for a few moments before mercifully changing the subject. "What is this crap you're listening to?"

"High School Musical Two . . . maybe three. Embarrassing, I know. Dylan and I used to watch the movies all the time. She had a crush on Zac Efron."

"I remember. I couldn't compete with a guy who could act, sing, dance, and look like that all at the same time."

"No. I think you won hands down." She felt her face flush. "Or at least that's what she told me."

He tugged on his ear and looked down at the yellow linoleum floor.

"Anyway, you won't tell anyone I was listening to it, will you?"

"No. I'm really good at keeping secrets." He looked around the interior. "I'd heard through the grapevine that you bought this thing, but didn't believe it."

"Surprise." Poe walked to the dinette, rested a knee on the couch, and tried to calm her nerves by biting her pinkie nail as she watched him take a few steps farther into the vehicle, lean forward, and closely inspect at a grouping of angels that she'd hung above the dinette. "What's with these?"

She shrugged. "They called to me for some reason." She pinched the angel pendent on her necklace between her fingers.

He glanced over his shoulder. "Called to you?"

"Yeah. You know, like they knew they belonged here or something. Angels became sort of our thing. Maybe they subconsciously connect me to Dylan somehow."

"Yeah."

She kept an eye on him as he scanned the dashboard, then looked at the bulkhead above the driver's seat where she'd taped a few articles about the disappearance of the other two girls.

"What's this?"

"Umm . . . research. I figured if I was gonna be spending so much time alone, I might as well spend it doing something productive."

He turned to her and cocked his head a little to the left. "What are you doing, Poe?"

"I'm just curious, that's all."

He raised an eyebrow and looked over at her, deadpan.

"Okay. Fine." She'd been caught and knew it. "I was at Brody's and heard his police scanner go off. I don't know, it . . . it just sort of took me back to sitting in the police car the day Dylan disappeared, and since I can't remember what happened in the bathroom, maybe if I dig around a bit and learn some more about the other girls, it'll dislodge something."

He walked to the kitchenette table, removed a stapler from the top of a file folder, and opened the flap. Inside were copies of all the articles written about her sister's disappearance.

"I haven't had a chance to hang those yet."

He picked up an article and closely studied the photograph of Dylan.

"So I've told you what I'm doing. Is it a secret as to why you're here?"

"No." He finally turned his attention back to her. "My mom had some questions about the flowers for the Norman funeral."

This time, she was the one not convinced, so she gave him the same cocked eyebrow, lifeless reaction he'd given her just a few seconds before.

He held his hands up in surrender. "Dylan would want me to check on you. Again. There. Happy now?"

"You're here because of Dylan?"

"Yes. And to find out about the flowers . . . and to make sure you aren't alone. At least not too much." They held eye contact for a brief moment before he looked back at Dylan's photo. "Do you plan on spending all your free time in here?"

"As much as my parents will let me. It's a lot better than hanging out inside the house, and they feel better thinking they're giving me a little more freedom, but in reality I'm just outside." She walked to the window and peered outside. "I even catch them watching me from the kitchen all the time. And I've seen Sheriff Jackson do a drive-by a time or two."

"Sounds about right." He carefully placed the article back on the table and picked up another. "I can't believe it's already been a year."

"I know."

She tried not to watch too intensely as he slid the articles back into the file and closed it. She found his sudden interest fascinating and a little unsettling. It came out of left field. Much like her attitude adjustment.

He surveyed the space. "It's kind of cool."

"It needs more work than I originally thought, and I want to make some new curtains and stuff. Dress her up a bit."

He lifted the cover of the stove and checked out the burners. "Need help with anything?"

The tingle in the tips of her fingers caused the roll of tape to slip from her grip, but she managed to catch it before it hit the floor. "You . . . you wanna help me?"

"Sure. We're both pretty much alone. Might as well be

alone together. Besides, what else have I got to do?" He opened the oven and peered inside. "Hearing her name—seeing her picture—makes me miss her even more . . . and all the fun we used to have together."

"Me too."

"Spending time with you reminds me of all of that. The fun we had."

Maybe if the two of them spent some time together, they'd miss her a little bit less. Or at least get to miss her together instead of suffering silently.

He looked over at her. "I think she would've liked Winnie. She'd be jealous you thought of her before she did."

"You think?"

"Yes."

"Maybe Winnie's like the angels, and I was drawn to her because I somehow knew Dylan would want her."

"It seems like you'll do anything to keep her memory alive."

"What choice do I have?"

"None. We don't have a choice."

Her eyes locked on his until she finally came to her senses and turned to hang another photograph. Her fingers tingled again, and it was nearly impossible to keep a grip on the tape. She wasn't sure why he was having such a crazy effect on her, but she chalked it up to Dylan needing her to keep him close.

"Are you any good with plumbing?" she asked over her shoulder.

"Why? What do you need done?"

"The kitchen sink is leaking. I don't plan to use it very much, but I don't want the wood underneath getting all wet and mildewed."

"I can look at it. See what I can do."

"That would be great. I don't wanna have to ask my dad. He and Mama think I made a mistake buying her. The last thing I plan to do is let them know I'm having any problems with her." She hung another photograph. "And I'd rather them not see all of this."

She heard him walk toward her. He stepped into the bathroom, stood behind her, and looked over her shoulder at the photos of Poe and her sister throughout their lives. The photographs nearly covered the old linoleum stall.

"More research?"

"I guess you could call it that." She looked over her shoulder at him. "Don't tell. Okay?"

"My lips are sealed."

"Thanks."

He leaned forward and closely inspected several of the photos, and once he was finished, her shoulder cooled when he walked away. "I've got my toolbox in the car."

Once he stepped outside, Poe leaned against the shower stall wall and sucked in a deep breath. She couldn't remember ever having a full conversation with Cole, let alone one that felt so raw. But as awkward as it should've been, it felt nice.

She didn't feel quite as alone.

He walked back inside carrying an old metal tool chest.

"You always have your tools with you?"

"I was a Boy Scout. Their motto is be—"

"Prepared. Yeah. I know."

They shared a smile, but within seconds he was at work under the sink. And while he might have preferred to work in silence, Poe couldn't let him. As far as she was concerned, silence was torture.

"Even if you thought Dylan would want you to check on me, you wouldn't have to do it more than once. And you certainly wouldn't have to be this nice to me. So . . . why? Why are you being so nice to me?" She didn't give him time to reply before continuing. "I mean, you and Dylan were the item. All that hooking up behind the flower shop and all."

"It was completely innocent."

"Innocent?"

He lifted his head out from under the sink and shrugged as his face turned pink.

"A little innocent fun?" she asked.

He leaned his back against the wooden cabinets and brought his knees to his chest. "I'm crazy about her; you know that."

"You are?" She slid down the bathroom door and sat on the floor. She knew it was true. Always had been. But there was something about hearing him say it that made her heart beat faster until it felt like a brick in her chest. She'd never stopped to think about what he'd lost when Dylan went missing.

He'd suffered a loss that came with the same heavy heart she lugged around each day.

"She's all I think about. We dated for what, almost two years? I may have only been sixteen, but I loved her . . . as much as a sixteen-year-old can love someone. Still do."

"Tell me—what was it you loved most about her? I always wondered."

"What don't I love about her? She's a one of a kind. There's nobody else like her."

"You talk about her like she's still alive."

His jaw tightened and the skin on his chin crumpled. "That's because I believe she is."

CHAPTER 17

August 21, 2017
2:40 p.m.

Poe stood outside her last class of the day, stared up at the sign above the door, and let out a hefty sigh that sent her bangs flying.

Zoology.

It was one of the classes Poe picked in order to fill her class schedule with subjects colleges would smile upon, rather than a bunch of fillers like office aid and library assistant as so many other seniors did. Plus, the promise of lab time was a better offer than classes that were nothing but lectures. Especially for the last class of the day.

After a full day of being ignored, and eating lunch alone in Winnie, she mustered up all the fortitude she could, walked into the room, and took a seat at her desk. Luckily, the general lethargy ailing everyone in the room meant that they didn't have enough stamina left for snide comments about her rusty vehicle, crazy name, or the near heavyweight-level boxing skills exhibited in her fight with Joshua.

"I need you all to stand up and break into pairs," Mr. Stein announced, causing everyone around her to groan. "They will be your partners for the next few weeks as we work on our fetal pig

190

dissections. We've got an odd number, so one of you will need to be a group of three."

The room instantly grew loud. She listened as everyone called out a friend's name and tried to convince them to come to their table so they wouldn't have to exert the energy required to walk twenty feet. She didn't fail to notice that her name never got mentioned.

She laid her head on her table and rolled her eyes at the giddy laughter from girls who were either genuinely excited about the experiment or pretending to be a damsel in distress in an attempt to get the attention of a male suitor.

"I didn't say get loud," Mr. Stein announced. "Get your partner and grab a table."

Poe watched everyone around her pair off and walk to a station. They went out of their way to look around her or through her, but never at her.

"Payton still needs a group," he said.

"Don't you mean Poe?" someone teased.

Cole looked over at her, the only face in the room that revealed even an ounce of sympathy. He reached his hand out to get Poe's attention, but Lindy slapped it back down. He scowled at her and then turned back to Poe. "Poe, you can—"

"You know what, Poe?"

Poe turned to the teacher, a bit shocked. Partly because he spoke directly to her, but more because he'd started using her new name. None of her other teachers were as willing.

"We've got an extra pig, and I haven't done a dissection in a while. Would you mind if I was your lab partner?"

Poe straightened up and leaned forward as the dread that had collected in her body seeped out her toes, and relief poured over her. "I wouldn't mind at all." She'd reached such a low that being the teacher's lab partner sounded appealing. It was better than being alone.

"Why don't we do that, then?"

She ignored the snickers from around the room and rose from her desk. "Where do I go?"

"We'll just clear off the end of my desk and do it right here. How about that?"

One of the boys laughed. "He asked her if she wanted to do it right there."

"What are you, twelve?" Poe snapped.

"Mind your business, Nathan," Mr. Stein demanded. "Someone from each team, grab a pan with a pig in it and take it back to your table." In one fell swoop, he walked over, grabbed one, and sat it on the desk. Not wanting to see the contents, Poe pretended to study an animal classification poster on the wall.

"You'll notice that the arteries and veins of your pig have been injected with a colored latex. So, the arteries are red and the veins are blue."

Poe finally looked down at the small pig. It was flat on its back, legs stuck in the air like it tipped over in the middle of a snowstorm, froze to death, and was plucked out of the pigpen before it had time to thaw. Its glueish-white flesh tone and the smell of formaldehyde was familiar to Poe, yet overwhelming in a new environment. She slightly parted her lips, tried to breathe through her mouth, and again raised her eyes to find something else to look at as she felt her body turn clammy and watched spots form in her line of vision.

Mr. Stein placed a pair of scissors in her hand, like she saw surgical assistants do when she watched medical shows.

."Step one. One of you go ahead and insert a blade of the scissor through the body wall on one side of the umbilical cord." He looked over at Poe. "Go ahead."

Poe peered up through her eyelashes and caught Joshua at work. He stabbed the pig with a violent blow before he ripped the skin apart. He was heartless. Sinister, even.

She lowered her focus back to the umbilical cord and tried to drown out the image of Joshua and Misty's dead child with its own umbilical cord still attached, and the body being laid to rest.

She aimed for the center of the pig's abdomen with the scissors, and when she'd managed to get it within millimeters of the cord, she closed her eyes and slid the blade inside as gently as she could manage.

"Continue cutting"—Mr. Stein's instructions boomed through the room, and bounced off the walls in a menacing echo—"posteriorly to the base of the left leg. Then, once you get that done, go ahead and start back at the original incision and cut down to the base of the right leg. Basically, what you want to do is create a flap of skin so that you can lay it back and expose the organs within the abdomen."

Poe did as she was instructed, but with every cut, every tear of the skin, her awareness dimmed—until there was nothing.

"Poe?"

She opened her eyes and found herself staring up at the ceiling. She'd never realized that several pencils hung lodged in the acoustical tile above them.

"Don't move," Mr. Stein instructed. "Give yourself a minute to come to."

Smelling salt fumes burned her nostrils, gave her a severe

ache deep in her eye sockets, which made it even more difficult to take in her surroundings and recall what occurred. "What happened?"

"You passed out," Mr. Stein said.

"How much time passed?"

Cole stepped into view and hovered over her. "You were only out a minute or two."

Her eyes traveled up his long legs, up his torso, and focused on his gray eyes. "I think I need to lie down," she slurred.

"You already are," Cole said.

"Oh." She rolled onto her stomach and looked across the room. The last of her classmates filed out of the room but most took a long look or a photo as they went. "Where's everybody going?"

"I dismissed them. They're enjoying this too much." Mr. Stein screwed the lid back onto the smelling salts and placed it on his desk. "It's all a little ironic. I mean, forgive me for pointing out the obvious, but . . . Poe, your dad's a mortician. There are dead people in your house on a continual basis. That's a lot worse than what we're doing."

"She's not allowed in the embalming room," Cole explained. "She's never seen a dead body. At least not before it's in the casket. Her mom won't let her."

Poe rolled onto her back. "I'm still lucid, you know. Don't talk like I'm not right here, even if I am a blob."

Cole sat on the floor next to Poe and felt her forehead. "Are you going to be able to walk to Winnie?"

"I'll be fine. You go ahead. Don't bother with me."

"No. I'm not leaving until you're okay. Your mom may not like me, but she'll dislike me even more if she finds out I left you stranded."

"What about this, Poe?" Mr. Stein asked. "For the rest of the lesson, I'll do the cutting, you color the pictures and do the labeling. Do you think you can do that?"

"I think I could manage that."

"I'll bring a pillow, just in case."

"And keep a bucket nearby," Cole added. "She tends to throw up when she gets too grossed out."

"You sound like you've learned that from experience," Mr. Stein said.

"I have." Cole stood up and looked down at Poe. "I've seen that gray tone to her face before."

Mr. Stein laughed. "Oh yeah?"

"When we were in the fourth grade and working on a project for school together. We needed to cut some cardboard boxes, so we were using steak knives—"

"Brilliant, right?" Poe muttered. "And we were obviously at Cole's house, 'cause my mama wouldn't ever let me play with knives. We had to be at Val's to do the dangerous stuff."

"Anyway, she dropped the knife, and it stabbed her at the very top of the space between her big toe and the next one over. You would've thought she cut a major artery the way she was carrying on. There were only like two drops of blood, but she saw them, turned gray, and puked all over everything. And even after that, she needed to lie down to keep from passing out. I ended up doing the rest of the project by myself."

Mr. Stein stood next to her head and stared down at her. "Do you think you can get up now?"

"Is the pig gone?"

"Yep. I put her away for the day."

"Then I guess I can." Poe sat up and got her equilibrium

balanced before she completely stood, though she still needed to latch on to Cole's shoulder to steady herself.

"I've got to get to practice. The team's gonna be waiting for me." He looked over at Cole. "You'll make sure she gets home okay?"

"Yes, sir."

Mr. Stein rushed off to the gym, leaving Poe to walk slowly out of the classroom and down the hallway while Cole walked along beside her.

"Can't you park that thing somewhere else?" a student shouted as they arrived at the lot. "It's ugly as sin."

Poe rolled her eyes at the comments, but they didn't stop. She kept her head held high. Or as high as she could without it making her want to vomit.

"I can't believe we're gonna have to walk past this piece of garbage every morning."

"At least mine's paid for," she shouted, albeit a bit garbled, before she and Cole sailed the rest of the way on the wave of their insults.

Cole gripped her elbow and helped her stay upright as she slipped in the key and unlocked the door. "I feel drunk."

"You *look* drunk," he admitted. "Good news, though. You don't look gray anymore."

"Yay me," she slurred.

"You look green. And I look like I'm about to take you inside and hold your hair while you puke into the toilet."

"Don't give me any ideas."

He helped her up the steps and far enough into the living area for her to fall onto the couch. "I take it I'm driving?"

She slightly lifted her head up off the cushion. "Do I look like I can drive to you?"

"Right." She watched him turn and eye the decades-old dashboard. "At least it's an automatic transmission."

"Just take it slow."

Cole hopped into the driver's seat, and soon she heard the engine begin to turn over. The starter threw a bit of a fit, but eventually the vehicle hummed. He looked over at her, panicked. "Wait, there's no rearview mirror."

"Use your imagination."

She felt the vehicle slowly back up and then jolt to a stop before he threw it in drive. "How did you learn to drive this thing? It's huge."

"Not much longer than the hearse, really."

"You drive the hearse?"

"Only when Daddy's desperate."

Winnie came to a stop at the end of the lot with another lurch. Cole turned on the blinker, and waited for several seconds before he slowly pulled Winnie onto the street and headed toward Magnolia Road.

"You keep going over bumps and I really will throw up."

"Poe, this thing's forty-five years old. The road isn't bumpy; you just don't have any shock absorbers. I'm doing the best I can."

She pulled her feet off the ground to put them on the cushion, but just before they reached the couch, she felt the back tire hitch over a curb, and the jarring tipped her over and left her sprawled out on the floor on her stomach. "Cole!"

"Sorry." He glanced back at her for a split second and smirked, seemingly enjoying her misery. "Sorry."

She folded her hands one on top of the other and rested her cheek on top. "Par for the course."

"What do you mean by that?"

"Everything in my life feels off balance." She slowly pulled herself onto her knees, crawled to the front of the vehicle, and climbed into the passenger seat.

"Feel any better?" he asked.

"It was the smelling salts. They made me sick to my stomach." She somehow managed to look out the window without becoming nauseous, although the passing cars made it difficult. "Hey, can we make a stop real quick?"

"Sure. Where?"

She looked over at him and squinched her nose. "You won't judge me?"

"No."

"Or lecture me?"

"Uh . . . I don't think so."

"Okay. Turn left."

Cole followed her order and pulled Winnie onto the main drag. He glanced over at her. "I won't need to ask my dad to blackmail someone to get you out of jail again, will I?"

"Nope. Turn right at the corner."

"'Cause if you're going to do something that will raise eyebrows, I should at least get fair warning."

"Cole, I promise. It's nothing illegal or eyebrow raising."

Cole turned Winnie right at the corner, and the bus station came into view. His jaw turned granite.

"Pull in across the street."

"Why?"

She ignored his question. "Face the station."

He winced and shook his head, but did as she asked. "Please don't tell me you do this on a regular basis."

"Not at all." She pulled out her phone, opened her note

app, and tried to act completely unsuspecting. "I like to people watch."

"You like to people watch? Really? You're going to bring me here and then lie about why?"

She rolled her eyes toward him and shrugged. "It's a little twisted, I know."

"What do you hope to find?"

"I don't know. Something or someone that seems out of place."

"The photos, the news articles. You're really taking all of this seriously."

"I have to try to figure out what happened. I'll do whatever it takes."

"And that includes stalking the bus station?" Cole leaned forward, laid his arms across the large steering wheel, and rested his chin on his arm as he stared out at the station. "Any luck so far?"

"Truth be told, I've only been by once—on my way home from the hospital. Some people got off but got back on. I didn't recognize any of them."

"And locals?"

"Not someone who doesn't belong, or wouldn't have a completely justified reason for being here." She handed him the phone. "I wrote these names down last night. They're the people I remembered recognizing the other day."

Cole scrolled through the short list of names. "Are you planning to share this with the police?"

"There's nothing to share. It's just the names of people I saw at the bus station."

He handed the phone back. "You don't need to do this. They

199

just told us more girls have gone missing and they think the cases are connected. That means this is a hot case again. You may not see it, but they're working it."

"Good. So am I." Poe looked back at the bus, but her mind was elsewhere. There was a new determination sweeping through her body. She's been idle long enough. Feeling more and more comfortable in her skin helped her to find her fight. For the first time in a year, she felt energized rather than drained.

Once the bus pulled away, she turned to face Cole again. "What can it hurt for me to see what I can find out?"

"You. You could get hurt."

"I won't get hurt."

"You can't guarantee that."

He was right and she knew it, but that fact didn't matter. There was no way she could keep ignoring the voice in her gut telling her to search. "Then just trust me."

Cole put Winnie in reverse and pulled out of the parking lot. "If you feel like you need to watch, text me. We can come in my truck."

Poe looked over at him again, startled by the fact that he was volunteering his time to help. For someone who'd hardly spoken to her in well over a year, he'd availed himself to her more and more the last few weeks.

"Why are you doing all this, Cole?"

"I want her back too."

CHAPTER 18

August 23, 2017

6:50 a.m.

Poe was a woman on a mission. On a search for answers. And since she couldn't go unnoticed in a contraption like Winnie, she parked in the alley behind the coffee shop, slipped inside to grab a cup of coffee, and then casually walked to the bakery that sat cattycorner to the bus station. There, she could sit in one of the white wicker chairs beside the front window and witness all the travelers' comings and goings.

She realized that if her mission wasn't so morbid, it could've been an interesting, and maybe even beautiful, field trip. Life for Payton had been busy, each obligation and event another wave she got caught up in. For the last year, she'd kept so close to her family and friends that she'd almost forgotten that there was an entire civilization of people who went around and lived their lives outside the Brave funeral home doors.

Poe had just adjusted her oversized sunglasses when a woman with a small child on one hip, and pushing a stroller with her free hand, suddenly ran toward the bus and arrived in time to see another woman exit. They greeted each other with an excited squeal and all-encompassing hug that looked like it could nearly squish the breath out of the child in her arms. The sight caused Poe to raise an eyebrow. She was so desperate to bury the bad that she'd kept failing to see any good.

The new arrival smothered the small child in kisses, then reached into the stroller, pulled out an infant, and repeated the smooch fest.

I bet they're sisters, and she's seeing her niece and nephew for the first time.

The thought caused an ache in her chest. Momentarily, her mind reminded her that there was a great likelihood she would never have such a moment with Dylan. She might never have nieces and nephews to smother in affection.

A pebble of a lump started to form in her throat and she felt the tears try to break through. She quickly put on her sunglasses, cleared her throat, and stared intensely at the bus, hoping that her hyper-focus would shove her emotions out of the way.

As the Atlanta bus passengers made their way inside, and out of her view, Poe forced her eyes to wander over the building's exterior. Just as the image of the two sisters greeting each other started to reenter her mind, she turned her thoughts to the bus station. It hadn't changed much since it was built in the fifties. The town took special care to ensure that it kept its nostalgic charm. It reminded her of a Norman Rockwell painting, only it was being trampled on by modern-day citizens going about their day, most with no clue as to what took place in the rear bathroom stalls.

How could they? Poe herself wasn't even sure.

Lost in thought, she startled when her cell phone vibrated on the chair next to her. *Lemme guess. Mama.*

Sure enough, when she checked her phone, it was a text from her mama. Where are you? I missed you at breakfast.

As annoyed as she was by the fact that it was her mama, she appreciated the interruption.

Needed some help on Calculus. She winced at her lying. Came to school early to work on it.

Poe stared at the three dots on the screen and anticipated her mama's response. Okay. Btw—you missed your dentist appointment again.

Poe rolled her eyes. Sorry. I didn't get the reminder for some reason.

That part wasn't a lie. The appointment completely slipped her mind. Again.

I give up. See you when I get home.

Poe winced at the disapproval hidden in her mother's words, then turned on her calendar app and looked for the appointment. *Not there.*

She thought back to her argument in the kitchen with her mama and remembered adding the appointment to the calendar, but where it went from there, she had no idea.

Readjusting her sunglasses, she looked back out at the bus station and watched the Charleston bus pull in. Three men got off and quickly went inside, then a male in his twenties climbed down the bus steps and stood on the pavement.

Poe sat forward and peered over at him. The young man wore blue jeans and a sweatshirt, which made no sense whatsoever. August was one of the hottest months of the year, and he had to be sweltering under all those clothes. She squinted her eyes, trying to improve her vision well enough to see his eyes. They would tell her a lot. She wanted to see if his focus darted around the parking lot, or stayed fixated on anything in particular.

He was bulky enough to be able to commandeer a teenaged girl. Especially one that wasn't paying attention, or didn't find him the least bit alarming.

In a quick moment, Poe raised her phone and took several photographs of the visitor.

Through the screen on her phone, she saw him turn her direction. Her bones froze. Her heart thumped in her chest. She stood, and took a step his direction, ready to get a closer look and ask questions if necessary.

"Imagine finding you here."

Poe's phone slipped out of her hand and dropped to the ground. She looked over her shoulder with a frightened grimace. "Cole," she squeaked. "What are you doing here?"

"Sightseeing." He took a swig out of his bottled water, and looked proud of himself, like he'd figured something out that he could be haughty about. Even if only for a few seconds.

As she reached down to pick up her phone, her attention turned back to the guy from the bus. She caught his line of vision shift as he swung around, held up his arm, and assisted an elderly woman as she stepped down from the bus. He even held on to her hand and walked carefully alongside her as they made their way inside.

Although she couldn't see what they did once they made it into the air-conditioned building, she imagined that he helped the woman purchase a snack, and waited for her as she used the restroom. The normal things a grandson or aide would do.

"I'm not doing anything wrong," she muttered.

"Never said you were." He spun the white bottle cap around his finger and watched her with a smirk. "Correct me if I'm misremembering something here, but I thought we agreed that if you were going to start doing this, we'd come in my truck."

"I didn't want to wake you."

"I was already up for school."

"And I didn't want you to be late for class."

"Nice try, but you're not as good a liar as you think." He looked across the street and watched the travelers for several seconds. "Well, since we're going to be late anyway . . ." He fell into the seat across from her at the small table. "So tell me, what were you going to do if you actually saw something . . . or some-one? Chase them down? Call 911? You don't even know what you're looking for."

Seeing as how she couldn't argue, she took a long, loud sip of coffee and stared at the line of people loading back onto the Charleston bus.

"You're over here taking photos of people like you're with the CIA or something."

She scowled over at him. "How long have you been standing there?"

"Long enough to make sure you weren't about to do some-thing really stupid. Looks like I showed up just in time." He leaned across the table. "Let's just say, for the sake of argument, that this guy is here and roaming around, and he sees you sitting here and realizes you're trying to figure out who he is. How do you think that's going to go down?"

Another long sip.

"You don't think that might tick him off? And, I don't know, cause him to lash out at you . . . or someone else."

She set the cup down and turned to him. "I don't know, Cole. I'm a little new at this."

"Exactly my point."

A truck backfired across the street, causing Poe and Cole to scoot farther down into their seats, and her heart to briefly stop beating, or at least feel like it did.

"This is crazy," he muttered. "What are we doing?"

"We're looking for something that will dislodge my memories. I'm locked up in more ways than you could possibly imagine. It's like the majority of my life is gone. Hidden away somewhere . . ." She picked up her coffee and took another long sip, but it was more to gather her thoughts than avoid his line of questioning. "When I was here the other day, I felt the fog lift a little bit. Like maybe there's a chance I can remember if I just put myself in the right situation."

"Danger? Is that the right situation?"

She sighed. "Not if I can help it." She held her coffee cup to her bottom lip and let the steam warm her face even more than the Mississippi heat managed to do. "But if I don't figure this out, I don't know if I can survive it."

"Poe, I'm on your side. I just don't think you're going about this the right way. You're putting yourself out there. At risk."

"If he's out there, I'm already at risk."

He bent over at the waist, rested his elbows on his knees, and stared at the ground. She wondered if he was watching the ants that scurried out of an anthill situated between his tennis shoes. They seemingly had his full attention.

She stared at him. Really studied him. They hadn't held more than a handful of conversations in all of their seventeen years, yet here he was, again. "You want her back," she eventually said. "That's why you're suddenly around all the time?"

He looked up at her. His eyes were tight and his forehead became heavily grooved. "What are you asking me?"

"I'm asking you if you're hanging around so much because you want to help find my sister."

"Or . . ."

"Or if you have ulterior motives."

He sat up and fell against the seat back with a thud. "Are you accusing me of something?" There was a tone in his voice that was so new to her that she couldn't make it out. Possibly anger, or hurt. Maybe a mixture of both. "Do you think I could've hurt your sister?"

She tucked her ear to her shoulder and partially shrugged. "No."

He walked away from the table, toward his truck. "That didn't sound convincing."

CHAPTER 19

August 13, 2016

6:00 a.m.

It felt cooler than usual. Low seventies that early in the morning meant a storm was about to blow through. Dylan could hear the wind pick up in velocity. An eerie echo, and what sounded like waves and slapping water, played in the background of her dream.

Certain she was having the start of a weird nightmare, she snuggled deeper into the softness surrounding her. *Odd, I can even smell a storm coming.*

Dylan's phone rang, forcing her awake, and she realized what she'd sensed wasn't part of a dream at all; the fabric against her legs had the familiar scratch of the cushions often in the back of Cole's truck, and the pillow beneath her head felt a lot like Cole's chest. On the third ring, she reached out to where she figured her phone must be, but Cole didn't budge. Without his hearing aids in, he probably hadn't even heard her squeak when she awoke.

Barely opening her eyes, Dylan held the phone to her ear and answered. "Yeah?"

"Mama's going to kill you if she finds out you stayed out all night with Cole." Dylan reluctantly sat up and wiped her eyes as she listened to her sister somehow scream and whisper simultaneously. "We have to leave for the bus station in less than an hour, and I hear Mama up and moving around downstairs."

A groggy and only half-listening Dylan checked to make sure Cole still hadn't woken up. He hadn't.

"We wanted to stay up to watch the sunrise. Must've fallen asleep. No big deal. Nothing happened."

"No big deal? She'll be up here any minute!"

Dylan carefully reached for her flip-flops and slipped them on her cold feet. "I'm heading home right now. Okay?"

"You best hurry!"

"I am."

"I will not cover for you, do you hear me? I won't lie for you."

"You won't have to. I'll be right there." Dylan hung up the phone, collected her belongings, then leaned over and kissed Cole on the temple.

She was just about to climb out of the truck bed, but stopped and turned to write "I love you" in the moisture on the rear window before she slipped out of the back and disappeared into the mist.

10:07 a.m.

Cole stood at the counter of his mama's flower shop, added up the receipts from the day before, and then looked at his to-do list for the day. Two small weddings, a funeral, and three birthday parties meant that he'd spend most of his time making deliveries. But a crazy-busy day was good for such a small business, so the hours behind the wheel were worth it.

He felt a smile grow across his face as he thought about the night before, and the note he'd found from Dylan on the truck window when he'd woken up that morning. Though he could have done without the momentary jolt of fear when he'd rolled over to talk to Dylan and found she was no longer in the truck bed with him.

The front door opened, and a chime alerted that someone entered the small, flower-filled shop.

Cole placed the receipts in the drawer of the cash register, closed it up tight, and turned up his hearing aids. "Sheriff Jackson. How can I help you?"

"Cole, have you seen Dylan around today?"

Cole cocked his head and furrowed his brow. There was a slim chance Laurie Brave found out about the accidental sleepover, but he doubted she'd call the sheriff if she did. Laurie may hate him, but she'd come over herself to chew him out and make sure to bring Dylan to witness it. "Dylan? No. She's heading to Charleston with Payton and Nana."

"Right."

"They left this morning on the bus."

"Were you there? When they left?"

Cole shook his head, then placed his pen on the glass counter and walked to the refrigerator. "No." He opened the cold door, pulled out a small bouquet, placed it on the counter in front of him, and started to wrap the neck of the vase with gingham ribbon.

"Unfortunately, I'm not here to make small talk about your girlfriend. I'm here on official business."

Cole stopped working on the flowers and looked up at the sheriff. "Something wrong?"

"Could be."

Cole tried to swallow again, but discovered his throat refused to cooperate. Soon, the anxiety rushed through his veins, leaving his body feeling hollow and empty. "What? What's wrong with Dylan?"

"We don't know if anything's wrong. We just need to find her."

"What do you mean, 'find her'? She's with Payton and Nana."

Sheriff Jackson shook his head. "No. Payton and Nana are at the bus station, and have been since this morning, when Dylan somehow disappeared from sight."

"Disappeared from sight? Where'd she go?"

"That's what I'm here to find out."

"I haven't actually seen her today. I—"

"Did you talk to her at all? By text, maybe?"

Cole pulled his phone from his pocket, unlocked the screen, chose the stream of texts with Dylan, and handed it to the sheriff. "We texted a few times this morning."

The sheriff scanned the messages, which Cole knew were nothing but small talk. Dylan had grumbled about having to take the nasty bus, so he'd encouraged her to enjoy her time with Nana, seeing as how she might not be around in a few years, and there were a few *I love you*s and hearts. "Can I make copies of these? Email them to myself?"

"Of course." Cole wiped his moist hands on his jeans. A mixture of the condensation from the vase just out of the refrigerator and the sweat that now formed all over his body. "You're serious? She just up and disappeared?"

"I'm serious."

"And she was definitely at the bus station with her nana and Payton?"

"That's what we've been told."

Cole finally managed to swallow and blinked in shock.

The sheriff was still focused on the phone as Cole rushed toward the door.

"Son, where do you think you're going?"

"To look for Dylan."

"No sir," Sheriff Jackson barked. "You'll stay here to answer questions."

"But—"

The sheriff's jaw tightened, and his eyes narrowed. Cole considered heading for the station anyway, but thought better of it and slowly walked back to the counter.

"This is all the communication you've had with her this morning?" He pressed a few buttons, then handed the phone back to Cole.

"Yes, sir. I couldn't see her off at the station because my mom had some appointments with customers. I had to open the store."

"Can anyone verify that?"

Cole's mouth turned dry. The room grew spotty. "Um . . ." His mind was suddenly blank. "Um . . . We've had a few customers." He opened the cash register drawer, pulled out the day's receipts, and laid them on the counter. "I think someone was here around eight."

The sheriff slid the receipts off the counter and shoved them into his small notebook. "I'll make copies and get them back to you." He turned and marched toward the door. "We'll talk again soon."

"Yes, sir." Cole looked around the shop, stunned and not even sure what to do. As his eyes darted around, he spotted the surveillance camera in the corner. "Sheriff Jackson."

The sheriff turned to him, still wearing an expression Cole couldn't read, as hard as he tried. "Yeah?"

Cole pointed to the camera. "If you need proof I was here, we have footage. I swear, I've been here since seven this morning."

The sheriff let out a sigh of relief. His face softened. It was the first moment since he entered the store that showed any hint of concern . . . or empathy. "I can't tell you how glad I am to hear that."

Cole took a few steps toward the sheriff. "She's really gone?"

Sheriff Jackson offered a single nod. "Don't go lookin' for her. If you happen to come across her in a bad state . . ."

Cole felt the room begin to wobble around him. "A bad state? As in . . ."

"It just wouldn't look good. Stay put."

Cole shoved his hands in his pockets and nodded.

"Just pray, Cole. That's all we can do right now." He opened the door, causing another cheerful chime to ring out. "I'll be in touch." He walked out the door and left Cole standing alone.

He pulled his cell phone out of his pocket and dialed.

A voice on the other end answered. "Hey. What's up?"

"Misty?"

"Yeah?"

"Dylan's gone."

CHAPTER 20

August 23, 2017

8:28 a.m.

Within minutes of their argument at the coffee shop, Poe pulled Winnie into her parking spot at school, hopped out, and jumped in front of Cole as he walked by on his way inside the school building.

"I wasn't accusing you of hurting her, Cole. I never would."

He lowered his eyes to the ground and drank the rest of his water, but slowly, as if he couldn't swallow.

"Honestly. You loved her—"

He swallowed. "Love. Present tense."

Suddenly, she was the one swallowing hard. She'd heard him talk about how there was no past for him and Dylan. As far as he was concerned, they were still very much in the present, but something about his insistence, his faith in her return, was striking.

"I wasn't accusing you of doing something, I was accusing Daddy."

Cole lifted his head and stared over at her with his mouth wide. "Your dad," he eventually managed. "What would he have done?"

"He asked you to watch over me, didn't he? That's why you're hanging around. He figures you're the only one who hasn't completely shunned me, and since Brody doesn't go to school with us, who better to keep an eye on me than you?"

Possibly a bit relieved, Cole managed a small, guilty grin. "Look, he did ask, but I planned on keeping you company anyway. Like I said, it seems like you're the only person who wants answers as bad as I do."

"Is he paying you?"

"No."

Poe glared over at him. She knew her daddy too well. He wouldn't hesitate to toss a little money someone's way if he thought it meant his girls would be happy . . . or safe.

"He offered . . . and it was a lot of money too. But I turned it down. I honestly want to help in whatever way I can."

The bell rang out across the parking lot.

"You really want to know how you can help?" she asked.

"Of course."

She watched the stream of people exit the main building in a race to get to their next class in one of the adjacent structures. "Can you help me survive them?"

"I can try, but they're pretty hostile."

"Tell me something I haven't already experienced."

"Well then, let's get to it."

"All right! We will," she laughed, and then turned and walked back toward Winnie. "In just a minute."

"Nope." He grabbed her by the arm and swung her around. "Why make them wait for the big show?" Cole lightly shoved her in the direction of the entrance and stayed close to her side as they walked toward the school building. He shoved his hands in his pockets and whispered into her ear, "Keep your head up. Never let them know they're getting to you."

215

She nodded, tilted her chin up a bit and forged ahead, looking people in the eye with a smile as she passed. The smiles were earnest. They weren't going to get to her, and her smile proved it.

In return, she mostly got an eye roll or sneer, but every so often someone would smile back, and she was able to find some humanity among her classmates.

It was only once they got inside the building that Cole removed his right hand from his pocket and placed it on the small of her back. Even through her T-shirt, his touch warmed her skin.

His gentle touch, and leading through the hall continued until they came to a stop outside her Literature class. He leaned toward her and put his lips to her ear. "Sit up straight, head high, and—"

"Hey, Poe, Cole." Kasi walked up with a wide, bright smile.

Cole turned to her with a glimmer in his eye. "Hey, Kasi. You're in Poe's lit class, right?"

"Yeah. I sit right in front of her."

"Perfect. Can you do me a favor?"

"Of course."

"Make sure she doesn't let them get to her and she keeps her head held high." Cole peeled away and walked toward his class without a look back.

Kasi looked over at Poe with wild, thrilled eyes. "I can totally do that."

Together, the girls walked into the classroom and took their seats just as the bell rang again.

Poe glanced down at Kasi's pants and realized that they, like the pair she'd noticed a few weeks ago, were stapled at the hem.

Kasi leaned back and turned her head to the point she could look over her shoulder at Poe. "I love your new car, by the way. I think it's the coolest thing I've ever seen."

Poe sat up, suddenly more comfortable. "Really?"

"Absolutely."

"If you like the outside, you'll love the inside. You should come check it out."

Kasi spun around and faced her. "Really?"

"Sure. Cole and I will be out there during lunch, if you want to join."

"That would be amazing." Kasi turned around in her seat, then immediately spun back to Poe. "You know? Dylan would love it."

11:50 a.m.

It took her the entire first half of the day, but Poe managed to figure out how to ignore everyone around her and just exist. School used to be a social event, now it was all business. Kasi or Cole checked on her between classes, and Kasi waited for her outside of Economics so she could walk with her to lunch.

She and Kasi walked over to Winnie and found Cole leaning against the faded burgundy-striped side panel. Several pouches hung on his shoulder.

"You found my daddy's pop-up chairs, huh?"

"Sure did." He swung them off his shoulder and tossed them to the ground. "They were a great idea."

"I didn't think so when he bought him. I figured I'd be eating alone every day."

217

Kasi practically beamed over at her. Her attitude, infectious. "Looks like you thought wrong."

Poe glanced around the campus at the hundreds of students milling around. "Why sit inside this thing when we can sit outside and enjoy the nice weather? Plus, it's more fun to endure ridicule when you can look right at the people when they're doing it."

Cole set up the pop-up chairs for the girls and then sat in Winnie's open doorway.

Kasi gave Winnie a long visual inspection. "You never really seemed like the old, rusty, obnoxious vehicle type of girl. This is so different than your other car."

"I never thought I was that type of girl either, but I took one look at her and knew we were meant to be."

Kasi laughed. "Really?"

"Yeah. She sat in the corner all by herself; almost like they put her over there knowing nobody would want to take a look. Part of me felt sorry for her and a part of me understood her somehow."

"It's a car," Cole said.

"Don't let Winnie hear you say that. You'll hurt her feelings." Poe glanced down at the hem of Kasi's pants as she brought her sandwich to her mouth. She stopped before taking a bite. "So, Kasi, what do your parents do?"

"My daddy works at the water treatment plant during the day. At night, he manages the coffee shop over on Main. And you may or may not know, but my mama left us when I was eight."

Cole and Poe exchanged a quick glance.

Poe swallowed hard. "You're right. It happened so long ago

that I'd forgotten. And . . ." She wracked her brain for more memories. "You have brothers."

"I have two little brothers." Kasi scooped out a spoonful of yogurt, flipped the spoon over, stuck it in her mouth, and left the spoon against her tongue.

"They were pretty young when she left. Right?" Cole asked.

Kasi pulled the spoon out and gave it a lick. "About six months and eighteen months old. Her note said she wasn't ready to be a mother. Course, neither was I, but that's what I ended up being anyway. An eight-year-old mother of two babies." She plunged her spoon back into the yogurt and gave it a stir. "That's why you don't see me around after school much. I'm usually dealing with the boys."

"That's tough," Poe said.

Kasi shrugged, seemingly not fazed by her reality. "They're older now, so it's getting easier. I can't wait until next year."

"What's next year?" Cole asked.

"College. Daddy said he's saved up all his coffee shop money and I can go to a school as long as it's in-state. He's gonna stop working the night job and be home for the boys. I don't know if I'll know what to do with myself, not having kids to look after all the time."

Poe focused on Kasi's pant hem as she talked. Much like those silver staples holding the material together, Kasi was keeping her tattered family from falling apart. Poe hoped Kasi was doing a better job at it than she could. All the maneuvering and acting in the world hadn't helped the Braves heal any faster. They were hanging on by a thread—or tiny silver staple.

Just as Poe did moments before, Kasi looked around the school campus, and her head paused in the direction of everyone milling around the picnic tables just south of the parking lot; except, unlike Poe, she seemed more in awe than disgust. "I've never actually eaten out here before."

"Why?" Cole asked.

"I wasn't ever invited." There wasn't a hint of disappointment in her voice. She said it so matter of fact that Poe couldn't help but take her in. Study her. Like Cole, it seemed Kasi accepted her place in life and didn't wish for different. Maybe she never pined away to be a part of the in-crowd like so many others did—and now that Poe was on the outside looking in, she understood why.

There was freedom in being on the outs. An exemption from the added expectations.

Kasi wasn't someone to be pitied, she was someone to admire.

Kasi scraped the last bit of yogurt out of the container and scanned the parking lot. "Oh, sweet baby Moses on a cracker."

"Who . . . on a what?" Poe asked.

"Alex Gates just drove by."

Poe stretched her neck to try to see the car drive past.

"Is that an old Chevy?" Poe asked.

"Yep," Kasi said. "He's elevated the social acceptance of Chevys just 'cause he's driving one. That boy is so good-looking that everything's sexier when he's associated with it. If he touches it, holds it, looks at it, eats it, drinks it, or in any way pays it a bit of attention, it's automatically freakin' earth-shatteringly amazing."

"Then he needs to hang out at Winnie. Maybe he'd make us acceptable."

Kasi frowned. "Sadly, the exclusion of us and Winnie were implied with that rambling list."

Poe scrunched her nose. "I should probably be surprised by that, but I'm not. I don't think we're redeemable at this point. But, you're right, that boy could wear a dog food bag and he'd still look good."

"Do you have to discuss this?" Cole barked.

Poe put her hand on her knee and turned to Cole with a fake glare. "What would you rather discuss?"

"Anything but that."

"Name one thing," Poe ordered.

"Nope."

"Just one, Cole. Humor me."

He stopped pulling chips out of his sandwich bag and turned his face to hers. "You're going to hate to hear this, but I wasn't put on this planet to humor you."

Poe thrust her hands onto her hips. "Wanna bet?"

They shared a playful grin, then went back to eating their lunch, but Poe snuck a glance at him from time to time. And at least once, she realized Kasi caught her.

"So, you said your daddy works at the coffee shop?" Poe asked, in an attempt to turn Kasi's attention away from noticing her attention on Cole. "Think he can get me a discount?"

"Sure. He could get you just about anything you want."

Poe started to throw the last of the chip crumbs into her mouth but suddenly stopped all motion when her brain latched on to an idea. One much more serious than scoring an occasional free latte. "Anything?"

"Within reason, of course." Kasi raised one eyebrow. "What?"

"Can he find out who ordered my coffee a few weeks ago?"

Cole perked up at the question.

"Why do you need to know?" Kasi asked.

"Yeah," Cole said. "Why do we need to know?"

Poe stared at Kasi for several seconds, contemplating whether or not she could tell her the truth, and quickly determined it was worth the risk. "I'm trying to remember what happened the day my sister disappeared."

"And how will a coffee receipt help that?"

Cole leaned even farther forward. His posture was curious. Anxious, even.

"I don't know for sure that it will. But . . . someone anonymously ordered me a coffee."

Kasi became almost as alert as Cole. "Okay . . . and . . ."

"And . . . I'm trying to find out if the person who sent it to me might have something to do with Dylan's disappearance."

Kasi's eyes widened. "You think he lives here? He was in my daddy's store?" Her body rotated back and forth in her seat as she inspected the school grounds. Only now did she appear intimidated by what surrounded them.

"I doubt it, but I would at least like to rule the person out. Ya know? Get some peace of mind."

"If it'll help figure out what happened to Dylan, I'm sure Daddy will try to get you the receipt. If he knew when and about the time the order was made—"

"I can tell you exactly." Poe pulled her cell phone out of her back pocket, opened her Twitter account, and found the tweet. It was easy to find, since she hadn't tweeted since. "August eleventh. Ethan delivered the coffee just before school started. He delivered a triple shot, half sweet, nonfat caramel macchiato."

Kasi's eyebrows jumped. "Wow. That's pretty specific."

"Exactly."

"Text all of that to me. I'll ask him to look into it tonight."

The bell rang overhead.

Kasi jumped to her feet and started a battle with the pop-up chair. It put up a great fight. "Stupid thing. I've got to get to my locker."

"You go." Cole walked over and took the chair from her frenzied hands. "I'll take care of this. We'll meet you at class."

"Thanks." Kasi scampered away and left Poe and Cole in a heavy silence as he folded up the chairs and slipped them back into their protective pouches.

"That morning I tweeted that I was running too late to get coffee, and someone anonymously had one delivered. A triple shot, half-sweet, nonfat caramel macchiato. Like Kasi said, pretty specific."

Cole's eyes were stone. Focused. Almost fearful.

"Someone would have to know me to know that order."

"What are you saying?"

"Okay." She pulled him to Winnie, opened the door, ushered him inside, slammed the door back, and then stood in front of the bulkhead where the articles about the two missing girls were hung. "Remember at the funeral when I told you that ten people didn't sign the guest book?"

"Yes."

"Joshua is one of those people."

"Poe—"

She stopped him before he could scold her. "Please, just listen."

He nodded, although reluctantly, and took a seat.

"I've been racking my brain trying to figure out what's come over Joshua. He went from nice and trying to get me to go out with him to publicly ostracizing me. All-out emotional assault."

223

"You turned him down, then hit him in public. That's not going to appeal to his softer side."

"If he even has one."

"He's embarrassed and mad."

"I thought that might be it too, but then I realized that it also lined up to about the same date that Dylan went missing. Within a week or so, one year later. And then I remembered that the day before I went crazy and punched him in the nose, Joshua and I were in Lincoln County. At the state park."

Cole didn't respond. Just stared over at her. She took it as a sign to keep talking. "We went on a walk through some trails. I got a little creeped out."

"By the trails or by him?"

"Both."

He hitched an eyebrow. His jaw tightened.

"Anyway, he wanted to go farther—" Cole's eyebrow hitched higher. "Down the trail." His eyebrow relaxed. "But I didn't want to go. It didn't feel right, so I headed back up the trail and left him to keep exploring."

Again, Cole stayed quiet. Seemed to soak in every word.

"As I walked back up, a girl bumped into me. She looked a little bit like me, and she was jogging. The same direction Joshua was walking."

Cole's brow furrowed. "Are you saying what I think you're saying?"

"Doesn't it make sense? Dylan and Joshua had a history."

"A brief one. Very brief."

"She picked you over him."

He shook his head. "Long before she disappeared."

She waved him off and kept right on spilling her newfound

224

theory. "A day before she went missing, she beat him at King of the Mountain."

"She beat everybody."

"Still . . . And he tried to pull me down the trail. He got mad when I didn't go. And Melissa. Her hair was brown. She went for a run. You heard Sheriff Jackson. She—"

"Poe, Joshua's a jerk, but he's not a kidnapper. Or a murderer."

"Are you sure about that?"

He slipped his hands into his hair. His head drooped. "I don't know anything anymore."

"Joshua told me that I'd regret not being with him. My car was keyed. Then the Twitter storm of accusations, and my missing shoes. All during the anniversary week of Dylan's disappearance. Don't you think that's quite a coincidence?" Her words felt frantic. Desperate. Her heart raced. "Then he shows up at Mrs. Thomas's viewing? The boy hasn't ever been to a viewing, or a flipping library. Cole, why would he be there? Why would he suddenly have compassion for an old librarian that he probably met once or twice in his entire life, if even that? It makes no sense."

Cole swallowed hard. "Unless your mom was right and Dylan did go to the library. To see Joshua. And he got to know Mrs. Thomas there."

She strongly shook her head. "No way. Didn't happen."

Cole's relief was evident. His body relaxed a bit before his eyes scanned the RV walls.

"He has no compassion. His child just died and he didn't blink an eye. Who does that?" She waited for some sort of reaction. "I know I sound crazy—"

"You're not crazy." Cole leaned back against the seat and took

225

a long, deep breath. "I've never been a fan of Joshua's, but . . . possible murderer?"

"When he put his arms around me at the trails, my body tensed up. Maybe my subconscious mind knows what my conscious mind doesn't. What if I'm repelled by him because somewhere in my brain I know what he did?"

"Shouldn't you just leave this to the investigators?"

"I care more than professional investigators. And I know my sister. That library hunch is stupid. She wouldn't walk into a library, let alone use a library computer. And even if she were chatting with someone, I would know. We kept each other's secrets and didn't keep secrets from each other."

"True." Cole probably knew that too well. She'd been privy to each and every detail of his and Dylan's relationship since day one, and often helped orchestrate ways for Dylan to escape their mama's attention and spend time with him.

For years, she'd come to know Cole through Dylan's point of view. She never knew him outside of Dylan's descriptions, or narrative. But there, in Winnie, she was seeing him as he truly was, and with each growing moment, she understood what it was that attracted Dylan to him.

He leaned forward and placed his elbows on the table. "Okay, what else have you got?"

She had to force herself to snap back and move her focus off of him and back on their discussion. She went back to business.

"Here's what I know so far. Both girls have medium-length to long brown hair. According to the articles I found, Melissa was nineteen and Kennedy was seventeen. Almost eighteen. They were both born to single mothers, although Melissa's mom married a tax attorney from Lincoln County; and they both lived within an hour and a half or so away from the bus station. Melissa to the east and Kennedy to the north. Melissa was actually closer than Kennedy."

His eyes widened. He nodded. "Impressive."

"Button up, I'm not done."

"Yes, ma'am." He pressed his lips tightly together and watched her with a gleam of amusement in his eyes.

"They both had active Twitter and Snapchat accounts. I can't see who follows them on Snapchat, but get this, Joshua and Kennedy follow each other on Twitter."

"Why would they be friends if she lives so far away?"

"That's what I'm wondering. I scrolled through his Facebook account, but he opened it in middle school, and hasn't really used it since. I didn't find her tagged in anything. And she isn't in any of his Twitter pictures."

"Did they ever tweet each other?"

"I'm still looking." She slipped back into the dinette and rested her chin in her hand. "Problem is, even if I mention Joshua to the sheriff, he won't see any reason to look into him."

"Why's that?"

"So far all I have is a Twitter connection. That's pretty weak. And he was sixteen when Dylan went missing. Seventeen now. There's no way they're gonna think a senior in high school abducted three girls within a year."

"Why not? They thought I did, at least right after it happened."

"They didn't know about the other two then, and you were her boyfriend. It wasn't as unreasonable."

Cole stood and walked to the bulkhead. She watched him slowly study the girls' photographs. He seemed to take in every

227

detail. "Other than the hair"—his attention didn't waver from the photos as he spoke—"they don't look much alike. It can't be just about the hair color."

He turned his face to hers. "There's got to be more that connects them."

"Melissa was on her school's cross country team; Kennedy was a cheerleader. Melissa went to Catholic Mass every Sunday; Kennedy traveled for cheer competitions. Their worlds didn't intersect."

"How did you figure all of that out?"

"Twitter. You'd be amazed what people share with the world. We tell everyone where we are, what we're doing . . . anything someone might need to know if they wanted to find us."

Cole sat back down in a stunned silence.

"Look, I could be totally wrong."

"Let's hope so."

"Let's just wait and see what Kasi's dad can find out. If Joshua didn't order the drink, then I'll back off and let the cops do their thing."

"But if he did?" Cole asked.

She looked back up at the articles. "It's possible he's a murderer."

CHAPTER 21

August 24, 2017

12:00 p.m.

Poe hadn't eaten in the cafeteria since freshman year, and less than sixty seconds of standing in line to get a piece of pizza reminded her why. The old air-conditioning units couldn't keep up with the rising temperatures outside, and the heat combined with the steam coming from the kitchen left it feeling stuffy and smothering.

"Remind me to never forget my lunch at home again."

Kasi stood behind her and carried a lunch tray that already held three chocolate milks: one for Kasi and the other two for Cole.

The room went silent for a good thirty seconds before it returned to its near-deafening roar. Poe looked up to figure out what caused the sudden lull in conversation and spotted Misty walking through the crowd. If there was anyone higher on the list of people to be shunned than Poe, it was Misty.

Her eyes watched her feet as she walked, and she only glanced up a few times to look for a seat—eventually finding a chair at an empty table in the back of the cafeteria.

Poe handed Kasi her tray and some money. "Here, get me a slice of pepperoni. I'll meet you at Winnie."

Knowing all eyes were now on her, Poe marched through the crowd and straight up to Misty.

Relief covered Misty's face. "Poe!" She jumped to her feet and greeted her friend with a hug. When they looked at one another, tears threatened to overflow Misty's eyes, but Poe knew that if anyone saw her crying, they'd be ruthless.

She offered a quick change of topic. "How'd you know about my name change?"

Misty's eyelashes fluttered as she stepped back a bit. "Seriously? I may not be at school, but I'm still on Twitter. Payton becoming Poe has been the talk on social media for days."

"I tried not to look."

Misty shrugged and her round eyes widened. "I like the change. Not as much as I liked seeing you beat the tar outta Joshua, but I like it."

They shared a smile.

"Welcome back to hell," Poe offered.

"Thanks. I think."

"Want to get out of here?"

Misty hugged Poe again and then released her. "Absolutely."

"Grab your stuff and come on. You're eating with us."

With her head held high and a smile on her face, Poe led her fellow outcast through the room. As they passed Joshua, he glared at them, made a gun with his fingers, and pulled the imaginary trigger.

"So mature," Misty snapped.

"Misty, meet me at the RV." Poe waited for her to walk away, then put her hand on the back of Joshua's chair and placed her mouth to his ear. "The gesture you just made could be considered a threat, and seeing as how I'm under the protection of the police force right now, you're lucky I don't have your butt arrested for threatening my life."

"Nice try. It wasn't a threat."

"For all I know, you're as much a suspect in my sister's disappearance as anyone else."

"I wouldn't do something like that and you know it."

"Do I?" She stood up and glared at him. "Talk your trash and spread your rumors, but stay away from my friends."

Poe walked away, immediately regretting her end of the conversation. The last thing she wanted was to alert him to her suspicions. If he truly was an honest suspect, now that he knew about her theory, he could try to cover his tracks.

She walked out of the cafeteria and tried to re-center her mind as she caught up with Misty.

"Set him straight?" Misty asked.

"That, or did more damage. Hard to say which just yet."

Misty stopped a few feet away from Winnie and dropped her backpack to the ground. "This is so cool."

"Welcome to our tailgate party," Kasi squealed.

"Poe," Misty gushed. "I'd heard about this car, but oh my word, it's more than I imagined."

"Do you like her?"

"Like her? She's amazing!"

"You're one of the few who thinks so."

"No way," Misty said. "People love her—they're just too scared of Joshua and Starr to admit it."

"Well, Brody has big plans to fix up the outside."

Cole stepped out of Winnie, opened up another pop-up chair, and placed it next to Kasi. "Have a seat," he offered.

Misty gave him a hug and then made herself comfortable. "Are you gonna sit out here every day?"

"When it's nice outside. On bad-weather days, we can sit inside at the table."

"There's a table? Oh, I gotta see this." She hopped up and made her way inside as if she were entering a palace. Poe was close on her heels. "This is the most awesomely amazing piece of vintage crap I've ever laid eyes on."

"I know, right?" Kasi hollered from her chair outside.

"Oh my gosh, I wish I would've thought of it." She ran her fingers over the gold linoleum counter and opened the tiny oven door. "Have you ever cooked in here?"

"Not yet."

"We seriously need to."

Poe tried to suppress a smile. "I don't really cook."

"I do. There's even a bathroom! I needed something like this when I was kicked out of my house. You could live in here."

"I practically do."

Misty pointed to the loft. "Is that a bed?"

"Yep."

"How many does this thing sleep?"

"Well, it's supposed to sleep four, but I don't know how. I guess you could cram one up there and then once you fold these couches out, fit three or four more. But they'd have to be small people."

Misty took a brief moment to read the newspaper articles taped to the bulkhead. "What are these?"

"Just doing some research."

"What kind of research?"

"Don't ask."

"Okay. Well, I have an idea. We're camping out." Misty jumped out the door and called, "Did you hear that? We're camping in this glorious piece of garbage."

"When?" Kasi asked.

Everybody stared at Poe and waited for an answer. "Um . . . any time you want."

"Friday?" Kasi suggested.

"I don't see a problem with next Friday." Hopefully, that would give her enough time to talk Daddy into saying okay.

Cole shook his head. "I don't think you girls need to be camping out by yourself. It's too dangerous. Plus, that Friday's homecoming."

Misty chuckled. "Look around, Cole. Does it look like any one of us are going to homecoming?"

"Nobody I know is going," Kasi said. "That's more for the elite, and I'm dang sure not elite."

"Who'd want to be?" Misty asked, then looked over at Poe. "Sorry, I hope that didn't offend you. Given, well . . ."

Poe almost laughed. "Don't worry about it. I'm certainly not one of them now, and don't want to be."

Misty visibly relaxed. "We should have our own homecoming then. You know, for all the normal people."

"And by normal, you mean outcasts?" Poe asked.

"Exactly."

"Wait. You wouldn't camp out with us?" Kasi asked with a look at Cole.

"Who, me?" Cole asked.

"No, your imaginary friends Manny, Moe, and Jack. Yeah, you."

"No way. I'm not camping with three girls."

"Why not?"

"Because you're three girls. I'm a guy."

"The world is full of guys. Be a man," Misty said.

Kasi sighed. "Best movie line ever written."

"What movie?" Cole asked.

"*Say Anything*," the girls answered.

Inspiration shot into Poe's mind, and she stood and climbed onto her chair.

"You're going to fall," Cole warned.

"I'm not going to f—" The chair tilted.

Cole thrust out his arm and pushed the chair back down before the entire thing flipped. "Watch yourself!"

"I said, I'm not going to fall." Poe held her pizza high over her head while carefully balancing on the chair edges. "John Cusack," she said, hardly skipping a beat. "You know, holding the boom box over his head at what's her face's window—"

"Diane Court," Misty said.

"Yeah, her, while 'In Your Eyes' played. The best movie scene in the history of eighties movies."

"We get the point, now get down before you kill yourself," Cole ordered.

"I don't know, Poe," Kasi said. "Any scene with Jake Ryan tops that one."

Misty nodded. "True that. John Hughes was a genius." She crossed herself. "May he rest in peace."

Cole kept his eye on Poe, who still perilously held her pizza above her head. "You can come down now."

"I got it!" Misty yelled, falling into her seat. "We have our own retro eighties rom-com-inspired homecoming."

Kasi squealed. Cole rolled his eyes. And Poe chuckled as she carefully climbed down.

"It would be epic," Misty gushed.

"I'm out," Cole moaned. "As if camping with a bunch of girls wouldn't be bad enough, you've got to make it a dance?"

Poe cut her eyes to him. "If we got the word out, it would be interesting to see who showed up." She pumped her eyebrows, hoping he'd somehow understand her own form of Morse code.

He nodded. Rubbed his temples. "I guess that's true."

"We could hold it at the cove. Bonfire. Dance. Camp out. All done eighties-style. It would be the most epic homecoming to ever happen in Cornwell. One for the record books. And the memories."

Cole groaned and hid his face in his hands. "Okay, okay. I'll do it."

Poe snuck a grin over to the other two girls but quickly turned serious before Cole looked back up. "You're a trooper, Cole."

Poe unscrewed the cap on her water bottle and spun it on her finger. "Cole, I would think that with a rumored seasoned hussy like Misty, a rumored-to-be newly deflowered slut like myself, and a quote-unquote hot mess like Kasi, you could very well go down in local history as having the best homecoming experience of any Cornwell Condor ever."

"That's right," Misty said. "I mean, if you add onto that the fact you hang around strippers all day, aren't you pretty much an icon?"

"I don't hang around strippers all day. I don't even go in the place when it's open."

Kasi laughed. "Since when does the truth matter around here? This is about presumption and gossip, which in Cornwell is treated as fact—you know that."

Poe pat Cole on the knee several times. "Don't you worry

about a thing. You hang around with us long enough and you'll have no redeeming qualities left whatsoever. At least as far as anyone else is concerned, anyway."

"I don't even know what to say," he muttered.

"If we get too loud and obnoxious, just turn your ears off. You won't know the difference."

He eyed each of the girls in their state of giddiness and then his head fell back. "Why am I agreeing to this?" Cole asked as he looked up at the heavens.

"'Cause you love us," Kasi said.

He lowered his head and glanced at Poe, then at Kasi. "I what?"

"You love us. You can't help yourself. We're very loveable."

"Look, you need to drop it with the homecoming thing for now or I'll—"

Poe stood, hands on her hips. "You'll what?"

He held a straight face, but it only lasted a moment. It cracked and he laughed.

"You're harmless, Cole."

"Wish you were," he admitted.

"Little ol' me? What harm can I do?" She raised one brow.

"A lot."

"See that, girls, Cole's scared of me."

"So am I," Misty laughed. "After seeing what you did to the boy who shall remain unnamed, I wouldn't mess with you."

Cole stood and folded up his chair, while Misty and Kasi continued to talk about homecoming.

Poe folded her chair and handed it to Cole with a grin. "Are you really scared of me, Cole? I can't do much physical damage to someone as big as you."

"It's not physical damage I'm worried about." He threw the chairs into Winnie's loft and started the walk back to the school.

Misty watched him walk away and then turned to Poe with a grin. "So this is what we do?"

"What do you mean?" Poe asked.

"We spend each lunch ignoring the fact that you two are totally into each other?"

"We aren't *into* each other."

Misty looked at Kasi. "Do you believe this crap?"

"Not a bit."

"He's Dylan's," Poe said.

Kasi shrugged. "I don't know . . . I mean, if you did like him, that would be okay. You have to start living your life. And so does he. I think Dylan would want that."

"Maybe, but like I said, he's Dylan's. Always has been and always will be. Ask him if you don't believe me."

Misty somehow managed to frown and pout at the same time. "Well, that sucks. You two would be good together."

"That might be true," Poe said. "But he and Dylan are perfect."

CHAPTER 22

August 29, 2017

12:00 p.m.

News quickly spread that any and all outcasts were welcome at Winnie. Soon twelve new friends joined them regularly for lunch. More laughter filled the parking lot, and every person who sat in a pop-up chair appeared to feel a little bit less alone. Poe certainly was in that number, and her daddy told her that he loved buying more chairs to accommodate her growing circle of friends.

And luckily for Cole, several of the newcomers were guys, so he was no longer the only one with a Y chromosome. He seemed relieved and a little less awkward during conversations.

As Poe sat eating her peanut butter and apple jelly sandwich, Cole walked to her and presented her with a large cardboard box.

"What is it?" Poe asked.

"Open it up and look," he said.

Poe cut through the tape with one of her car keys, opened the box flaps, and peeked inside. "What are . . . Are these old eight-track tapes?"

"They sell them at thrift stores. So anytime I'm delivering flowers in surrounding towns, I run in and see what they have. There are some good ones in there."

"Oh my gosh." Poe picked up a stack and sifted through them. "Gordon Lightfoot, Waylon Jennings, Bread, Captain and Tennille, Billy Joel, the Carpenters. Cole, this is amazing. I can't believe you got these."

She handed the stack to her left, and the rest of the group took turns looking at them.

"I figure you might as well put Winnie's stereo system to good use. Maybe add to the nostalgia."

Poe caught Kasi and Misty glancing and grinning at each other, something they seemed to do a lot more often. She thought back to Misty's comment late last week about Cole, and again dismissed her friends' romantic assumptions. Some things just couldn't be, and it was best to keep it that way. They were spending so much time together because it's what Dylan would want, and because they had a common mission.

To find out everything they could about her disappearance.

She looked over at two of her friends and watched them inspect the tapes for several seconds before Joshua walked into her line of vision. His eyes cut to her and he glared at her, his jaw set, as he walked away from his car and toward the picnic table. His hand tightly gripped the fast food bag.

Poe straightened her back and set her shoulders, refusing to wilt under his hostile scowl.

"This is the coolest gift ever." Poe bumped her shoulder against Cole's arm and looked over at him with a smile as if Joshua never existed. "I've never had a friend do something like this for me." She took a deep breath and allowed herself to be in the moment. "Honestly, Cole, I can't thank you enough."

He dipped his head and scratched his ear. "You just did. We're all good."

Just then, another guy slowly wandered up to the group and offered a small, insecure wave. One that said he thought he was welcome but wasn't completely sure. Cole walked over to greet the lanky, strawberry blond–headed boy and shook his hand. "Hey, Finn. Glad you could make it." He turned to face the rest of the group. "You guys know Finn?"

Poe eyeballed Finn as he greeted the rest of the lunch crew and then turned to her. "Hey, Poe," he said with a grin.

"Hey, Finn. Good to see you. Are you gonna join us for lunch?"

"I was hoping to. I heard this was the place to be."

"You heard right," Misty said, offering him a chair. "So what brings you to the land of the lost?"

"I'm the preacher's kid who actually doesn't mind being one. How well do you think I fit in?"

"Not at all?" Kasi asked.

"Bingo."

Misty sat in her chair and crossed one leg over the other. "Well, welcome to the trash heap. Make yourself at home."

"I plan on it." Finn took the chair Misty offered him, and Poe observed him carefully as he sat it next to Misty. "Sorry about your baby. How are you holding up?"

Misty, Kasi, and Poe exchanged quick, wide-eyed looks. He'd brought up the elephant in the parking lot that everybody pretended they didn't see. Or the second elephant: the first was the subject of Poe's sister.

"I'm . . . I'm good." Misty re-crossed her legs. "Your dad conducted my son's funeral."

"He told me. Sorry I couldn't be there. My mom and I had to go out of town. It was a boy, right?"

"Yeah."

"What was his name?" he asked.

"Benjamin."

"Benjamin. That's a great name."

Poe watched them talk for a few minutes and then stole a glance at Cole. He looked back at her, shrugged, and then dipped his head and dove into his lunch sack with a small grin.

"Cole?"

He swallowed his grin and looked up. "Yeah?"

"How 'bout we try out one of these eight-track tapes?"

"Uh . . . now?"

She jumped to her feet and grabbed his arm. "Yep. Right now." She dragged him inside and closed the door behind her.

"What was that about?" she barked.

"What was what about?"

"Don't you 'what was what' me. You know exactly what was what. Are you trying to set them up?"

"Who?"

"Misty and Finn."

"No, I just thought he might want to join us, that's all."

"And?"

"And . . . I vaguely remembered he mentioned her a while back."

"Mentioned her how?"

"This was a long time ago, while she was with Joshua even. I think."

"Mentioned her how?" she said again, now drawing out each word.

"Like how he thought she was wasting her time with Joshua."

She stepped toward him. "And?"

"And . . . maybe he thought she was cute or something. I don't remember the specifics."

"He thinks she's cute?" she gasped.

"He thought she was cute. Whether or not he still does, who's to say?"

"Well, he showed up here for lunch, didn't he?"

"He did."

"At your invitation."

"Yes."

"And . . ."

"I might have mentioned the fact she ate with us."

"Holy crow!"

"Now don't get all excited. It could just be that he wanted to have some people to eat with."

"At first I was skeptical, but if you think he's genuinely interested . . . And out of fifteen people, he sat right next to her."

Cole shrugged.

"His daddy's a preacher. Surely you don't think he'd let Finn date a girl who had a baby when she was seventeen?" she asked.

"Don't know for sure. But he lets him hang out with a guy whose dad owns a girlie bar. Maybe he actually does what the Bible says and doesn't judge."

She clutched her hands to her chest. "I sure hope he likes her . . . unless he's going to hurt her. Then I don't want him to, 'cause she doesn't need to be hurt anymore. Do you think he's coming to the dance? Oh, I hope so."

"Good lord, Poe. He sat next to her at lunch. You're acting like he's about to pop the question or something. Settle down already."

"But if he's good, Cole. If he's a good guy—"

"He is a good guy."

"And she *needs* a good guy. Deserves a good guy."

"I know that. Why do you think I invited him?"

"You did!" She hopped around Winnie in excitement. "You did invite him for her!"

He opened the door, jumped off Winnie's step, and walked toward the school building behind their friends, who'd already started back.

"Coleman Rhodes." Poe stopped hopping, ran out, then slammed the door and locked it before chasing after him. "I only *thought* the eight tracks couldn't be beat. I was wrong. Inviting Finn to lunch was the best gift ever."

He stopped and looked over at her with a smirk. "What if I didn't do it for you?"

"It still is. It's the best gift ever." She stood back and watched Cole and their group of friends head toward the school entrance, and for a brief moment felt complete joy. Devoid of any negativity, she could see light at the end of the tunnel and wanted to sprint toward it before it dimmed.

9:10 p.m.

Poe sat on the floor next to Cole, and stared down at her cell phone as she drummed her fingers on the linoleum.

"A watched pot never boils," Cole sighed as he worked on the leaky faucet. His face stayed hidden in the shadow of the cabinet.

Poe wasn't sure if he knew what he was doing, but was impressed by his effort and determination. And she'd be more impressed if she weren't so preoccupied. "Could this take any longer?"

"Phillips screwdriver."

She dug through his toolbox, pulled out a screwdriver, and handed it to him.

"That's a flathead. I need a Phillips. It has four grooves. A cross head." He sat up and reached for the tool as she grabbed it, causing their hands to briefly touch, and a zap of low-voltage electricity to race up her arm.

He ducked under the sink and went back to work. Poe stared at her fingers. "Kasi said she'd call by nine with the information about the coffee order. It's ten after."

"Don't drive yourself crazy."

"I wouldn't have far to drive."

"Give yourself a break, and give Kasi a break while you're at it. She'll get you the information as soon as she can." He handed her the screwdriver. "Wrench, please."

She grabbed the wrench and handed it over. Careful to keep from touching him again. "So anyway, um . . . I've been meaning to talk to you."

"About what?"

"I just wanted to say thank you for being my friend. For sticking up for me, looking out for me, that kinda thing."

"No worries."

"I mean, I haven't been the nicest to you since Dylan's been gone. Or maybe ever. I don't have an excuse for that. And, honestly, you and I both know I don't deserve you being so nice."

"Sure you do."

She slid the angel pendant back and forth across the chain around her neck. "People are so wrong about you, it's crazy."

"They're wrong about you too. At least now, anyway."

"Thanks, but they're really, really wrong about you . . . and your daddy. You're so much more mature than all the other guys. They act like they're twelve, and you manage to act like an adult. You're so levelheaded and kind."

His head emerged from under the sink. "What's all this about?"

"It's not about anything." Her heart raced. "I just wanted you to know how much I appreciate you, and that I realize how lucky I am to call you a . . . a friend."

He stuck his head back under the sink. "I'm glad to call you my friend too."

"Good." She rolled her eyes at herself, thankful he couldn't see her, and then bit the inside of her lip and tried to think of something else to say. "I thought maybe . . ."

"Maybe what?"

Instead of answering, she stood, walked to the bathroom, and momentarily lost herself in the photos of Dylan and Cole that hung on the wall.

"Poe?"

She turned to him. Cole had pulled himself out from under the sink and stood looking at her with eyebrows arched high. "Maybe what?" he asked.

"I don't know."

He set the wrench down inside the sink cabinet and walked to her. "I know you wanted to say something."

She looked down at her hands, noticed she was fidgeting with her fingers, and pressed her palms to her sides as he took two more steps toward her. They were now less than an arm's length apart.

"What?" he asked. "Just say it."

"Say what?"

"The truth. Whatever you're thinking," he encouraged.

Her lips cinched together and she stared down at the yellow linoleum.

"All right then." He turned back around and was just about the climb back under the sink when she unhinged her lips and spoke.

"My truth is that I d—"

Poe's phone rang, catching them off guard and startling them both.

She cupped her hands close to her chest and stepped farther away from the dinette table, suddenly afraid to hear the news. "You do it."

"Are you sure?"

She nodded. "Please."

Cole took a deep breath and answered her phone. "Hey, Kasi." He stared into Poe's eyes as he listened to Kasi speak. His jaw, already tight, practically became like rigor mortis. "Thanks," he managed. "We'll see you tomorrow."

She watched his hand place the phone on the table. He seemed to be at a loss for words. Either that, or afraid to speak them out loud.

"What?" Poe asked. Her voice shook, and her knees wobbled. "It was Joshua, wasn't it? I was right."

Cole took another long, collecting breath and turned to look at her. "It was you. You ordered the coffee."

"No. I di—"

"Poe. It was your name. Your credit card number."

"Cole, I couldn't have. I—"

246

"Let's just call it a night. Okay?"

Panic overcame her. Her mind raced. She searched for an explanation, but nothing materialized. "I went straight from the house to the school. I didn't stop. And I didn't call in an order." She picked up her phone and scanned through the list of recent calls. "Mama . . . Daddy . . . Mama . . . Cole, it's not here. I didn't call."

"Poe—"

"I need you to believe me." She looked up at him. Her heart beat wildly. "Please."

His face softened and his eyes filled with compassion. "I do. All right? I believe you . . . I just think we need to dial all this back some. Like you said. Let's let the cops do their job and wait and see—"

"But—"

"Poe. Give it a rest." He walked to the door and opened it. "I'll see you tomorrow. Lock the door behind me."

Poe watched Cole walk out. Her heart snapped in two when he closed the door behind him.

I didn't do it.

Tears streamed down her face. Her body shook.

I don't remember doing it.

11:30 p.m.

Poe sat in Winnie's driver's seat. It was as far back as it would go and her feet were perched on the steering wheel, her knees at her chest. It was a near-fetal position, only she was lucid. Thinking. Worrying.

Thanks to the light from the back patio and the strategically placed streetlights that lined the alley, she could watch the moss hanging from the trees above the cemetery as it blew in the gentle push of the wind. Small wisps floated in the air and caught a moment in the spotlight when the moon illuminated it as it fell to the brown earth.

The gentle scene did nothing to calm her mind.

It hadn't ended well with Cole. She was almost certain she'd completely freaked him out with her odd behavior and the revelation that she somehow ordered the coffee.

After more than an hour of regret, Poe's forehead was red from all the pounding it took. Every time she thought about the look on his face when Kasi gave him the news, her palm made contact with the delicate skin of her face.

"How could I be so friggin' stupid?" She slapped herself. "I'm going crazy." *Slap.*

She slipped out of the driver's seat, walked to the bathroom, and stood in front of the photographs that hung in the shower stall. Her and her sister's faces looked back, possibly trying to tell her something, but she couldn't pinpoint what. The images were intermingled with each other. No rhyme or reason to their placement.

With each photo, she carefully examined the people in the background. Was there anyone unusual? Anything out of place?

Was Joshua present?

She pulled her cell phone from her pocket and opened her list of names of people she'd seen at the bus station. She read each name individually and then looked for their face in the photographs.

It was a waste of several minutes. The names and photographs never matched up.

Car lights swept across the cemetery, turning her attention from the memories in front of her to the front windshield, then the lights dimmed. She walked to the dashboard, leaned against it, and peered into the darkness, where she could see the orange parking lights still illuminated, and casting an eerie, faint glow onto the ground.

She watched someone walk around the front of the vehicle. Their shadow moved toward the middle of the cemetery.

Who are you and what are you doing in my graveyard?

She quickly walked to the couch, slid her feet into her flip-flops, grabbed a hammer from Cole's tool chest, then quietly opened Winnie's door and stepped outside onto the moist grass.

Crouching down, she slowly walked toward the dim light. The closer she inched, the closer to the ground she got.

Just a few yards away from the vehicle, which was parked in the narrow driving path between sections of the cemetery, she hunkered down behind a headstone.

The car door opened then shut.

She stood, the hammer in a fist at her side, ready to fight, but the car suddenly backed up, the wheels spinning in the mud and tossing it into the air.

The car turned slightly, the headlights shining directly into her eyes—but she stood, unmoved. Her heart pounded.

The brights flipped on, momentarily blinding her. She blinked to try to clear her vision and focused on the shadowy figure that sat behind the steering wheel. Poe squinted, trying hard to make out their face, but before she could recognize their features, the car finished backing up and quickly drove off.

Who comes to a graveyard in the middle of the night?

She turned to head back to Winnie and realized that with

the interior RV lights on, anyone from her current vantage point could see what she was doing inside.

Poe swallowed hard, realizing she was being watched, and could've been for days. Her worst fear was true: Her enemy was in town, and possibly keeping a watchful eye on his next victim. Her only question now was if that person was Joshua.

CHAPTER 23

September 1, 2017

7:20 p.m.

Poe stood in front of a full-length mirror attached to the bathroom door and inspected her black Gunne Sax tuxedo cocktail dress. A simple white bow sat just below her chest and wrapped around to the back in a simple white line. Another strip of white ribbon hit mid-thigh. She found it on the Internet and selected it because it looked the most her of all the eighties dresses she had to choose from, and it could be shipped overnight. If she was going to go to a homecoming dance, she figured she'd do it right, and look the part. Her overly backcombed hair sat in a loose bun on her head, and looked so good that she wished teasing was back in style.

"The bigger the hair, the closer to God," she muttered, and then glanced at her bare feet and wiggled her toes. Rather than wearing fancy shoes, she'd painted her toenails black. It seemed more fitting and was much more comfortable than slipping on old patent leather pumps and trying to walk on the sand. Plus, she was Southern, which meant shoes are never mandatory.

Staring at the reflection in the mirror made her feel more distant, even from herself. She didn't feel like herself anymore, and she didn't look like herself either. And it was more than the vintage garb.

Poe layered on hot pink lipstick, shut the bathroom door, and exited Winnie. The cove parking lot was full, so she'd been forced to park up the road and walk about a hundred yards on the dark road that lined the perimeter of the woods. With every step, she wished she'd reconsidered going barefoot. The pebbles and seashells layering the road dug into her feet like needles. The pain, combined with the uneasiness of being alone in the dark, enticed her to walk a little faster.

"Though I walk through the valley of something death . . ." she whispered, "I will fear no evil . . . something, something . . . yada, yada."

It was a Scripture she'd heard before. Or at least parts of it. Her mama muttered it incessantly whenever she hung new crosses. She'd collected about every decorative version she could find, and hung them from crown molding to baseboards on every wall that backed up to the cemetery. There were hundreds.

Just like her mama thought the crosses and Scripture would keep evil away, Poe hoped for the same as she made the walk to the cove. Even if she didn't remember all the words.

"Though I walk through the valley—"

A rustle in the woods stopped her cold.

She looked into the shadowy foliage and squinted, trying to pierce the darkness. "Yada, yada . . ."

Another crinkle of tree limbs.

"I will fear no evil."

She stood silent. Listening. Waiting. Wondering if someone looked back at her. "I will fear no evil!" she shouted, and then ran toward the homecoming dance.

She slowed and worked to regain her breath as she reached the beach.

The trees surrounding the waterfront were lined in bright, twinkling Christmas lights, making it appear that the deep woods were alive with lightning bugs. A bonfire raged in the middle of the beach, and eighties music blared through the speaker system and poured out over the fifty or so dance-goers who mingled on the beach. They'd reportedly raided every thrift store within a fifty-mile radius and clothed themselves in the best eighties attire they could find, almost all of which included jewel-toned dresses with plenty of poofs and bows. At least for the girls, anyway. The guys either wore tacky old suits or tuxedos, or nice dress pants with a button-up shirt just like they did for every other school dance.

Those lucky enough to have vehicles with four-wheel drive parked their cars on the perimeter of the beach, and their headlights shined across the white sand, which caused it to sparkle like diamonds and light a makeshift dance floor.

The entire event had been thrown together in a matter of days, but nobody seemed to mind. The crowd was more interested in a good time than the appearance of it all, which was completely the opposite of those who attended the official Cornwell High Homecoming Dance.

Poe approached Kasi, Misty, Cole, and Finn, who stood on the beach in front of the refreshment table, downing bottles of water.

"Okay, boys, so give us a guy's perspective on this whole Joshua thing," Misty said.

"What whole Joshua thing?" Finn asked.

"Not owning up to getting me pregnant and not even bothering to say anything to me when the baby died."

"He's a jerk. What more is there to say?" Cole asked.

"Do you think all guys would think that he's a jerk, or just you two?"

"A lot of guys would—" Poe caught Cole's eye, stopping him cold.

"But not all?" Misty urged.

Poe and Cole's eyes met for a few brief moments before he dropped his eyes and then turned his attention to the beach.

"Not all," Finn said.

"That's why we're all single. Cornwell's full of Joshuas. You're two of the few who aren't, but of course Cole's still pining away after Dylan."

Poe watched Cole reach for a pretzel off a small snack table and inspect it. She sensed his discomfort with the conversation. "We're not the only non-Joshua sorts. You just have to look for them."

"What do you think I've been doing? I *was* looking. Stalking, practically. Or maybe not stalking, but lurking at least."

"If you've got to stalk a guy, he's not the one," Finn said.

"What about you, Kasi?" Misty asked.

Kasi looked up from her plate of finger foods. "Who has the time for a guy? I can't keep up with the three I've got at home, let alone one that I'd have to give extra attention to."

"And Poe?" Misty asked.

"My daddy's a mortician."

Misty winced. "'Nough said. You'll be single a while."

Misty grabbed a fistful of pretzels and turned to Cole. "So, how long are you planning on holding out for Dylan?"

"Why are you focusing on me?"

"Because my life is depressing," Misty admitted. "Wallowing in other people's crap keeps me from wallowing in my own."

"Losing a baby's a big deal," Kasi said softly. "Maybe you need to wallow a little."

"Trust me, I'm wallowing. I just don't want to do it at homecoming." She turned back to Cole. "So, you gonna answer the question? How long will you hold out for Dylan?"

He pushed the pretzels around in his hand. "Please change the subject."

The opening bars to "Girls Just Want to Have Fun" blared across the beach, and brought squeals and giddy dancing with it. Misty gripped Kasi by the hand, and they took off toward the beach to join the other girls who were already well on their way to staking a claim to their new theme song.

Poe sat on a downed tree limb eyeing the woods around them. She was on full alert. On the job and completely focused. Or at least almost. She couldn't help but glance Cole's direction from time to time, until midway through the song when he turned and slowly walked to join her.

"Hey," she said meekly upon his approach. "Thanks for coming. Even though you didn't want to."

He studied their surroundings. "Did you walk here?" he asked, as if he hadn't heard a word she said. His eyes bearing into her.

"No. I drove Winnie. Parked up the street."

"You walked down here in the dark by yourself?"

"Uh . . . yeah. It was fine. I was totally safe."

"Do I need to remind you that a possible murderer is lurking around?"

She thought back to the car at the cemetery. "Nope. You don't need to remind me. That's why I'm here. To see if he makes an appearance."

Cole shook his head and stuffed his hands in the front pockets of his black tuxedo pants. "I don't know what gets into you."

She took a deep breath. "Look, I'm sorry. I didn't mean to mislead everyone earlier. I— I don't remember ordering the drink."

"Poe. Stop. Okay? I believe you, but it's starting to be too much. For you, especially. You're starting to see suspects where maybe there shouldn't be any."

"I'm not starting to see anything. He's here. I know it."

"Poe—"

"You think I'm making all of this up? Imagining that Joshua could've—"

He waved his hand at her, cutting her off before she could go off on a panicked tangent. "Of course not, but I'm worried that you're going to—"

"Drive myself crazy." She nodded. "Or crazier." It was too much, but she didn't have any intention of letting up. "He's close to overplaying his hand and I'll be there to see it when he does."

"That's what I'm afraid of." He squat down and took a deep breath.

"Can we just go back to acting normal?" she asked.

"Normal for us was not talking at all."

"Okay, then maybe we should try to redefine normal." She sighed, threw her head back, and let it hang there so she could look into the dark sky. "I feel weird enough all the time. I'd rather not feel weird with you too."

"Don't feel weird on my account." He moved over and sat down next to her. "You don't want to get out there and dance with them?"

She lowered her head and admired the girls' inhibition as

they frolicked on the dance floor. "No. It's more fun to watch. Especially Misty. She needs this. She likes to act tough, but I know she's having a rough time."

"If there's one thing I've learned through all this, it's that people want to move on from tragedy pretty fast, and they expect everyone else to move on too. Even those of us who are most affected by it."

Poe smiled over at him. "Sounds like you need to have some fun yourself. Go." She flapped her hand, shooing him toward the dance floor. "Dance with them. I'll be fine."

"I've already done my duty when it comes to being their partner. Three dances. And I hate dancing."

They laughed, easing a little of the awkwardness.

"Yeah," she laughed. "I know."

"Do you?" He looked over at her, his head at a tilt. "Come on." He gripped her by the hand, stood, and pulled her to her feet. "Here's a slow one. The least you can do is give me one dance."

"No. I—"

"Come on." He lightly tugged her out to the sand but didn't bother to go all the way to the crowded dance floor. "Do you remember how to do this?" he teased.

"Dance? Um . . . I think so."

It was as if they were at a middle school event and were paired up for their first dance ever. Neither seemed to know what to do. Her mind was completely blank. Dancing suddenly foreign.

He wrapped one arm around her, slipped his free hand in hers, and pulled her close. She became hyperaware of the sensations heightening on every inch of her skin. Her face felt warm, and her breathing forced.

"Relax," he urged. "You're safe."

Poe took a deep breath, then slowly exhaled. She wanted to melt into him and never leave. There, in his arms, she felt almost like herself for the first time in over a year. She fit perfectly. Belonged, yet felt guilty for it.

Screeching tires echoed across the cove. Car horns blasted continuously, and headlights swept around the parking lot.

Poe and Cole separated and sprinted across the beach. She heard footsteps behind them as they ran up the trail toward the parking lot, but didn't look over her shoulder. She knew it was Kasi and Misty. There was no doubt they'd have her back.

When they ascended the peak of the trail, Poe realized not only their senses were being assaulted. Each parked car was pelted with eggs and bags of flour. The rulers of the Cornwell High kingdom had left their crowning ceremony to terrorize the masses.

As she and Cole approached the parking lot, Poe saw Joshua standing next to his car. Starr, Spencer, Lindy, and a few others huddled around him, still wearing their formals. A crown sat on Lindy's head.

"Poe! I was looking for you," Joshua yelled. He held up his arm to present a pair of Converse sneakers that hung from the tips of his fingers. "Found these a while ago, and thought you might want them back."

Just as she predicted, Joshua had just overplayed his hand. Poe picked up steam and moved toward him.

"Didn't anyone ever tell you that you shouldn't go walking on a beach alone?"

She shoved him against his car.

"Be careful there, Poe. I kind of liked that. You'll get me worked up."

Poe shoved him again. Cole pushed past Spencer, but his progress was thwarted when Misty jumped in front of him. "Let her handle this."

Poe stood squarely in front of Joshua. "The only way you win is if I lose control again and show how crazy I am, right?"

Joshua grinned. "Wrong. I've already won."

She tightly clenched her fists, and could feel herself shaking with hatred as she stared at Joshua. His smugness was almost too much to take.

Out of nowhere, she swung a fist toward his face, but stopped just before she made contact with his jaw. "You're not worth it."

"Okay, Cole, get her outta here," Misty whispered.

Cole moved to one side of Poe and Joshua, and his features relaxed back into their typical calm as he gripped Poe's hand in his. "Let's go."

Before he could pull her toward the beach, she yanked her hand out of his grip. "No!" She leaned her body against Joshua's and placed her mouth to his ear. "You talk big in front of your friends, but you and I both know the truth. I know who you are and I know what you've done."

Joshua stood as if frozen. His face turned bright red.

She pulled away and glared at him with such an intensity that she could almost read into his soul. But there was nothing to see. He was dead inside. Nothing redeemable.

Poe turned and walked toward the road.

She saw Cole turn to Misty, Kasi, and Finn. "Misty and Finn, you guys stay here. Make sure nothing gets out of control. Kasi, come with us." They followed behind Poe as she walked back to Winnie, but kept a small distance. Poe's head was spinning. She wanted the proof that Joshua was guilty and she wanted it right then. She didn't have any more patience for his games. Dylan deserved justice and she deserved it now.

They stepped inside Winnie and within moments, Cole pulled the door shut. "We've got to tell the sheriff about Joshua."

"No. Not yet."

"What about Joshua?" Kasi asked.

"He's violent. A possible murderer." He looked at Poe. "You shouldn't be egging him on."

Kasi stumbled backward and practically collapsed onto the side couch when her legs made contact. "You think Joshua took Dylan? How? Why?"

Poe crossed her arms over her chest and leaned against the back of the driver's seat.

"That's what we're trying to figure out," Cole said. "It's time we told the sheriff. I'm going. Are you coming with me?"

Poe shook her head defiantly.

He thrust his hands on his hips and looked down at the floor. "You're too pigheaded sometimes."

A swarm of vehicles rushed by Winnie and caused a gush of wind to rock her back and forth for several seconds. Honking reverberated against Winnie's exterior and stung Poe's ears. She covered her ears and waited for the shaking to stop.

"We've got to end this," Cole shouted over the noise. "Don't you see that? Look at what they're doing to you. I'm going to get the sheriff. We're going to give him all of your research and let him handle it."

She didn't respond.

He lowered himself so their eyes were level. "Okay?"

She knew he was right. Joshua and his minions were growing

more aggressive. He had to know she was on to him, and he'd cranked up his attack tactics.

Eventually, she nodded.

"Okay. I'll be back." He looked over at Kasi. "Don't leave her alone. Lock the door behind me. I'll be right back." He stood and walked to the door. "From here out, we're going to let the police handle this."

8:35 p.m.

Poe sat at the dinette, bit on her fingernails, and stared up at Kasi as she studied the research Poe taped to Winnie's walls.

"I can't believe Joshua could've done something like that." Kasi slowly shook her head. "I mean, he's a horrible, miserable human being. But this?" She turned to Poe. "Is he even smart enough to pull something like this off? And get away with it?"

Poe shrugged.

"Poe, we've known him our entire lives. How would we not see that he could do something like this?"

"We see what we want to see," Poe muttered.

A knock at the door stunned them both, and sent Poe's heartbeat into heavy thuds.

Kasi reached over with a shaking hand and unlocked the door, which immediately swung open, causing her to cower against the passenger seat.

Sheriff Jackson bounded inside, Cole close on his heels.

In full police mode, Jackson marched around the small space and took it all in before he stopped and studied Poe's research. Like Cole had, he took his time inspecting the photographs. "Care to explain all of this?"

"I'm doing a bit of an investigation."

Her turned to her. "I see that. Why? We're working on—"

"It took you a year to start," she blurted, then quickly glanced over at Cole, knowing she'd said the wrong thing. His eyes were wide.

"Cole, you're in on this?" Sheriff Jackson barked.

Cole shifted his eyes to the floor. Kasi sat on the couch with her knees pulled to her chest but her eyes peeled and focused on the sheriff's every movement.

"No. Cole's been trying to talk me out of this the entire time. It just, it . . . it seemed like nobody was doing anything," Poe added, a little more timidly.

"Do you kids seriously think I would advertise everything I've been doing?" She shook her head. "We did the work we could until we ran out of leads. Now, we have new leads, and we're working on—"

"Is Joshua Toobin a suspect?" Poe asked.

The sheriff raised an eyebrow. "Joshua Toobin?" He said the name like it was a joke; the *T* snapped off his tongue. "I've kept your parents updated on any new news I've had. I—"

"But are you looking at Joshua?"

"Why? Should we be?"

She slipped out of the seat and stood under the bulkhead.

"Did you know that Kennedy and Joshua follow each other on Twitter?"

Sheriff Jackson folded his arms across his chest but didn't answer back.

"I searched and searched his account for any sign of her

but couldn't find anything. Then, the other day, I realized he would've erased anything . . . but she wouldn't have. So I spent the other night scrolling through her Twitter feed and found something."

The sheriff's forehead twitched a bit, but if he were the least bit intrigued by her words, he hid it well.

"She . . . she retweeted two of his tweets." Poe walked to the oven, opened the door, and revealed its new function as a filing cabinet. She removed a file and closed the door with a bang. "One was on February eighth." She opened the file and handed him a printout of the screenshot she took of the tweet. "That's his Twitter handle, @SavageJosh2016." The tweet was a photo of a black bag full of trash, and the accompanying words, *Actual photo of me from class this morning.*

Poe pulled out the screenshot of the second tweet, dated February twelfth at three forty-seven in the afternoon. *Whenever life sucks, remember . . . you're gonna die someday. Hopefully sooner rather than later.*

"This was Friday. Kennedy disappeared the next day."

"Payton, we looked at her Twitter. She retweeted people all the time." His voice softened and slipped to the side of compassion-filled.

"Did you see his? Even know that was him?"

The sheriff kept his lips tightly sealed.

"Okay . . ." Her eyes darted around the room, ready to find the next piece of information that would convince the sheriff to consider the possibility Joshua was involved in her sister's disappearance.

"A few days before you told us about Kennedy and Melissa going missing, I was with Joshua. He took me to the same state park Melissa was at when she went missing. Out to the middle of nowhere, he tried to pull me down the trail, but I didn't want to go. He got a little ticked about it and went without me. As I walked back up the trail . . . there was a girl. Brown hair like me. A runner. It could've been her. It could've been Melissa."

"Payton, there are young girls with brown hair running all over the area."

"He got Misty pregnant and wouldn't pay for the baby's funeral. He threatened me at school. He was here tonight and threatened me again in front of everyone. He had my shoes. The ones that went missing that day we talked at the house. And I think I caught him spying on me from the cemetery. I think he's been watching me in the RV. Sheriff Jackson, he—"

"They have a suspect in Lincoln."

Poe blinked hard. Shocked by his words and believing she may have misheard his statement. "They what?"

"A transient. Found him staking out a gas station bathroom. They're questioning him now; and then we'll bring him here, sit him down, and see what he says."

"A transient? But anyone could stalk a bathroom. Anyone—"

"And anyone can retweet something."

She stepped back and partially hunched over like he'd punched her in the gut. Her insides churned and her thoughts spun in circles.

"I'm not saying your concerns have no merit, okay? Just keep an open mind— Payton, it probably isn't Joshua."

"But—"

"I'll talk to him. All right? I'll talk to him." He walked toward the back of the RV and pulled out his walkie-talkie. "Dispatch, this is two-eight-five. Do you copy?"

264

Poe closed her eyes. Again, her mind flashed back to those moments sitting in the police cruiser, the moments after the disappearance of her sister.

"Two-eight-five, this is dispatch. Go ahead."

"Yeah, I'm gonna need someone to pick up a possible person of interest and get him to the station. Tonight."

"Copy, two-eight-five. Name?"

The sheriff's eyes cut to Poe. "Joshua Toobin."

"Ten-four."

The sheriff placed the walkie-talkie back in its holster and turned to Cole. "Take them home, Cole."

<hr>

10:00 p.m.

The closet was so dark that all the clothes took on a gray hue. Poe's hands trembled in her lap, and her vision jetted around the small space at the now depressingly drab skirts, pants, and blouses. Her reality felt overwhelming.

She stared up at the dead light bulb. Let her mind enter the fog. She saw her and her sister sitting in the closet, clinging to one another while a tropical storm raged outside and rattled their bedroom windows.

"One thousand one, one thousand two, one thousand three . . ."

They could've run downstairs and jumped into bed with their parents, like most kids did when they were scared of the thunder and lightning, but Dylan and Payton never needed anyone but each other.

265

"One thousand four, one thousand five . . ."

She looked up at the clothes around her. "Are you here?" she whispered. "Is that why I come here all the time? I somehow know you're here?"

"It's where we wait for the storms to pass." She heard Dylan's voice as if she were sitting right next to her.

She rearranged herself, knelt onto her knees, and started to rummage through the items on the floor. "Are you here?"

Her search was frantic. Futile, and she knew it, but her hands didn't stop scraping the clothes and shoes from the floor, tossing them out of the closet and into the bedroom. "Where are you?" she screamed, then stood and yanked Dylan's clothes off the rod and threw them outside the door. "Don't come to me all the time if you aren't going to tell me where I can find you!" She threw another load of clothes onto the bedroom floor and then fell into a heap on the closet floor. Her energy drained and her fight, waning.

Poe looked up and studied the light bulb another long moment.

She stood, reached up, and twisted it a half turn in the opposite direction. It immediately brightened the space.

She slowly lowered her hand while continuing to stare up a moment more, and then loosened the bulb again. The closet returned to its state of darkness. She lowered herself back to the floor and leaned against the wall just as her daddy appeared around the corner.

She watched him look at the mess she'd created. He scratched his head and then reached down and picked up one of Dylan's retro concert T-shirts. Def Leppard. "We often thought about removing her things from the room so maybe you could

266

have a little peace, but . . . I just couldn't bring myself to do it. I wanted it to be ready for her when she came home. But . . ." She watched the shirt slip from his fingers and fall back to the floor, and Poe believed that he let his hopes for Dylan's return fall with it. Maybe he was starting to let go just as Poe was trying to hold on with all her might.

"Rough night, huh?" He sat down next to the heap of clothes. "I heard what happened at the dance."

She cocked her head. "You did?"

"It was just a dance. I cannot for the life of me figure out why people can't simply leave you be. What did it accomplish to have it shut down?"

"It's Joshua. He's trying to pay me back."

"Pay you back for what? For the fight?"

"Yeah. And he knows that I know he's the one who got Misty pregnant. I found out right before he showed up at the house that day."

More sadness covered her daddy's face, to the point that his tanned skin was shrouded in it.

"I was upset and . . . not really thinking. I just acted out of—"

"Disgust. Rage."

"Yeah. He refused to take any responsibility for the burial. He left her to deal with it on her own."

"Like your mama was left to deal with you two on her own?"

"I needed to fight back at something, and I think he became my outlet." She took a deep breath and laid her head against the wall. "Maybe Cole's right. I'm finding pieces of a puzzle and forcing them to fit what I think happened."

Daddy didn't respond. He picked the T-shirt back up and clutched it in his hand as he looked over at her.

267

"But it made sense, Daddy. The pieces did seem to fit. I mean, he's out there spreading lies to the point that everyone thinks I'm crazy. Which, maybe I am. I know I feel crazy."

"Is crazy so bad?" He slipped into the closet, sat down next to her, removed a hand from the T-shirt, and ran the palm over her hair. "I think people like to believe they would handle a situation better. But nobody can know how something will affect them." He regripped the T-shirt again and wrung it in his hands. "It's not like you can plan ahead and put together some type of game plan for a tragedy. Especially not one like your child . . . or sister going missing. I think we're doing the best we can. Don't you?"

"Honestly, I don't think we're doing much of anything. We're just existing."

He tightened his grip on the shirt, rested his head against the wall, and stared out across the bedroom just on the other side of the closet door. "Everything happened so fast that we didn't have any time to stop and think." He shook his head and chuckled a bit. Not the type of laugh with joy, but the kind filled with disgust. "All that chaos. Police asking questions and the press asking questions and everybody taking part in the search, but . . . from time to time, they'd look at me like . . ."

"Like you'd done something wrong."

"Yup." He again removed a hand from the shirt and wrapped his arm around her shoulder.

"I think about her all the time and what she went through . . . or is going through."

She allowed her gaze to travel the length of the closet ceiling, and land on the light bulb. "I have moments where I think I'm having a memory, but it doesn't line up with anything the police are saying, or it's something I wouldn't do. At least not normally, anyway. For a second it feels so real, but then it feels . . . counterfeit."

"Maybe you should stop trying to remember. Let your mind go there when its ready. We can't change what's happened. All we can do is somehow find a way to cope."

She placed her hand next to his on the T-shirt and squeezed it tight. "I don't know if I can."

"And I can't tell you how because I'm still working on it myself. We all are." He leaned over, kissed her on the head, and started to stand.

"I just need answers," she cried.

He tossed her the shirt. "We all do."

CHAPTER 24

September 2, 2017

5:50 a.m.

Wearing the Def Leppard T-shirt and a pair of cutoff shorts, Poe walked aimlessly along the road. She didn't have a plan. No idea where she could go or who she could talk to. Even if she did find someone, what would she say?

She kept her focus on her flip-flops and didn't look up until she hit grass.

She was met with a modest, bungalow-style house that sat at the end of Magnolia. Poe took a deep breath before she walked across the lawn and knocked on the back door.

It was early. Chances were that nobody would answer or she'd be shooed away and told to come back at a more agreeable hour.

Inside, the kitchen light turned on. Poe watched Kasi walk through the room and open the door.

"Hey, Poe." She was amazingly chipper. Nothing unheard of for Kasi.

"I'm glad I didn't wake you."

"Are you kidding? I haven't been able to stop thinking about last night. Oh, and Misty's here too. We didn't have our camp-out at the cove, but we're sort of camping out here. Want to come in?"

"No." Poe suddenly felt horrible for dragging someone else into her craziness. "You know, never mind. We can talk about it at school on Monday." She turned and ran across the yard.

"Poe? Poe, wait."

She slowed but didn't turn around. "No. You two have fun. I shouldn't have come."

"Are you going to make me chase you all the way home? Come on back."

Poe stopped walking and allowed Kasi to catch up with her. "We'll go inside and talk."

Poe shook her head, panic rising in her chest.

"You came all this way. You obviously need to talk to someone. I'm here."

"Me too."

Poe looked back to find Misty standing on the front porch. "And I've had coffee, so I'm capable of thinking." She stepped into the grass. "Is this about the Joshua stuff?"

Kasi looked over at Poe and winced, perhaps feeling a bit guilty. "I told her what happened tonight and what you said about Joshua. I hope you don't care. I wasn't gossiping."

Poe shook her head. "It's fine."

"It's actually helpful," Misty said. "Makes me grateful he didn't want to be involved in my life." She dropped to the ground and sat on the grass. "Can you imagine being in a relationship with . . . a monster?"

"It may not be him," Poe admitted. "But that doesn't mean he isn't still a horrible person."

Kasi sat down next to Misty, and with a deep breath Poe came over to join them.

"He's beyond horrible." Misty picked up a blade of grass and wrapped it around the tip of her finger. "A master manipulator."

Kasi's eyes were focused on the tip of Misty's finger, which was turning white from the pressure of the grass noose around her finger. "How's that?"

"I mean, look at him. I got knocked up, which he played a part in. He's trolling Poe hard . . . Yet he's managed to convince everyone else we're the crazy ones. No matter what he does, he's got this ridiculous fan club that cheers him on. It's twisted."

"And one minute he's sweet as pecan pie, the next he's slamming you on social media, and then back to sweet again." Poe rubbed her temples. "He gives you whiplash."

"The whole time we dated, he'd talk about how much he hates drama, but in reality, he loves it. Creates it."

"Thrives on it," Kasi added.

"It's all so heavy," Misty sighed. "We're seniors in high school. We're supposed to be doing crazy, fun things—"

"Not seeing lives end."

Misty and Kasi looked back at Poe with shocked, widened eyes.

"You just had to go there . . ." Misty tossed the blade of grass into the air, laid back, and looked up at the sky. "God, this year has sucked."

"Yep." Poe crossed her legs at the ankle and looked up at the heavens. "Speaking of God . . ."

Misty groaned. "Now we're going there too? We should've invited Finn. He could handle the God stuff. I'm not up to speed on all that."

"Speaking of God, what?" Kasi asked.

Poe had too many questions about him to even ask, but there

was one that raged on each and every day. "If he lets bad things happen, do you think he makes people suffer through it too?"

Poe heard Kasi fall onto the grass beside her and groan. "Heavy stuff."

Poe lowered her head and looked out across the yard. "Benjamin. Dylan. Melissa and Kennedy. They're gone—"

Kasi shot her hand into the air. "Hold up, Poe. We don't know if the girls—"

"Sheriff Jackson doesn't think they're alive."

Her arm fell back to the ground. "I'm so sorry."

"I mean, I get it. He allows suffering. I've been suffering for a year, but does he allow that sort of pain—her level of suffering—to last a long time?"

"I've wondered stuff like that about Benjamin too."

"What kind of stuff?" Kasi asked.

"Like Poe said. Was he ever in pain? Did he feel sick? Did he feel loved or cared for . . . Did he know . . . did he know how much he scared me but how much I loved him?" She rolled onto her stomach and rested her chin on her hands. "Did he suffer? Physically or emotionally? Because I did."

"You did everything you could for him," Kasi encouraged. "You went to all your doctor's appointments. You ate right. You found him a family that could provide for him. You did that out of love, Misty. He didn't suffer from your choices, because you did what you thought was best."

Poe nodded. "He was surrounded with love, and I bet it protected him from all the negative."

"But you don't believe the same thing about your sister?" Misty asked.

"I don't know. I don't know anything anymore."

"She hated pain," Misty said. "She couldn't stand the sight of blood or guts. Even if she just stubbed her toe, she acted like her arm was cut off or something."

"But she loved scary movies," Kasi added.

"And musicals," Misty said. "If she made me watch *High School Musical* once, I swear she made me watch it a hundred times. And often all three, in order."

"I was telling Cole the same thing the other day," Poe said with a small smile. "He caught me listening to one of the songs. My music was on shuffle and it started playing."

"That's a magical moment, right there," Misty said. "Maybe she's trying to reach you through Troy and Gabriella."

The girls laughed.

Misty sat back up and looked over at Poe. "But you. You don't really like horror movies or being scared, yet you're willing to look a monster like Joshua straight in the face."

"He doesn't scare me. What else can he take from me? My life? I don't feel like I have much of one anymore, anyway. I just think if he was going to take one of us, it obviously should've been me. Maybe I could handle it better than her. Maybe I was meant to."

"I don't know if anyone could handle that, Poe. Not even you."

"Maybe not, but still . . . I hear it all the time at the funeral home. 'At least they didn't suffer' or 'I hope they didn't suffer.'" Again, she looked directly at Misty. "Right?"

Misty nodded.

"That's what tortures people and makes them crazy in the head. It's all that wondering about how much their loved ones suffered. It's what I think about. It's what you think about."

Kasi reached out and held Poe's right hand. "Your sister

wouldn't want you obsessing about that. She'd want you to remember her as she was when she was with you; with us. Laughing and talking up a storm. Giving Cole a hard time."

"The mess." Misty chuckled. "Such the mess."

"My parents and Nana are so out of it. They're doing everything they can to escape thinking about it or talking about it . . . but I need to talk about her. I miss her," Poe whispered. "And I'm starting to forget her. What she sounded like . . . all those quirky things she'd say, and wear."

"Is that why you became Poe?"

Poe felt as if the world suddenly started spinning faster around her.

"Trying to be more like Dylan? Taking on some of her personality? The way she dressed? You're trying to stay connected to her somehow?"

Misty's questions felt like a revelation. Tears immediately developed in Poe's eyes. "Is that what I'm doing?"

"It makes some sense, actually," Kasi said. "You're trying to hold on to her. You're escaping as much as your parents are, you're just doing it in a different way."

"I don't know what I'm doing anymore," Poe admitted. "Ever since the sheriff showed up and said other girls went missing, I've felt lost in a really dark place."

"Remember the light she was," Kasi encouraged. "Please don't let the darkness you're feeling take away the light that she gave while she was here. If you do, then evil wins. It's stealing your joy. It's winning. Evil is winning in you, Poe. Don't let it. Don't let that man, and the need to avenge Dylan, destroy your life anymore."

"Yeah." Misty took Poe's left hand in hers and squeezed it tight. "Stare it down."

7:00 a.m.

The wind flowing through Poe's hair seemed to take some of the chaotic thoughts with it. Her mind no longer raced, and from her spot at the playground, she felt a little more at peace. Even her grip on the swing chains loosened.

"Poe?"

She opened her eyes. Drug her feet on the ground to stop the swing, and turned toward the voice. "Brody! You scared me to death."

He stepped a bit closer. "Did you not hear me pull up? I said your name a few times."

"I was sort of out of it. Sorry."

He walked to the empty swing next to her and sat down. His wide girth barely fit between the swing's chains.

"What are you doing out so early?" she asked.

"I had to pick up my sound system from the cove."

She shook her head, feeling stupid for not thinking. "We left a mess. How bad is it?"

"By the time I got there, it was all picked up."

"I appreciate you donating the speakers and everything."

"No problem." He waved it off, but sat in complete stillness. "Forget about me. What are you doin' out so early?"

"I was at Kasi's. Talking some things through."

"Gotcha."

"I went out for a walk and ended up at her house. It was good, though."

"You walked? Need a ride back home?"

"Naw, I'm good."

He stood up. "I don't think it's safe for you to be out all by yourself like this. Please let me give you a ride."

"Um . . ."

"Come on. I'll get you back."

Seeing as her feet were still on fire from almost a full day of walking on hot Mississippi pavement, she acquiesced and followed him to his truck.

"You okay?" he asked as they climbed into the cab.

"I guess so."

"You seemed kinda out of it when I pulled up." He checked the side mirror, made sure nobody was coming up behind him, and pulled onto the road.

"I was just thinking."

"'Bout what?"

"Oh, you don't need to crawl inside my messed-up mind."

His eyebrow cocked as he glanced over at her. "You think your mind's messed up?"

"I know it is."

"Don't be so hard on yourself."

"I'm not being hard on myself. I'm being honest."

"Okay, so why do you think that?"

She looked down at her hands, which had begun to fidget. "'Cause I'm doing things that don't make sense. I'm going crazy."

"You seem pretty sane to me. Who's telling you you're crazy?"

She gulped. "Nobody, I guess. Or just me telling myself."

He didn't respond.

She turned to face him. "Can I ask you a question?"

He laughed, which slightly improved the mood inside the

truck cab. "You always say that to me before you ask a question, and I always say yes. Might as well quit askin' and just get to the question."

He had a point. "Okay." She took a few moments to find her wording. "How . . . how did your dad die? Did he suffer at all?"

He blinked hard. "Oh. I wasn't expecting that."

Poe grimaced. Regretted she'd even asked. But no matter how carefully she tried to word the question, it would never be an easy one to answer.

The mood in the truck returned to feeling morose.

"Um . . . overdose." Brody scratched his head and readjusted his position in the seat. "Some think he did it on purpose," he added.

"I'm sorry."

His fingers gripped the steering wheel, and he stared at the road in front of him.

"How did you find a way to cope with it?"

He shrugged. "Just did."

"Wish I could."

"I guess we all gotta find our own way."

Poe thought over her conversations with Misty and Kasi, and now Brody. So many people lost so much.

Loss surrounded her. She wasn't as alone as she'd thought.

"I'm sorry, Brody."

"For what?"

"For never asking you before now." She sighed and leaned her head against the window. "For being so wrapped up in my own stuff that I didn't even see that you had stuff too."

"You've got nothin' to apologize for. We're family. We're good."

They stayed quiet until he pulled the truck to a stop in front of her house and put it in park.

She exhaled and then looked toward her house. "Thanks for the ride."

"Anytime. Oh, and Winnie's paint came in yesterday. We need to plan a time for you to bring her in. Give me a call later, and we'll set it up."

"I'll do that."

She opened the door.

"Hey," he said before she hopped out. "I heard last night on the police scanner that they were looking for Joshua. Know what that's about?"

"Yeah. They wanted to ask him a few things. They're probably questioning him now."

"Naw. I just saw him down at the cove. He was getting there when I left."

"Did you talk to him?"

"Just for a minute. He was drunk, saying something about an angel and the platform. I was afraid he was gonna try to swim out there. Made him promise he'd stay on land." He shrugged. "Aw well. I'm sure the cops will find him." He smiled over at her. "You best get inside. We wouldn't want your mama to worry."

She sighed. "No. We wouldn't. Thanks for the ride."

Poe shut the door, watched Brody drive away, and started the walk across the yard. Her mind raced at the same speed she ran the pendant across her necklace.

"That platform sure has seen a victim or two." She heard Joshua's voice in her head. His words on the day of the King of the Mountain Championship.

She stopped walking and looked down at her necklace. A gold angel.

7:45 a.m.

The waters of the cove were calm. Its surface, smooth like glass.

Poe stood on the edge of the shore and stared out at the platform peacefully floating in the middle of the water.

"Are you out there?" she yelled across the water. "Is that where you're waiting for me?"

She took several steps into the water. "I've looked for you everywhere. Why won't you talk to me? I waited in the closet, but you didn't come. I counted . . . but the storm is still right here. I sat out in the cemetery with the twins, thinking you might tell me, but you didn't. What are you waiting for?"

She closed her eyes and focused on the sounds around her: the birds, the leaves ruffling in the wind, and the tiny waves that rolled onto shore. She walked into the water until it reached her shoulders and swam to the platform.

It was the first time she'd been in the water since the day her sister went missing, but it felt familiar. Like the time hadn't passed, a year hadn't been spent waiting, losing herself.

She took a deep breath and plunged deep into the water and underneath the platform. Her eyes opened as she strained to see through the murky water. Her arms flailed around as if she would eventually touch her sister and be able to pull her close, but her skin only made contact with the algae that covered the yellow barrels.

She ran out of breath and broke through the surface. Her nose and mouth barely had enough room to take in air beneath the slats of wood. Tired of kicking her legs under the weight of her wet clothes, she threaded her fingers through the spaces between each board and grabbed ahold with her fingertips.

"Talk to me. It was Joshua, wasn't it? Please, talk to me."

She tilted her head back as far as possible, kept her face close to the moss-covered planks, and moved along the perimeter.

Poe took a deep breath. Submerged herself deep into the water.

Moments before running out of breath, she swam toward the surface and broke through with a deep inhale.

Over and over again, she immersed herself in the water, waited until the last moment, then fiercely kicked her legs and returned to the surface.

Becoming desperate, Poe sank as far as possible, then kicked her way to the surface again. When her head popped out of the water, it smacked into a metal barrel. She surfaced, opened her eyes, and ran her hands across it.

"No algae," she said. Her voice sounded thick to her ears, as if it was drowning in the water that seeped into her mouth.

After clearing her head and her airway, Poe slipped her fingers through the slats above her and moved along underneath the platform until she bumped into another large piece of metal. Again, she ran a hand over it. It was completely smooth.

She searched again. Found a third barrel and ran her hand across it.

Smooth.

Poe felt along every inch of the barrel. Every ridge, every seam. At the mouth of the barrel, she cupped her hand over the circular rim and tried to twist the cap, but as she turned her fingers, a small metal chain wrapped around the nozzle and rotated under her grip.

With the fingers from one hand gripped between the planks, she felt along the chain as it drifted in the water until she came upon an item that hung from the end.

She knew the piece of metal well. Her fingers traced it several times a day. The pendant was identical to the one that hung from the thin chain around her neck.

"No!" Her fingers lost their grip. She slipped under the water and guzzled a mouthful of water.

She surfaced again. "No!" She spit the water out of her mouth and wrestled the chain off the neck of the nozzle. Once it was free, she plunged back into the water and emerged outside the platform, slipped her arm through the ladder and hung, exhausted and unable to tread water or swim toward the shore.

She pressed her cheek against the wooden ladder and sobbed.

Cole sped down Cove Trails Road and screeched to a halt in the parking lot next to Winnie.

He jumped out of the truck, raced around to the RV's side, and threw open the door. "Poe?" He could hear his voice shake and feel his heart pound in his chest.

"Poe!" He slammed the door shut and raced down the trail and onto the beach. As soon as his feet touched the sand, he spotted her clutching the platform ladder. "Poe!"

He pulled out his phone, dialed, then anxiously paced in a tight circle. As soon as Mr. Brave answered, he shouted, "I found her. She's at the cove again. Bring an ambulance. She looks hurt."

Cole yanked off his shoes, ran through the water until it reached his thighs, and then dove in and swam quickly toward the platform, working to keep his head above the water so his hearing aids wouldn't get wet. His soaked clothes weighed him down, but he kept his arms moving and sliced through the water, pulling himself closer to her.

"Poe!" Cole finally reached the ladder. "Poe!" He skipped the steps and used his arms to thrust himself onto the platform and then pulled her out of the water.

He sat down, scooped her into his lap, and wrapped his arms around her. "You scared us. The police went looking for Josh and couldn't find him. Brody told your mom that he dropped you off at the house, but you weren't there. We—"

"I found Dylan's necklace." Poe slowly reached up and gripped onto his wet shirt. He noticed the familiar chain and pendant hanging from her fingers. "I finally found her."

8:30 a.m.

Poe and Cole stood huddled together, sharing a blanket. It was a hot day out, but they both continued to shiver. Probably more from the shock than the temperature in the air.

Cole looked around the perimeter of the beach. It was cordoned off with yellow police tape, but that didn't stop the gawkers. News must've traveled fast, because they stood by the dozens and watched the dive team retrieve the three barrels, place them on the platform, haul them back to the beach, and inspect them one by one.

283

After hours out on the water, Sheriff Jackson and three other officers finally disembarked from the police boat and silently walked to Mr. and Mrs. Brave, who stood a few feet away.

An aura of sadness hung in the air like a dense fog. "David, Laurie," Sheriff Jackson said as he walked up to them. He paused, fumbling as he searched for the words.

"Just say it," Mrs. Brave sputtered. "Just tell us."

He took a deep breath. Glanced over at Poe. "Three bodies."

Her mom gasped and threw her hands over her mouth. Poe stood motionless. When Cole looked down at her, her eyes showed no sign of life.

He slipped his hand in hers and gripped it tight.

"No . . . no, no, no," her mom whimpered.

"I'm so sorry," Sheriff Jackson said. "We don't have positive identifications yet. We'll run DNA tests. But—"

"But what?" her dad asked.

"All brunettes. Mid- to late teens. The remains are at different stages of decomposition, which would point to their deaths taking place at different times."

"Cause of death?" he asked. He acted more mortician than father. He snuck a peek at Poe, then shook his head and grimaced. "How did she die?" he corrected.

"Looks like blunt force trauma on the back of the skull."

Cole recoiled at the description but noticed no movement from a still-petrified Poe.

"I pray she didn't suffer," Mr. Brave added, then clumsily wiped at one eye.

The officers stood quietly and let the family absorb the information. The silence of the beach and parking lot was overwhelming. A solemn moment that everyone feared would come but, sadly, expected.

Mrs. Brave began to walk toward the water's edge, but only made it a few steps before she dropped to the sand in sobs. Her husband fell to her side, and Cole saw them embrace for the first time since meeting them back in the eighth grade, when he showed up at the Brave Funeral Home with his first flower delivery.

"Cole? Can I talk to you?" Sheriff Jackson asked.

Cole nodded, removed the blanket from his shoulders and wrapped it around Poe, then followed the sheriff to the center of the beach.

"What sort of state was she in when you found her?"

Cole shook his head, not even wanting to recall what he saw. "She . . . she was clinging to the platform's ladder. She was in shock. Just staring across the water. I don't even know if she saw me swim up to her."

"And she had the necklace?"

"Yes. She had a tight grip on it, but it was obvious that it matched the one she wears every day."

The sheriff sighed and he rubbed his temples. "Did you look? Underneath?"

"No, sir. I just sat there with her until you showed up."

Sheriff Jackson turned toward the beach and watched two officers in the direction of the boat. "I best head back out. We've got more evidence to collect." He placed his hand on Cole's shoulder and squeezed tight. "Stay close to her. She'll need you. I'm not so sure her parents will be able to comfort her. They're grieving enough on their own."

Cole watched the sheriff walk to the boat, climb in, and head back to the platform. The man's head hung in defeat.

He's got to be close. The realization hit Cole like a ton of bricks. If the bodies were found under the platform, that meant that the kidnapper was close and knew the importance the platform played in Cornwell.

For the first time since Poe mentioned the possibility, Cole knew she was right.

Joshua was a killer, and there was no telling what he would do next.

He turned to walk back to her but only saw the blanket lying in the sand.

The streets of Cornwell were nearly empty. With the storm moving in, some citizens took shelter in their homes, while others were still at the cove.

Poe drove through town and looked for Joshua's car. She was tired of playing cat and mouse. He killed her sister, Kennedy, and Melissa, and she was ready to do what the police hadn't managed to do so far: catch him and make him pay.

She parked Winnie in the alley behind the Suds 4 Duds and walked up and down the alleys of Main Street. Thanks to her past connection with the in-crowd, she knew all their favorite spots, where they could slip inside and hang out to avoid going home for the afternoon.

Her pace was quick and her heart beat even faster. At each location she checked, Joshua hadn't been seen. But as much as she wanted to find him, fast, she stopped checking shops when she got tired of being asked questions about Dylan being found.

News had already spread through town, which meant it

would soon get back to her parents and the sheriff that she was on the hunt for Joshua Toobin.

Poe raced back to Winnie and started to head toward the trails Joshua boasted about spending so much time scouting, but as she reached the city limits her eye caught his car at the end of a rural road and heading south.

Poe waited until the car drove out of sight. There was no need for her to hurry; the street led to a dead end at Brody Wynn's Body Shop.

She pulled Winnie onto a small dirt road hidden in the trees, climbed out in her still-wet clothes, and ran through the woods and onto the property as Brody pulled the garage door shut behind Joshua's car.

Poe snuck toward the building and placed her ear to the garage door, but only heard muffled words.

She moved beyond the garage door and toward the corner of the building, then slid along the side until she came to a door at the back of the building.

As the voices inside grew louder, she slowly turned the knob and was surprised to hear the latch release. She took a deep breath and then crept inside.

"Why did you ask me to come?" Joshua said.

"I heard on the police scanner that the police are lookin' for ya," Brody said. The voices moved toward her. "Figured you needed a place to collect your thoughts."

"Looking for me? What for?"

Poe slipped into the dark, dingy bathroom, left the metal door slightly open, and looked through the crack between the door jamb and the door.

"You tell me," Brody said. His voice was gruffer.

"Hell if I know."

"Probably all the messing around you've been tryin' to do with Payton." The sound of Brody's voice moved closer. She could see their legs down the hall.

"Wh-what are you talking about?" Joshua sounded less than sincere.

"I've been watching. I know you're messin' with her."

Poe backed away from the door, moved deeper into the bathroom, stepped inside the bathroom stall, and slid the latch in place behind her.

A heavy thud sounded against the outside of the bathroom wall.

"Hey, man!" Joshua shouted. "Cut it out. I was just joking around, trying to give her a hard time."

Another thud.

"Brody! Stop."

A slap.

Poe pulled her phone out of her pocket and typed a message for Cole. I'm at Brody's. Joshua is here!

She sent the message, slipped the phone back in her pocket, and peered out of the slit between the stall and the door. Her reflection looked back at her. Only . . .

Poe studied it more closely. She didn't see a reflection. It was her class picture from junior year. She placed two hands on the door in front of her, leaned forward, and stared at the wall across from the stall. Photographs covered the wall. Photographs of Poe and her sister. Kennedy. Melissa.

She gasped, placed her forehead to the door, and studied the wall with one eye.

An enlarged photograph of Lady Bug caked in mud. Another

of the Bug in the early stages of the fire. A third of her parked in the cove parking lot. Brand-new scratches marred the paint on the door.

Snapshots of Winnie's interior. The bulkhead covered in research. Poe's files opened on the table.

The shower stall, blanketed in memories.

Photos of Poe inside Winnie. Photos obviously taken from the cemetery.

Joshua broke through the bathroom door. Quickly, she looked over more photographs. Interior shots of her closet. Her bedroom and bathroom.

Poe jumped onto the toilet seat and crouched into a ball.

Joshua's head slammed against the stall door. His hair flew through the slit, then slid down the door as he fell to the floor.

She stared at the latch and prayed that it would hold. She listened to her deep breathing. Her eyes darted around the stall until she closed her eyes and tried to concentrate on staying conscious.

CHAPTER 25

August 16, 2016

5:35 p.m.

Cole was glued to the television, and all the news only made matters worse. When he tried to make a run to his daddy's house, he didn't make it three steps outside before a reporter stuck a microphone in his face. His only option was to turn back around, head inside, and hide in his room alone.

He'd pretty much stayed there or at the flower shop since the news about Dylan's disapperance spread and reporters flooded into Cornwell. First the vans pulled up outside the Brave Funeral Home, and lights, sound equipment, and cameras filled the sidewalk across the street as each station vied for the perfect shot of the morbid house that sat on the corner of Magnolia and Main.

Those with the best camera angle managed to get the side view of the house, along with the loading bay of the funeral home and the cemetery. The perfect setting for a girl-gone-missing story.

Within hours of the disappearance, the press caught wind that the missing girl was in a relationship with a boy who lived in the trailer park on the edge of town. Less than thirty minutes later, reporters set up camp at Cole's mama's house, her flower shop, and his daddy's club.

It was only a few minutes more before a station reported an anonymous source saw Cole rush to work on the morning Dylan disappeared. His hair was a mess, and he was wearing the same clothes he wore to the bonfire the night before. There was a quick trial by gossip, and Cole was found guilty.

He sat on the edge of the bed and kept a stern eye on his laptop. Live streaming coverage of the prayer vigil for Dylan started just a few minutes before, and the high school football stadium was almost full.

Nineteen eighties hair band music played over the announcement system. It was loud and distorted, but obviously "Living on a Prayer" by Bon Jovi. One of Dylan's favorites.

"You aren't gonna go?"

Cole looked over at his mother, who stood in the doorway. She wore her favorite dress and heels. Unusual for her, but this was an unusual occasion.

"You look nice, Mom. Dylan loves that dress."

"I know." She smiled slightly. The kind of smile an anxiety-filled mother might give if she doesn't have words, but somehow wants to make you feel better. But in this particular case, there was no feeling better. "Your dad and I thought we'd go together. He'll be here in a few minutes. Please come with us. It'll look strange if you aren't there."

"And it'll look strange if I am. Everybody already thinks I did something to her."

"The sheriff released a statement. Said you're not—"

"Since when do people care about the truth?" Cole slammed his laptop shut. "I see the way they look at me. They think I did something."

"Which is why you have to go." He kept a stern eye on her

as she walked into the room and sat down next to him. "I think that since you can't help in the search—"

"I wanted to." He felt his frustration level soar. His temples throbbed. "They wouldn't let me. They said if I found her, it would only make me look more guilty."

"I know that. I'm just saying that I think you need to walk into that stadium with your head held high and show them that you're there because you want her back."

His body relaxed a little. "My head held high, huh?"

She playfully bumped her elbow with his. "Yeah. It's what all the cool kids do."

"I don't want to be cool, I just . . . I want her back more than they ever could."

He heard the front door open. Footsteps sounded on the mobile home floor until Carl appeared around the corner. "Are we ready?"

Although his parents never lived together, Carl always made himself right at home when he was over—which was often.

"He's not going," she said.

"Yeah, you are."

"Dad, I—"

"You're goin'. Get your shoes on."

Cole swung his legs over the side of the bed and reached for a shoe as his relieved mother glanced over her shoulder at his father. "Thank you," she mouthed.

"I was trained to read lips, you know," Cole quipped as he tied his shoe.

Carl shoved his hands in his freshly pressed Wranglers. "You're too smart for your own good, that's for sure."

Cole stood and adjusted his hearing aids.

"What are you doing?" his mom asked.

"If they're going to talk about me, let them talk. But I won't be listening."

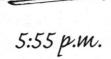

5:55 p.m.

Cole and his parents climbed out of the pickup truck under the watchful eye of those who were already walking through the parking lot. There were murmurs, but that was nothing new. People from town had been murmuring about them for years.

Cole followed his parents through the gated entrance and turned his hearing aids back up when they came face to face with Dylan's father, who stood in a receiving line so he could personally welcome and thank each person who came to pray for the safe return of his daughter.

A visibly distressed David Brave hugged Cole's parents, and then looked to Cole and placed a hand on each of his shoulders. "Hey, son. How are you holding up?" The gentleness and sincerity in his voice brought Cole to tears.

Mr. Brave reached out, pulled Cole to him, and held him close as they both lamented her disappearance. In their tight embrace, they ignored the flash of cell phone cameras and the rush of reporters who wanted video of the moment so it could be the opening image of their newscasts that evening.

Eventually, he released Cole, draped an arm over his shoulders, and led him across the football field to the fifty-yard line and onto the stage.

To the awe of the more than five thousand people collected

on the football field and in the stands, Dylan's family, along with Cole and his parents, stood on the platform together.

Cole focused on the crowd in front of him and did as his mama suggested; he held his head high. He felt every muscle movement, every breath that left his body. Hyperaware. Hypersensitive. It was impossible to act natural when appearing normal was the goal. The situation was anything but.

Finn's father, Pastor Downs, walked to the microphone. "Thank you for joining us today . . ." The pastor's voice faded out of Cole's mind as he worked to concentrate on standing upright. The overwhelming circumstances, combined with the heat, left him reeling, and he slightly swayed under the mounting pressure.

His pulse rate increased. Sweat collected all over his body and ran into the corner of his eyes. His fingers twitched. If he didn't move, let out some of the accumulating energy, he'd for sure keel over.

He slightly leaned forward and looked to his left, just past his mother and over to Payton. Her eyes were glazed over as if she were heavily sedated. Her face, completely blank. It was as if there was no soul inside. She was nothing but a shell of a person. Completely gone.

In a soul-stirring moment, she slowly turned her head his direction. They shared a long gaze. A gaze that made his heart beat again.

CHAPTER 26

September 2, 2017

10:15 a.m.

One thousand twenty-one. One thousand twenty-two. One thousand twenty-three . . .

Poe locked her limbs in place so she wouldn't tip over and squeezed her eyes tight. She was scared to open them. Scared to look out and see Joshua laying on the bathroom floor.

She feared that her recurring nightmares of finding herself in a bathroom stall standing in blood or perching on a toilet seat were more a premonition than a wild imagination.

Poe listened to the sound of bulky boots sticking to the ground as Brody moved around the room. He chattered gibberish at a feverish pace.

She listened as he pulled Joshua out of the bathroom and down the hallway. Joshua slid easily across the floor. Proof that he couldn't put up a fight.

Dizzy and lightheaded, she slowly lowered a shaking foot to the ground. Silence lay suspended in the heavy air around her. She peered through the slit in the door.

Brody's eye suddenly stared back at her. The pupil dilated to the point that it nearly covered his iris.

She screamed.

The stall door flung open, slamming her in the head with a violent blow that threw her back against the water tank and sent her cell phone into the toilet bowl.

He yanked her out of the stall with so much force that she crashed into the sink and fell to the floor.

Her heart skipped wildly when she realized her cheek sunk into a small puddle of Joshua's blood.

"What are you doin' here?" Brody's shout was more of a demonic growl.

"I-I-I came to warn you about Joshua." Her mind tumbled thoughts. Searched for something to say. "It was self-defense," she blurted. "Joshua attacked you. He's dangerous and hiding from the police. You protected yourself. I saw it."

Brody clenched her arm. Drug her down the hall, past Joshua and into the office at the back of the building.

He tossed her into a metal chair.

Restlessly paced like a cougar.

She tried to breathe but hardly took in air. She couldn't catch her breath.

Couldn't believe her reality.

Joshua lay in the hallway just across from the doorway. "Joshua's been following me." Her eyes darted around the room. "Messing with my head." She searched for a way out. "Doing things to make me think I was crazy." Or something she could use as a weapon.

Brody took a deep breath in through his nose. "He shouldn't have been doin' that." His pacing slowed but continued. Hands relaxed out of fists.

"I'm on your side." Pain shot through her back as she spoke. "He's horrible, and you and I both know it. Everyone in Cornwell knows." She didn't care what she said, just that she kept talking. Anything to calm him down.

Brody stared at the floor as he marched from the doorway to the desk. Back again. And again.

She eyed the desk. Spotted a razor lying next to a picture frame. When he turned to stomp toward the door, she grabbed it and hid it in her hand. The double edges cut into her closed fist.

"What are you lookin' at?" he shouted. Suddenly agitated again.

"This picture." She pretended not to notice the white powder that clouded the glass surface. "Is . . . is this you and your daddy?"

He glanced up at her. "What do you care?"

She thought of Cole. Regretted sending the text instead of calling 911. She now feared he would show up and fall victim to Brody's rage-filled wrath.

"Like . . . like I said in the truck, I'm sorry about your daddy's death."

"He was a drunk. Nothin' to be sorry about."

She suddenly became aware of the razor cutting into her palm. She felt the blood fill her tightly gripped hand and ooze between her fingers.

"He looks familiar. I think I recognize the smile."

Brody's gaze shot over to her, a look of disgust on his face. His pacing stopped. Then began again.

He laughed. Its tone sent chills across her body.

"It's crooked. Same as you and your sister."

The pacing stopped yet again. He stared down at her. "He left me with this hellhole and bills I'll never catch up on." With every word, his throat tensed, his voice turned colder. "All while you and your sister are over there living in the lap of luxury."

His breathing was so rapid, he was nearly hyperventilating. "You want for nothing! The cars. The trips. The clothes. I don't have anything!"

Poe's vision went spotty. The room started to spin.

"You're just like your mama. Followin' in her footsteps with Joshua. You're gonna end up knocked up just like she was." He continued to pace. "If you would've just burned along with Lady Bug . . ."

Poe watched Joshua open his eyes and blink while she tried to choke down Brody's words. "You . . . you did that."

Brody kept pacing.

"The carburetor. You told me it was all about combustion."

He cocked his head toward her. "Trust me. If I wanted you dead, you'd be dead."

She watched Joshua slowly blink and struggle to focus on her.

"You wanted to scare me? Mess with my mind? You keyed my car and made me think I somehow did it . . . The light bulb in my closet, the mud on the car . . . The coffee . . . all of it. That was you."

"You're crazy."

"No, you wanted me to think *I* was crazy!"

"We are crazy!" He instantly calmed himself. "It runs in the family." His voice was low. Dead-sounding.

She observed the tattoo on his calf, and really looked at the image for the first time. A Celtic angel, one that closely matched her and Dylan's necklaces. Seeing it made her sick. She swallowed to keep bile from rising into her throat.

The angel tattoo. She must've seen it in the bus station bathroom. That's why angels called out to her. She was drawn to them because her mind was trying to remind her of what she saw.

298

Of *who* she saw murder her sister.

With every step Brody took, more pieces of her crazy thoughts fell into place.

"You told me Joshua was at the cove so I would go there. To the platform. And you left the necklace where I would find it." Her vision turned to static, and her heart pounded vigorously in her chest. "You made me believe Joshua was a monster."

"He is a monster!" Brody's voice boomed, but quickly lowered to a whisper. "He's just a different kind."

"We trusted you. Treated you like family. My daddy took you in!"

"Your daddy?" He pointed to the photo. "That man is your daddy." He picked up the photograph and shoved it in her face. A cloud of white powder briefly hovered behind him in the air. "Look at him! Let that soak in. You're the daughter of a drunk ol' fool." He thrust the photograph backward and slammed it on the table, shattering the glass.

"He'd drive by your house every stinkin' day and watch you playing outside with your sister. I couldn't figure it out . . ." Brody's stride intensified. "He was obsessed. All he wanted was to see you girls, and your mama kept him away. He'd come home angry and take it out on *me*!" He picked up the frame and threw it against the wall.

Poe pulled her body into the fetal position as the remaining glass flew around the room.

"He left me nothin' but this stupid shop. You got everything."

"We didn't, Brody. We didn't get anything. We didn't know—"

"Just cause your mama didn't tell you, doesn't make it untrue." She gulped.

His face hardened. His eyes closed to slits. "I found out

about you in a will. He wasn't even man enough to look me in the face to tell me the truth!" He furiously swept his arm across his desk. The computer and many small objects went airborne and crashed to the ground around her.

"If it was about revenge, why the other girls?"

"Dylan was for revenge." He squatted down, picked a hammer up off the floor, stood, and gently placed it on the desk. "The others . . . for sport, I guess." He noticed the surprise in her eyes. "Like I said, crazy runs in our family."

He crouched down in front of her. His eyes bearing into hers. "Does that make you proud? Wish you would've known who your father was?"

She stiffened her back. Clinched her jaw. Stared right back at him. "David Brave is my father."

Brody backhanded her across the side of the head. She fell to the ground, and hit her forehead on the desk leg as she went. The razor dug deeper into her hand.

He shoved her body with his foot. When she didn't respond, he walked out of the office, kicked Joshua on the side of the head as he passed, and headed into the shop.

Poe lifted her head and watched Joshua as she listened to Brody throw tools around the garage and chatter recognizable words, but the sentences made no sense.

Joshua's eyes were dead. Lifeless.

She jumped to her feet and ran. Drips of blood left a trail down the hallway and out the back door.

The heavy door closed with a bang.

Within seconds, Brody's work boots pounded on the dirt road behind her, and she could hear keys rattle in the pocket of his cargo pants.

She ran toward Winnie. Her chest heaved with every breath.

Poe shoved through tree limbs. The branches sliced into her skin like the blade still gripped in her hand.

Brody caught up to her just as she reached for Winnie's side door. He grabbed her by the hair and yanked her backward. Lifting her off the ground.

She turned to face him. In desperation, she retrieved the blade from her bloody hand and sliced his wrist.

He recoiled. Released her hair.

Poe threw the door open.

He lunged for her again. A growl surged out of his throat.

She backed up the step.

Brody's arm thrust through the doorway as she pulled the door closed, catching him on the injured wrist. He groaned in pain.

She fell and turned her body away from the door. Scrambled towards the back of the RV.

She wasn't even halfway past the dinette before he grabbed her by her right ankle and pulled her toward him.

"Brody, no! Don't do this! Don't do this!"

He grabbed her left ankle. Flipped her over onto her back. Threw his body on top of hers and held her to the floor so she couldn't take another swing at him.

She screamed.

"Shut up! Shut up! I'll kill you right now if you don't shut up!" He punched her in the face. Her eye socket felt like it would explode with the impact.

Brody pulled a cushion off the couch, covered her face, and pressed down with one arm as he held her to the ground with the other.

Poe struggled to turn her head. Tried to find a way to get air as she thrashed around and slashed his arms with the razor.

Her neck tightened. She tried to keep air in her burning lungs.

When the pressure on her face momentarily lifted, she sucked in quickly. Inhaled air and dust from the decades-old cushion.

She continued to struggle. Continued the fight until the air left her lungs and the razor fell from her hand.

With no breath or energy left, she accepted her fate. Stopped fighting. Calmed.

Her mind was at peace. Fear completely gone. Her sister's voice seeped into her thoughts.

"Though I walk through the valley of the shadow of death . . ."

Dylan walked into the kitchen and immediately laughed at her sister. She was helping their mama hang another cross on the kitchen wall. Their collection, growing. The Scriptures, flowing.

". . . for thou art with me. Thy rod and thy staff they comfort me."

"Something, something . . . yada, yada." Dylan ignored their chanting, as she always did, and dug through the refrigerator. "Ghosts in the graveyard and corpses in the basement. We're surrounded by death. If you think some verse is gonna save us, you're crazy."

"This isn't just some verse, Dylan," Payton scolded. "And if you'd ever come to church, you'd know that."

"I think I'll pass." Dylan grabbed a pickle out of the jar. "I'll let you be the good girl." She walked out as they started the Scripture again.

"Though I walk through the valley of the shadow of death . . ."

. . . *I will fear no evil.*

She vaguely heard someone bound into the RV, and felt a weight leave her body after what felt like a sharp impact above her.

A large gush of oxygen filled Poe's lungs. She coughed at the dust still lodged in her chest. Her eyes flew open.

She realized Joshua had entered the RV, and as he and Brody wrestled on the yellow linoleum beside her, Poe's left hand fumbled around the floor and to the cabinet under the sink.

She opened the door, slipped her hand inside, and gripped the wrench. "Joshua!"

Joshua rolled Brody in her direction. With no hesitation, Poe swung her arm and struck Brody across the back of the head.

He went limp. His arms fell to his side.

Joshua rolled off him, sat up, and took several deep breaths.

Poe dropped the bloody wrench, grabbed the bottom of the stove, and pulled herself away from her half brother.

"Joshua, are you okay?"

"I've been better."

A shout from Brody assaulted their ears. He reached for the wrench and swiftly swung it at Joshua. The strike to his jaw threw him onto his back.

Adrenaline surged through Poe's body. She pulled herself away and crawled toward the bathroom, and when Brody again grabbed her leg she pulled it from his grip and kicked him in the face over and over.

As he grabbed for his nose, she shifted to her hands and knees and scrabbled toward the only remaining space: the tiny shower stall.

Backed into the tight corner, she set her sights on her sister's murderer. Visions of the boy she grew up with scrolled through her thoughts. The young man she drove the streets of town with, who Dylan defeated in the King of the Mountain.

Her brother.

He stared back at her. Nothing but rage reflected in his eyes.

As he rose to his feet, she pulled her leg back. Her knee touched her chest. "I will not fear you."

She kicked him in the knee. Hyperextended it.

Seconds later, Joshua jumped onto his back, linked his arms under Brody's, and tried to pull him away.

It was no use; Brody was too strong. He dropped to his knees as if Joshua were a small gnat and grabbed her by the neck.

Brody slid his fingers around the sides of her throat and increased the pressure. Poe watched Joshua fight the beast, madly attacking him at every angle.

Through the blood pounding in her ears, she vaguely heard a voice call, "Poe!" *Could that . . . be . . . ?* She worked to focus her eyes as Cole appeared in the bathroom with the wrench in hand. After pulling Joshua out of the way, he slammed the tool against the back of Brody's head.

He swung several more times until the monster finally went limp and fell forward onto Poe.

She fought to breathe as Cole grabbed Brody's shoulders, pulled his head back, and tossed him to the floor.

Cole stood with the crimson wrench, ready to strike.

A police officer pushed his way through the side door. Gun drawn, pointed toward the boys. "Get away from her!"

Cole and Joshua backed up.

"It wasn't them!" she rasped as loudly as she could. "It was

Brody. Just Brody." The effort stole all the small gasps of air she'd managed to take, and she became numbly aware her head was rapidly tipping back, taking the rest of her body with it.

"Payton? Are you all right?"

She slowly opened her eyes to find the sheriff squatting in front of her. "Payton, talk to me or move and let me know you're okay."

Her left eye throbbed with pain, and only allowed a small slit of vision.

"Why don't you come out of there and let the paramedics check you out?"

She shook her head as much as she could and huddled more closely to the farthest shower wall. Closer to the photographs of her sister. "I'm not sure I can." Her jaw barely moved, and she realized her words slurred.

"You're safe. They've gotten Brody out of here. He can't hurt you anymore."

"He killed my sister."

"I know he did. The good news is we've got him, and you three did as much damage to his face as he did to yours."

She turned her eyes back to the wall.

"You won't come out?"

Poe instinctively reached up for her pendant and felt that her shirt was ripped open; she tugged on it, trying to cover herself.

The sheriff snapped his fingers. "Jacket." Within seconds, an officer handed him a coat.

Sheriff Jackson draped it over her. "What do you need? Tell me what I can do."

She processed the question. Looked up at him. "I want my mama."

He motioned for one of his men to do what he needed to fulfill her request, and then he focused right back on Poe. "She's right outside. They got here almost as fast as we did."

Poe slowly nodded.

"You did it, Payton. I'm so proud of you. You did real good." He reached over and peeled a strand of hair off her face and tucked it behind her ear.

She felt the floor quake as her parents bounded into Winnie.

"She's in here. Please don't touch her." The sheriff moved out of the way and allowed her mama to pass by.

She took one look at Poe and started to cry. "Oh, baby girl."

She climbed into the tiny shower stall, sat down next to Poe, and used the arms of the police jacket to pull her close.

Daddy knelt down in front of Cole and looked him over as Poe ran the tips of her fingers across the dozens of photos that hung above her head in the shower.

She swallowed hard. "I haven't remembered much about my life. Everything's a fog. But this . . ." She looked back at the photos, pulled one down. It was a photo of Payton and her sophomore homecoming date, Trig. "This isn't my memory."

She pulled down a photo of Dylan and Cole at the same dance.

"This is."

CHAPTER 27

August 13, 2016

6:00 a.m.

The sun rose outside the window, tossing an orange light through the spotless third-story window. The color clashed with the pink walls and left a peach hue hovering in the air, which mingled with the scent of fresh coffee that traveled up the stairs.

The intoxicating wake-up call that roused Payton out of a deep sleep.

She rolled over, rubbed her eyes, and found her sister's bed empty. "Dylan?" She sat up, scanned the room, but saw no signs of her. "Dylan?" She looked back at her sister's bed. Stacks of clothes still covered the bedspread. Her laundry from the day before hadn't been touched.

Payton groaned, and grabbed her phone off her nightstand. "Hey, Siri. Call Dylan."

"Just confirming. You would like me to call Dylan Brave?"

"Yes."

"Calling Dylan Brave."

Within seconds, the phone rang.

"Yeah?"

"Mama's going to kill you if she finds out you stayed out all night with Cole." She kicked her covers off her legs with a violent shove and jumped to her feet. "We have to leave for the bus station in less than an hour, and I hear Mama up and moving around downstairs."

"We wanted to stay up to watch the sunrise. Must've fallen asleep. No big deal. Nothing happened." Dylan sounded groggy and completely unfazed by the fact she'd just spent the night sleeping somewhere other than her bed, or the fact that if Mama found out, she might never sleep anywhere again.

"No big deal? She'll be up here any minute!" Payton picked up her brush and ran it through her hair in rapid, painful strokes.

"I'm heading home right now. Okay?"

"You best hurry!"

"I am."

"I will not cover for you, do you hear me? I won't lie for you."

"You won't have to. I'll be right there."

Payton hung up the phone, tossed it onto the bed, and quickly threw on a bit of blush and lip gloss. "That girl's lost her mind." She checked herself in the mirror and took a deep breath, then rushed out of the room, down the stairs, and into the kitchen.

"Good morning."

Mama looked over at her and smiled. "Hey, Payton. You ready for Charleston?"

"Ready as I'll ever be." She grabbed a bag of trail mix out of the drawer and tried to act as nonchalant as possible. "I'm packed and ready to go." She dumped the mix into her hand and threw the bag in the trash.

"I hope that sister of yours is ready too. Knowing her, she'll be throwing whatever is in arm's reach into a bag at the last minute."

Although she'd sworn she wouldn't bail Dylan out this time, Mama's tone convinced Payton she had no choice. "Actually, Dylan's going to bring my stuff, and she and Nana will meet me at the station."

"Why? Where are you going?"

She gulped. "Starr wanted to meet for coffee real quick. Boy problems."

"Again?"

"Always." Payton headed toward the back doorway.

"Payton?"

She turned to her mama. "Yes, ma'am?"

Her mama walked over and kissed Payton on the forehead. "I love you. Have a great time."

"I love you too. I'll see you in a few days." Payton slowly walked around the corner, glanced over her shoulder to make sure she wasn't being followed, then raced to the front door. She opened and closed it back, and then quietly ran up the main steps and to the third floor.

She was barely back in her room before she heard, "Dylan Brave!"

Payton rolled her eyes. "Yeah?"

"Coffee's ready!"

"Yes, ma'am!" She rushed over to Dylan's bed, grabbed a sweatshirt and sweatpants, and threw them on over her T-shirt and shorts. "I hope this idea works . . . Hey, Siri, call Dylan."

"Just confirming. You would like me to call Dylan Brave?"

"Yes."

"Calling Dylan Brave."

Payton began placing clothes into Dylan's weekender bag and waited for her to answer.

"Yeah?"

"Where are you?"

"I'm running home." She was practically out of breath.

"Don't come home!"

"What, why?"

"I'm covering for you."

Dylan laughed on the other side of the phone. "I thought—"

"Yes, well, you thought wrong. Meet me at the bus station. That back bathroom."

"Why there?"

"Because I'm about to go downstairs, make an appearance, and leave this house as you. That's why. I'll change back later."

"You're too good to be true, Payton."

"Yeah. You remember that."

Dylan laughed. "Okay, I'll see you in a few."

Payton grabbed a hair tie, swept her hair into a ponytail, then rubbed the lip gloss and blush off her face. "The things we do in the name of love."

She took another deep breath, collected herself, and then marched right back down the stairs.

"Hey, Mama." She slurred her words and acted groggier. Typical early-morning Dylan.

Her mama looked her up and down. "Well, hey, Dylan. Need coffee?"

"Always."

Her mama slid her cup over. "Black. Just as you like it."

"Awesome. Thanks." Payton took a sip and tried to hide her disgust at the bitter, rubber-like taste.

"Hit the spot?"

"Yep," she sighed, attempting to sound satisfied as she grabbed a chocolate-covered granola bar out of the drawer, peeled the wrapper off, and left it laying on the counter surrounded by crumbs.

"Payton just left. Said you were taking care of getting the bags to the station for you two and Nana?"

"Yep."

"Okay, well . . . I've got to get to work." She walked to Payton and kissed her on the forehead. "Love you. Have a good trip."

"Love you too."

As soon as her mama disappeared from the kitchen, Payton fell onto the counter in a heap, took a deep breath, and smiled.

6:45 a.m.

Dylan stopped at the street corner, placed her hand on the wall, and collected her breath. The cove wasn't very far from the bus station, but running at full speed was exhausting.

She turned and leaned against the wall and looked out across Main Street. The sleepy town was awake, and the streets were already busy. With this many people out and about, she was positive someone had spotted her at the cove with Cole.

She pulled out her phone, opened Twitter, and scrolled through her feed. Surprisingly, there was no mention of her and Cole's activities. For once, people were more interested in their own lives to bother with reporting on Dylan's.

Once she could breath and walk simultaneously, she collected herself and entered the Donuts To Go, walked straight to the front, and threw a five dollar bill onto the glass counter.

"Hey, Gert."

The elderly woman, in her classic diner waitress uniform, glanced over her shoulder. "Hey, Dylan. What'cha doin' here so early on a Saturd'y?"

"Heading to Charleston with Payton and Nana." She tried to sound like she was looking forward to it, but wasn't sure it worked.

"Sounds like fun." The woman turned and walked toward her with a coffee pot in her hand. "What can I get ya?"

"A glazed, a chocolate-covered, and a black coffee, to go, please."

"You got it." She slowly turned back to the work station, pulled out a tall paper cup, and poured Dylan's coffee.

Dylan returned her attention to her phone and read a text from Cole. You shouldn't scare me like that. I woke up and you were gone.

She glanced up, watched Gert grab the donut most covered in chocolate and shove it into a paper sack, then texted him back. Sorry. Payton called freaking out. Oops. ;)

Okay. Well . . . have a great time. Call me if you get bored.

I plan on it.

Love you.

Love you too.

"Here ya go." Gert placed a cup of coffee and bag of donuts on the counter. "Can't get a receipt to print, but it'll be three dollars."

She placed her fingers on the five dollar bill and pushed it to Gert. "Keep the change," Dylan said with a wink.

"You know I will." The woman sauntered away with a smile on her face and her hand firmly attached to the coffee pot.

"Can I take the back door? I need to meet my sister out back."

"Course."

Dylan walked around the counter, pushed through the

312

kitchen door, and walked through the back room where Gert's daughter, Millie, and her husband, Dennis, rolled dough. "I love seeing where the magic happens."

Millie laughed. "You're welcome to help."

"Don't have time. Nana will be waiting for me." Dylan pressed her hip against the door bar, pushed it, and opened the back door. The bright sunlight almost blinded her, but she somehow managed to open the sack, pull out the chocolate donut, and shove it in her mouth.

"Hey, Dylan."

Startled, she spun around, nearly spilling her coffee. "Brody? What are you doin' here?"

He pointed to a Ford Taurus parked in the alley. "Mr. Monroe had a flat tire. Left it here for me to fix last night, but I'm just getting 'round to it."

She looked him over. He wasn't wearing his usual work coveralls. Instead, he was in his dressy Wranglers and a polo shirt. The shirt was wrinkled, the collar stained, but it was his eyes that fully gave him away. They were bloodshot, and his eyelids were heavy. "Rough night?"

"Naw. Just havin' some fun."

"Bet you were. Here." She handed him her coffee. "Looks like you need this more than I do."

He took the coffee and inspected it. "Black."

"As always."

"Least you don't get the frou-frou drink your sister does."

"On that note, I've gotta go. I'm meeting her and Nana at the station. We're off to Charleston." This time, she didn't bother to act excited. She rolled her eyes and gagged after *Charleston* rolled off her tongue.

"You should be more grateful." The tone in his voice caught her off guard. It was weighted, full of sudden aggitation.

"Grateful to go to Charleston?" She laughed in an attempt to lighten his sudden sour mood. "It's not like Europe or anything. But okay, I'll get a better attitude about it."

"Some people don't ever get to leave this town. Ever thought about that?"

She swallowed hard, realizing she'd hit a raw spot. She straightened her back a bit and nodded. "You're right. Thanks for the attitude adjustment."

Dylan looked down at the coffee in his hand. She noticed his fingers tighten around the cup, causing the sides to bend inward. "Well, uh . . . you enjoy that coffee, Brody."

When he didn't respond, she pulled the glazed donut out of the bag and walked toward the bus station employee bathroom not too far away.

A loud slam of the car trunk brought her attention back to Brody just as she placed the bag on the door handle and turned. Brody was leaned over the trunk, his hands were curled into fists and resting on the vehicle, but his eyes were fully on her.

"See you soon," she hollered, before stepping into the bathroom.

7:05 a.m.

Acting as Dylan, Payton arrived at the bus station where even for an early Saturday morning, the area was crowded. The bus pulled in, and its passengers milled around the station

314

purchasing drinks and snacks as she led Nana through the crowd and to an empty seat.

Payton looked around the room and noticed the line to the bathroom spilled out the door.

She set all but one of the bags at Nana's feet. "I'll be right back, Nana. Just gonna run to the bathroom."

"Where's Payton?"

"She'll be here any minute." She crouched down in front of her impeccably put-together grandmother and placed her hand on hers. "You gonna be okay? I'll be right back."

"Don't you bother over me. I'll be jus' fine, Dylan. You go right on ahead."

Payton pat her hand and then stood, pushed through the crowd, exited out the side entrance, and walked to the alley. As she approached the little-known restroom, she grabbed the bottom of her red T-shirt and placed it over the grungy metal surface before turning the door handle and throwing open the door.

Dylan sat on the sink edge with a single bite of a donut left in her hand. "It's about time you got here."

"Very funny."

"I've been in this disgusting bathroom for fifteen minutes. It stinks to high heaven."

"Yet you're managing to eat a donut. Cry me a river." She reached into her bag, pulled out a maxi dress, and tossed it to Dylan. "Put this on."

"Why? We've got time. You put it on, and I'll change into what you're wearing. Let's just be ourselves."

Payton shook her head. "No, ma'am."

"What do you mean, 'no, ma'am'?"

"I just covered for you. You owe me."

"Payton, please. I'm exhausted. We stayed up and—"

"I don't want to hear your sob story." She pulled Dylan off the counter, removed a comb from her bag, pulled the elastic band from her sister's ponytail, and started brushing her hair. "Nana's so excited about this trip, she's going to talk like a mad woman all the way there."

Dylan's hair got tangled in the comb, causing her head to jolt backward. "Ouch," Dylan screeched. "Watch it."

"If you'd just hold your head still . . ." Payton started to back-comb the roots. "Anyway, the least you can do is listen to her, and Lord knows Dylan wouldn't ever give her the time of day. So . . ." She backcombed another section, causing Dylan's hair to grow in volume and look much more like a Payton hairstyle than one Dylan would ever wear. "She's all yours, *Payton*."

Dylan groaned. "Fine. But only on the ride to Charleston. You get her on the way home." She shoved the rest of the donut into her mouth. A bit of donut glaze coated her lips.

Payton finished Dylan's hair, dropped the hairbrush into the bag, and then leaned against the sink, careful to make sure her hands didn't make contact with the disgusting surface. "So . . . what did you two do last night?"

Dylan mimicked her sister and leaned against the sink. "Just talked about our trip next year and stuff like that."

"You really are in love, aren't you?"

Dylan's grin couldn't have been larger. "Totally. Like I told him last night, he's dreamy."

"You're lucky to have him. There aren't many guys like Cole. If any."

"Yep. He's the real deal."

"Well, then all the chaos this morning was worth it," Payton said. "Operation Parent Trap was a success."

"It better have been." Dylan walked into the bathroom stall, used the fabric of the dress to cover the dingy handle to shut the door behind her, then pulled her T-shirt off and tossed it over the door, where Payton caught it and threw it into the bag. They did the same for Dylan's shorts. "You've played me enough times to get good at it."

Payton laughed. "Nobody's ever caught on."

7:10 a.m.

The dress was pinned between her fingers and the door, hanging limp, draped along the length of the stall door. The silver latch was broken and barely hung in place by a rusty screw. If it weren't for the pressure she applied, the door would swing open and reveal her sitting crouched on the toilet with her toes tightly perched over the edges of the horseshoe-shaped seat.

Perilously balanced on the ceramic throne, she was sweltering in the humidity and had her free hand resting on her knee. While it was early in the morning, the temperatures outside the thick, metal bathroom door were already in the high eighties. And inside the bathroom, with no air conditioning or circulation, she was starting to bake.

Although her skin felt clammy, sweat formed all over her body and caused salty liquid to enter her eyes with a sting.

When the lone working florescent bulb flashed off, she sat with her legs numb and her heart racing. The stench of bleach rose from the toilet bowl below her. The only illumination in the room came from the light seeping through the old exterior door frame.

She listened to her deep breathing as the blood ran out of her head, through her body, and pooled in her feet and calves.

She was frozen in place.

When her vision suddenly became tunnel-like and caused her to go wobbly, she tightly closed her eyes.

The darkness behind her closed eyelids was far more comforting than the semi-darkness of the bathroom stall. She could no longer read the vile words scraped into the black-painted metal walls, or see her reflection in the dingy mirror she could just view through a small opening between the stall door and the wall that barely held it in place.

Numerous voices mingled outside the bathroom door, but her throat was so dry, she couldn't open her mouth to call out.

Her fingers tingled. Her lips turned ice cold.

Dizzy and lightheaded, she slowly lowered a shaking foot to the ground and peered through the slit in the door.

The metal latch fell to the ground.

CLINK.

She blinked. And noticed the dress in her hand, and that she was only partially clothed.

With her mind in a fog, she pulled the dress on, placed the top of her foot on the bottom of the disgusting stall door, and pulled the door open.

She exited the dark, sauna-like bathroom and walked into the bright sunlight just as a dark-colored car peeled out around the alley corner and took off down the street.

She watched it drive away and then walked around the side of the building and entered the bus station.

"Payton!" Nana waved at her from across the waiting room.

"Hey, Nana."

"Dylan and I have been waitin' on you. It's not like you to be late."

"No, ma'am. I apologize."

"Your sister ran off to the bathroom. Will you go get her?"

She searched the room. Tried to think of what happened while she was in the bathroom. "Dylan? Um . . . I was just in the bathroom. She wasn't there. She's not here?"

"No. I told ya, she was in the bathroom."

"No, she wasn't." She walked off, and walked past the women standing in the line to the inside bathroom. None of their faces were her sister's. She walked into the bathroom, crouched down, and looked under each stall door. Nobody's legs or shoes matched her sister's.

She exited the bathroom and pushed through the passengers lined up to purchase a ticket. "Excuse me." She jumped in front of the person at the desk. "Hey, Lester."

The old man had worked at the station for more than thirty years. He knew everybody. "Hey, Payton! Never thought I'd see you in a bus station. How are your parents?"

"Same as always." She glanced over both shoulders, then back at the man. "Have you seen my sister?"

"Nope. Haven't seen her anywhere. Knowing her, she's getting in trouble somewhere or with Cole. Or both."

She forced a smile. "Or she could shock us all and not be doing anything troubling at all."

"Then she wouldn't be Dylan." He held the intercom to his mouth. "Charleston bus is loading," he announced, then looked back at her. "Grab your nana and get on the bus before it's too late."

"But I can't find my sister."

"Dylan Brave," he announced into the intercom. "Report to your nana."

She nervously knocked on the wooden counter. "Thanks, Lester."

She turned away from him and walked to Nana's side. Nana's pocketbook rest on her lap, held by tightly clutched hands. "I suppose we'll wait. She'll be back, and we'll take the next bus to Charleston."

She dropped into the seat next to Nana and closed her eyes.

Nana took in a long, deep breath. "We'll just wait for the next bus."

CHAPTER 28

September 2, 2017

11:30 a.m.

Cole listened to the police cruiser's wipers scrape across the glass in an attempt to keep up with the heavy rain that covered the windshield and coated the town of Cornwell in sparkling beads of water.

The sound helped drown out some of the thoughts flowing through his head. And the voice of Joshua, who sat on the bumper of a nearby police car, holding a black umbrella above his head while he answered questions from an officer.

Cole leaned against the open door of the cop car the second officer had directed him to, and adjusted the unopened umbrella in his hand. His clothes, still wet from the dive into the cove, were even more drenched.

"One of these vehicles matches the vehicle seen on the surveillance cameras at the state park."

Cole turned his attention to two officers standing near the row of cars parked outside the body shop.

"Looks like he might've been driving his customers' vehicles to hide his movements."

"Pretty smart, really," the second officer admitted.

"Cole? Son, did you hear the question? What did you encounter when you entered the recreational vehicle?"

He looked down at the blond officer, who sat inside the car taking notes in a small, spiral-bound notebook. "He—Brody—he had his hands around her neck. So I grabbed the wrench and hit him with it."

"How many times?"

"I'm not sure. It happened fast. Once. Twice, maybe."

"Okay. I guess that's enough questions for now. Just know we'll have more for you later."

Finally, Cole allowed himself to look behind him. There, Poe sat on a stretcher in the ambulance, staring past the boys as they gave their accounts of what happened in Winnie. Mrs. Brave sat silently next to her.

Cole turned back to the officer. "Can I go see how she's doing?"

"Not yet."

He kicked the mud with the top of his boot and sent it soaring into the air.

The officer looked at him with sympathy, but stood his ground. "Cole, you'll see her again in just a few minutes."

Cole turned to watch the officer walk toward the garage, where two other officers walked the perimeter of the body shop, hanging police tape and leaving a faint trail of clay and leftover sand that had collected on their shoes. Within seconds, each boot imprint filled with a layer of muddy water.

He followed the officers' progress, until his eyes settled on the cruiser that held Brody. Cole's jaw tightened and his hands formed into fists. Brody stared back. The whites of his eyes stood out against the blood that covered his face.

They stared at one another for several long seconds before Brody smirked.

Fuming, and feeling vengeful, Cole took two quick steps toward the car.

"Cole," Mr. Brave shouted.

Cole stopped his marched toward Brody and turned to Mr. Brave. "Yes, sir?"

"Come on; they'll let us see her before they take her to the hospital."

Cole pulled his attention away from the murderer and followed Poe's dad to the ambulance. "They said not to interrupt the questions or her answers."

Cole swallowed hard.

Together, they approached the ambulance. Cole was full of trepidation, and it only increased when he saw that her face was black and blue, her eyes practically swollen shut. A paramedic checked her blood pressure as another covered her hands in clear plastic bags and wrapped tape around her wrists to keep them in place.

She didn't look up at Cole or her dad. She focused on the sheriff. Cole couldn't even tell if she knew they'd approached.

". . . So you thought you were going to confront Joshua?" he asked.

She slowly nodded. "I followed his car to the garage. Came in through the back door." She spoke but barely moved her mouth. As if each word was a battle with pain.

"Did Brody talk about anything?"

"His father." Tears welled up in her eyes before she shook her head, as if she wished the subject hadn't even come up and she wanted to jar the thought out of her mind.

Mrs. Brave's back stiffened. She looked at her husband with heavy eyes.

"And he said that he had a lot of bills to pay, but we got to live a good life."

Poe—no, Dylan—closed her eyes. Opened them and, without moving her head, cut her eyes to her mother. "Is Brody's daddy my bio dad?"

Mrs. Brave lowered her gaze. Shame clouded her face. She nodded.

Dylan groaned a deep growl that seemed to rise from the depths. He knew the news was soul crushing and had to fight the urge to reach out and hold her, but understood that her mom wouldn't appreciate if he injected himself into the moment.

Silence took over and permeated the space until her father finally spoke up. "Don't you have enough for now? Can't you see she's in agony?"

"We're good for now." He motioned for the paramedics to take her. "We'll get the rest from her later."

She raised her hand to scratch her head and realized her hands were covered.

"They'll scrape under your nails during your exam at the hospital," the paramedic said. The tone was so matter of fact that there was no compassion in his words.

The sheriff stood. "So you're her?" There was awe in his voice. "You're Dylan."

She acknowledged his revelation with a nod.

The sheriff rolled back on his heels before slightly tipping. He readjusted his footing just in time to save himself from falling over completely.

"Our DNA is the same—I remember our Biology teacher

pointing that out in class when we were studying genetics. That must be why no one ever realized."

The sheriff nodded. "And your fingerprints never clued us in—"

"Because I never had them fingerprinted," Mrs. Brave added, obviously sick with herself.

"Did you two do that a lot? Change places?" the sheriff asked.

"All the time. Doctor appointments, dentist appointments. Tests." She eyed Cole. "Even a date once, but Cole caught on right away."

She looked at him, and they finally shared a small smile.

He knew her well and always had. As far as Cole was concerned, the twins had several things that made them individual. Maybe he noticed more than most because his lack of hearing forced him to rely more heavily on his other senses.

Payton, being the proper one, enunciated her words and spoke more slowly, which meant that her lips were often tense, leaving lines at the corners. Dylan's words tumbled out her mouth, but she spoke with a lazy dialect, and her relaxed lips rarely ever closed tightly together.

When Dylan disagreed, but didn't want to necessarily admit it, she'd cock her head to the left and shrug her shoulder a little. The shrug was faint, but enough for someone who watched closely to pick up.

And she had a small golden fleck in her eye that glistened when the sun hit it just right. He'd spotted it that day at the prayer service. It was the first glimmer of hope that the girl he loved was still alive.

There were hundreds of ways the girls were different, but only someone who wanted to see them might notice.

The sheriff led her to answer the next question. "So, when we pull her dental records to match her remains . . ."

"She took all the dentist appointments as soon as Mama trusted us to go on our own. Dental records would match starting after our sixteenth birthday."

Her mom gasped. "Is that why you never went to your dentist appointments?"

Dylan looked over at her mom. "I don't know. I . . . didn't miss them on purpose. I would honestly forget. The appointments were gone. Maybe Brody erased them to make me doubt myself. I don't know."

"If you would've made it to just one appointment . . ." Mr. Brave shook his head in disbelief. "We would've known."

"Or maybe if someone other than Cole would've just looked at me. Really, really looked at me." Cole felt his body relax at her proclamation. She'd somehow figured it out and come to realize that he knew all along, and seemed to be the only person who did. "I felt people staring at me all the time, but I don't think anyone was truly looking."

Her parents shared a glance. A silent acknowledgment of mortification passed between them.

"Like a real, earnest look." Tears filled her eyes. "We weren't completely identical."

"We saw who we thought we had," Mrs. Brave said, her voice heavy with grief. "We were so blind. To a lot of things."

Dylan shook her head, then winced. "Honestly, I didn't even suspect anything until Cole told Mr. Stine about that time I stabbed myself in the foot. I remembered it—his mama brought me a cup of apple juice and put a damp washcloth on my forehead. It smelled like vanilla."

326

She smiled a little at the memory.

"I couldn't wear flip-flops for a month. And later, Missy mentioned Dylan was the one who was afraid of blood." She glanced over at him. "And I realized that project is how she first got to know Cole. All of that is Dylan's memory. I wouldn't remember it if I were Payton."

"No, you wouldn't," her mom admitted.

"I still don't know what happened in that bathroom—"

"It'll eventually come," Mrs. Brave said.

"But if it doesn't? And these other holes in my memory. What if they don't come back?"

"We'll make new ones," Cole promised.

Dylan gazed over at him. Relief washed over her. "We get to make new ones. And that's what matters."

"Completely."

12:30 p.m.

The room was cold. Her feet, almost numb.

Dylan stared up at the white ceiling and folded her arms across her chest to try to warm her body. The thin paper crinkled below her. She readjusted the hospital gown to cover her thighs, folded her hands in her lap, and glanced over at her mama, who sat in the corner, talking to Sheriff Jackson and crying almost uncontrollably.

Dylan realized the news of Payton's remains being found, along with the revelation that she didn't recognize her own child, were too much to take. Even the sheriff seemed to be trying to make her feel better about it.

A police officer stepped in front of Dylan. "Just a few more photos and then we'll be done."

Dylan followed the officer's requests. Looked both directions so they could document the injuries to her head.

"We didn't find any traceable fingerprints in the bathroom," the sheriff was explaining. "And there was never any reason to doubt she was who she said she was—"

"She didn't say she was anyone." Her mom was adamant. "We told her. We told her who she was."

Dylan lifted her arms so they could photograph bruises. Almost every part of her body was examined and photographed. There wasn't much space on her body that Brody hadn't injured.

"She was dressed as Payton. She had her hair all fixed up. She even talked like her." Now he sounded more like he was trying to get himself off the hook than convince her distraught mama.

The second officer bagged her clothes and shoes into an evidence bag and left the room.

In the exam room, with all those people inspecting her, and her mama and Sheriff Jackson talking about her like she wasn't even in the room, she felt more violated than when Brody attacked her. Against Brody, she could fight back and maintain a little bit of control. In the hospital, she felt powerless.

". . . and that whole Poe thing. She was trying to connect with her sister," he added.

"No," Dylan blurted. "I think, deep down, I must've seen her die—that's why I blocked it out. I knew she was gone." She took a deep breath and let the tears come. "I just realized what all of that was. Winnie, the graveyard, the cove, the closet . . ."

"What?" Mama asked, with her chin trembling.

"I wasn't trying to connect with my sister, I was trying to *re*connect to myself." Now she was the one sobbing. The words found difficulty even forming in her throat. "I'd lost myself—Dylan—and I was fighting to find me again."

The medical staff stopped working. The police officer stopped taking photos. It was as if there was a moment of silence in the midst of a heartbreaking revelation. Both Dylan and her sister had been lost. One in body, the other in mind.

Once the exam was complete and the sheriff gone, her daddy was allowed in the room while they treated her remaining injuries and stitched up the cuts under her left eye and in her hand.

Her mama stood close and held her hand as a nurse sewed her up. "Um . . . about your birth father. I—"

Dylan's throat tightened.

"I didn't know he was married or that he had a son. And . . . I was young and impressionable . . . and . . . he wasn't in any shape to be a father. I told him that he'd need to clean up his act, stay sober if he wanted to be around . . ." She shook her head. "He couldn't manage."

"You were alone," Dylan whispered.

"I had Nana and my girls . . . and then your daddy came along."

"What about Brody?"

"Your daddy knew Mr. Wynn was your birth father, so when he died, Daddy tried to do the right thing and welcome Brody into the family. We didn't realize Brody found out that his father was also yours. It was supposed to be kept a secret until you were eighteen."

"So Daddy tried to do the right thing, but he actually brought a monster into the house."

Mama pressed her lips together, and continued to hold Dylan's hand while focusing on the physician's work.

1:30 p.m.

Cole leaned against the vending machine. His foot propped against the glass. Dylan's friends and family collected nearby but suddenly jumped to their feet.

Mr. Brave pushed Dylan through the double doors and into the waiting room in a wheelchair. Her mama quietly followed, as if in a trance.

Cole wanted to rush to her side like everyone else, but stood frozen solid in his spot on the tile floor as everyone else ran past him and showered Dylan with affection. He caught her eye after the initial rush, and was rewarded with a small smile.

As they made their way toward the emergency room entrance, several flashbulbs popped, and a flood of media began crowding the perimeter. Cole noticed police officers beginning to gather near the door, attempting to shoo people back.

"How'd they manage to get here so fast?" Dylan's mom asked. "It's barely been a few hours, and they're everywhere."

"Just wait," Cole's dad said as he approached the group. "These are just the local guys. It's gonna get even worse when the national ones show up. This town'll be crawling with reporters again."

Cole's cell phone chimed. He pulled it out of his pocket. Read the message. How is she?

He felt pressure mount in his jaw and realized he'd clenched his teeth. "They didn't care about her before; why do they suddenly care now?" Having no intention of giving them the time of day, he turned the phone off and shoved it back into his pocket.

"It's good gossip," Misty said. "People can't help themselves."

Dylan's mom placed her hand on her husband's arm. "Please go get the car. I want to get Dylan out of here."

Cole noticed Dylan shuddered at the name.

"I want Misty and Kasi to take me home," she announced.

Her mom scowled.

His body tightened. His chest ached. He'd waited a year to be reunited with Dylan, and here she was choosing the girls to take her home instead of him. It felt like the ultimate rejection. Maybe Dylan had returned, but her feelings for him hadn't.

"Will you?" Dylan asked, looking over at them. "Will you take me home?"

"If . . . if it's okay with your parents," Misty said.

"Dylan, we're going there anyway. We've got room in the car."

"Mama, I've been with you since it all . . . went down. I want to be with my friends."

"Of course," her dad soothed. "Whatever you want."

Cole backed away a bit, suddenly feeling apart from everything happening around him. Wondering if he should even be there.

Carl grabbed Kasi's arm. "Pull your car around to the service entrance where they make deliveries. That way the press won't see her and try to follow you."

Mr. Brave nodded. "Good idea. I'll go out front and answer

questions real quick, so they concentrate on me while you guys make your escape." He took off toward the front entrance with a bit of a limp. His body seemed to have aged several years in only a matter of hours.

"I'll . . . I'll go pull my car around back." Kasi was out the door before Dylan's mom could try to stop her.

"Dylan—" she started.

"Mama, please give it a rest."

The woman backed away, visibly upset but unwilling to argue any further. That one phrase proved she was dealing with Dylan, not Payton; and her mom knew as well as him that if there was anyone as stubborn as Laurie Brave, it was Dylan.

"I heard you got him good," Misty said proudly.

Dylan glanced up at Cole, and he allowed himself a grin. "I had a lot of help."

"Yeah. Sheriff Jackson said his nose is broken, among other issues. That's two broken noses in a month. Impressive."

"Where is he? Where'd they take him?" Dylan asked.

"County jail," Carl said. "One of the officers mentioned they'll transfer him out of there tomorrow. He's lawyered up already. I saw him talking with one of them in the hallway a little while ago."

"Here?" Dylan's mom screeched.

Carl stepped toward the wheelchair. "He was here just long enough to get patched up. And he was cuffed and guarded. He's gone now."

Cole's dad had arrived at the hospital within seconds of getting the call. Once Cole reassured him that he was fine and it was Dylan who'd been injured, they both set their sights on worrying about her.

Carl and Dylan had always been close. In the year before the abduction, she practically spent more time at Carl's house than at home. He always mentioned that he felt like she was the daughter he never had, but always hoped for.

The emergency room doors opened again and Joshua emerged from behind them. His face was swollen and bandaged.

Cole looked over to Misty, and saw that her eyes were locked on Joshua as he walked in their direction. And that she shuffled her feet as Mrs. Brave ran to him and embraced him like she owed him her life.

It was a bit hard to swallow. While he wasn't a murderer, Joshua went out of his way to make Poe's life miserable, and now he was being treated like a hero.

Mrs. Brave was wailing. "Thank you. Thank you for helping my daughter."

Her words stung.

Joshua peered over the woman's shoulder and made eye contact with Misty for a brief moment before diverting his attention to nowhere in particular.

Kasi emerged through the busy double doors. She stopped in front of the group and rubbed her palms on her jeans. "Nobody followed me. At least I don't think so, anyway."

Dylan's mom released Joshua, and he and his parents walked away without so much as a good-bye or another look their direction.

Carl placed his hands on the wheelchair handles and pushed Dylan toward the back exit. "Let's get her out of here. Get her home."

Cole followed Dylan, Misty, Kasi, and his dad down the hall and out the service entrance. Then, he watched his dad carefully load Dylan into Kasi's car.

Mrs. Brave stepped up to the car and kissed her on the forehead. "We'll hang out inside for a little while. Give you time to escape before we head out."

"Yes, ma'am."

Just before Carl closed the door, Dylan glanced back at Cole. "They'll follow you and my parents. They don't know about Kasi's car."

He nodded, his pride hurting a little less. "I'll make sure they follow us."

She stepped out of the car, walked to him, and kissed him on the cheek. "Thank you."

"You're welcome," he whispered.

"Now, go get some sleep. You look horrible," she teased.

"You still look beautiful."

"And you're still dreamy."

They shared a brief smile before she climbed back in the car and Kasi drove away.

Dylan leaned back against the headrest and closed her eyes.

"You okay?" Kasi asked. "Do you need anything?"

"I wanted a minute without Mama staring at me or Cole worrying about me. I just needed to breathe."

"Don't breathe too deep—it smells like stale french fries in here."

"Misty!" Kasi shouted. "It does not."

"It totally does. French fries and soured milkshakes."

Dylan couldn't help herself; she laughed. From the depths of her toes to the top of her head, her body ached from the vibrations, but she laughed. And the pain was worth it. She opened her eyes and looked over at Kasi. "Actually, a milkshake sounds really good right about now."

Kasi kept her eyes on the road ahead, but wildly nodded. "It totally does."

"I got money," Misty announced. "Nothing like some parental guilt to bring a windfall."

"Then I'll head to Clover's Dairy."

Dylan shifted in her seat and turned to face Misty in the backseat. "So, it's back to normal? Your parents are acting like they never threw you out?"

"No. They're acting like they threw me out and realized it was the worst decision ever, which is the better option of the two."

Dylan rested her chin on the back of her seat and slipped right into conversation with two of her best friends. It's exactly why she chose to ride home with them. She could be Dylan, and it wouldn't seem like a monumental achievement.

It simply felt normal.

She was sucking on her milkshake when Kasi pulled up in front of the house. Dylan watched her parents climb out of her daddy's truck. He wrapped his arm around Mama's waist and led her up the patio steps, past Nana, and into the house without a word.

"Do you want us to help you tell Nana?" Misty asked.

"We will," Kasi added. "If that's what you want . . . or need."

Dylan shook her head. "It needs to come from me." She turned to her friends. "Thanks for the ride."

"I'd hug you, but every inch of you looks like it hurts," Misty said. "I'll save you from the pain."

"I appreciate that." She carefully opened the car door. "I'll call you later."

Dylan climbed out of the car and slowly walked to the porch.

Nana sat upright in her rocking chair and watched Dylan approach. "Hey, Dylan."

"No, it's—" Dylan processed the words. "Hey, Nana."

"You got some news for me?"

"Yes, ma'am," Dylan's voice trembled and tears immediately fell. "What is it?"

Dylan dropped into the empty rocking chair. "They found her body."

"And they're sure it's her?"

"Pretty sure. They're running some tests, but . . . it was her. And the other two missing girls." She reached down and stroked Pugsley's head. Nana sighed, shut her eyes, and leaned against the back of the chair.

"Are you okay, Nana?"

She nodded without opening her eyes.

Dylan reached over and lightly squeezed her hand. "It was Brody. He killed her."

Nana opened her eyes. "The boy got his revenge."

She felt some shock at the words, but swallowed it down. "I suppose so."

For the first time in over twelve months, Nana looked over at Dylan with clarity in her eyes. "Well, sugar. Ya look beat up pretty bad. You okay?"

Again, Dylan swallowed hard and shook her head. "I don't think I'll ever be okay again."

Nana stood and kissed her on the top of the head. "Welcome back to us, Dylan. I was waitin' for you to return."

An amazed Dylan looked up at her. "You knew it was me?"

She kissed her again. "Of course I knew." The woman moseyed toward the door, Puglsey close behind. "There's only one Dylan Brave."

CHAPTER 29

September 6, 2017

7:50 p.m.

Storms rolled into town that night, and meteorologists claimed they were expected to stay for several days. The weather seemed appropriate to the mood in the Brave home.

Much like she did for those first months after the abduction, Dylan sat in their closet to breathe in the scent. She could never exactly figure out what the smell was. Maybe a mixture of soap and perfume? But unlike when her life first turned upside down, the smell was almost completely gone.

There in the darkness, and squished in among all the shoes and clothes that her mama had so carefully put back in place, Dylan felt like the two of them were still sharing a space, drawing energy from one another. Somehow the connection brought her some comfort.

When Dylan heard the roar of reporters outside her window, she crawled out of the closet, walked to the window, and watched her daddy approach a slew of microphones.

"We have a brief statement, but won't be taking any further questions." She watched him study the piece of paper in his hand and could faintly hear his words through the partially opened bedroom window. "Our family is again grieving the loss of a daughter. Payton Belle Brave. She was sixteen, full of life, and an absolute joy in the lives of everyone who knew her. We miss her greatly but are relieved to finally have some closure.

"Her sister Dylan's psychosis is difficult to understand, but we are seeking professional help to better understand all that she's been through. We ask you not to pass judgment on her actions since August fifteenth of last year. Instead, we encourage you to find compassion for a sixteen-year-old girl who was present in the bus station bathroom when Brody Wynn so violently took Payton from this world. She was under extreme duress and her mind did what it could to protect her.

"Thank you. No further questions." He turned, took Mama's hand in his, and they walked back toward the house. He looked up to her window and gave a brief nod.

As planned with her parents, while reporters screamed questions, Dylan snuck down the stairs, into the alley, and out into the world for the first time since she walked back inside the home as Dylan Brave.

Careful to stay off the main roads, Dylan walked downtown and waited outside Val's flower shop until Cole finished work.

Finally, at a few minutes past eight, he walked out the back door and spotted her leaning against his delivery truck. "Hey, Dylan."

"Poe."

Cole's forehead creased. His eyes squinted.

"I decided I want to hold on to her a little bit longer. She's both of us . . . and I'm not ready to let her go." She rapidly slid the angel charm back and forth on her necklace.

He nodded, shoved his hands in his pockets, and glanced around the alley.

"Sorry to bother you. I just . . . um, I mean, we didn't get a chance to talk at all . . . after . . . everything. And with Mama keeping me in the house and away from my cell because of the reporters and all the social media nonsense . . ."

He pulled a hand out of his pocket and scratched his head before he shoved it back in. "How are you holding up?"

"I'm okay." She fumbled with the necklace and shifted her weight back and forth between hips. "The flowers your mama sent were beautiful. I wanted to make sure she knew that. And I wanted to thank her."

"I'll tell her."

"No, I want to."

He shrugged and then looked toward the street. She followed his stare but didn't see anything in particular.

"Did you walk?"

"Yeah. The cops still have Winnie, and I didn't want to drive a hearse."

He glanced up at the sky and back to her.

"Can we take a stroll?" she asked.

He grinned, seemingly relieved. "Yeah."

They walked all the way to the playground in silence, his eyes continually scanning the area. His hands remained in his pockets.

Just as Poe stepped toward the swings, he grabbed her arm and pulled her back. Her heart rate accelerated as he gazed down at her, but then he walked past her and sat in a swing. "Sorry. I thought I heard something, and I'm used to being on guard."

She sat in the swing next to his. "He's gone. We don't have to be afraid anymore."

Illuminated by the streetlights, he reached over and stroked her cheek with his thumb. His eyes looked directly into hers. "I still worry about you. I can't help myself."

"I appreciate that. I truly do." She scuffed her foot back and forth in the dirt before gently swinging herself back and forth. "Is it odd that I'm relieved that he's locked up, but distraught that it's Brody?"

"No. He was like family, even before you knew he actually was. You've basically lost someone else."

"Or lost who I thought he was."

"Isn't it pretty much the same thing?"

"I suppose it is." Her choice of words and feelings of grief struck her as much more Payton than Dylan. Proof that she was still wavering between the two. Very much still Poe.

She leaned back and stared up at the sky. Thoughts and questions swirled through her brain. "I wasn't the only one living a lie. So many secrets." She looked back at him. "I was thinking back on everything, and, well . . . Why did you keep the truth a secret? Why didn't you tell?"

"I don't know. I mean . . . I knew you were you, but you weren't. You were there in body, but your soul seemed like it was gone. It's like Dylan went dormant. And you wouldn't do something like that without a good reason . . . or if you could help it."

She brought her swing to a stop and looked at him closely.

He looked over, his eyes questioning. "How is it that it wasn't obvious to everyone when it was so obvious to me?"

"I wonder the same thing, and I think my parents do too. Mama's beating herself up pretty bad. And Daddy's sick that he invited Brody in. It's all stuff we'll have to work through in therapy. I was there and they didn't see me for me. I can't lie, it hurts."

"Of course it does."

"Payton and I always used to laugh about how we could switch identities and nobody ever noticed." She shrugged. "I guess I got too good at it."

Now he was the one who brought himself to a complete stop. "When you finally came back to school, you never looked at me again. Not until last month."

"It's crazy. It's like I took on the identity everyone wanted me to have, and it dictated my existence. Every thought. Every move I made. It's like, live within the box . . . and the universe spins on its axis just like it's supposed to. People can go on living in the world they create for themselves. But if you dare to step outside your assigned identity, life stops existing as it's known; or at least that's what everyone's afraid of, anyway. We're all blind to a possibility that things may not be how they seem. Nor should they be."

Cole smirked.

"What?" she asked, taken aback by his response.

"You sound like you. Back to questioning everything. Raging against the machine. It's exactly what I've hoped for."

She couldn't stop herself from smiling. Her face flushed. "Can you believe it, Cole? I'm not actually crazy. In fact, I might be the sanest person we know."

He smirked over at her. "I wouldn't go that far."

She gazed back for several seconds. Awed that his faith never waivered. His love never faded. "Please tell me you're about to kiss me," she whispered. "I think there's a part of me that's been waiting a long time."

He grinned, and shook his head.

"Why not?"

"I want to take you on a date first."

"A date?" She'd failed at keeping the disappointment from her tone. "When? What kind?"

He shrugged. "Europe, maybe?"

"Europe?" She laughed. "How would we manage that?"

He turned serious. "When I saw you at the prayer vigil, I knew you'd be back. I didn't know when, but I knew you'd come home. So, I asked the tour company to put a hold on the tickets."

"They were willing to do that?"

"Under the circumstances. And for a small fee."

She pushed off the ground. Set the swing back into motion. "Wow. You still want to take me to Europe?" She felt as if she could fly away that very moment. "That's unreal."

He stood, stepped backward, and lifted off the ground. His swing matched hers.

"But what makes you think my mama's gonna let you do that?"

"I just saved your life. I sort of think she owes me."

Poe laughed. The deepest, most sincere laugh she'd experienced in more than a year. "I think maybe you're right about that part."

"Just that part?"

"Yeah, but I can promise you one thing. I'm not gonna be willing to wait for that date for you to kiss me." She watched him as he let himself be free, and felt an amazing peace and happiness flow over her. "You know what?"

"What?"

"This is like . . . the first moment I've looked at you with my own eyes."

"Oh yeah? What do you see?"

"The boy I love."

He smiled.

"The boy I'd do anything for."

They brought their swings to a stop and faced one another, like perfectly matching bookends.

Cole's eyes became soft. "It took every bit of my strength to keep from grabbing you in my arms every time I saw you. For over a year, I was forced to go along with it, and I didn't even know why. But if I did what I wanted . . . if I touched you, if I grabbed your hand . . . or . . ." He shook his head. "Even though I'd know it was Dylan I was touching, everyone would think I was betraying her. Betraying you. I couldn't stand being so close to you all the time and having to pretend you weren't the girl I love."

She climbed out of the swing, walked to him, and placed her hands on his face.

"I saw you and knew you'd be back," he whispered.

Her fingers slid through his hair as she pulled him to his feet, and his head toward her. Their foreheads touched.

She quickly put her lips where her forehead had been. He didn't protest, so she moved her lips to his right temple as she settled her hands on the sides of his neck. When he didn't push her away, she allowed her lips to slowly travel to his.

"Poe. What about our date?"

She leaned in and erased the gap between them.

For the first time in over a year, Dylan and Cole were back together, but as Poe and Cole, they were perfect.

CHAPTER 30

September 9, 2017

8:30 a.m.

Poe walked to the closet and flipped the switch. The light immediately came on, illuminating the two sides of the closet. One side was filled with creams, whites, pastels, and the brightest tones of the color wheel. Fabrics of every sheen and texture.

Then she inspected the opposite side. Mostly dark colors. Blues, grays, browns, and denim. Lots and lots of denim.

She'd spent a year entering the closet and walking to the rainbow-inspired side. Today, she made the conscious effort to walk to the side diametrically opposed in every way.

Poe ran her fingers over the rough denims and cotton blends, and then selected a black pantsuit. The choice was still a little dressy for her taste. But the day called for it.

Once dressed, Poe stood in front of the mirror and stared at herself. Her clear eyes closely inspected every inch of her freshly washed face.

"We see what we want to see," she whispered. "What we need to."

She stared a bit longer. What looked back at her left her unsettled. She didn't feel like herself. Her line of vision moved from her reflection back to the closet behind her, and directly to the rainbow of light.

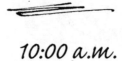

10:00 a.m.

Poe sat beside her parents and Nana on the first row of the First Presbyterian Church. It was filled to the brim with the people of Cornwell. Every pew in the sanctuary was filled, and she was told an overflow audience watched on video from chairs set up in the church gym.

She raised her head and briefly looked at the large photograph of Payton that sat beside a small urn on the large stage covered in pink and white flowers. Val did an amazing job on the flower arrangements. Poe was convinced they were some of her best work.

Poe lowered her eyes back to the handwritten speech in her right hand as she ran the charm across her necklace with her left. With every second that passed, she was grateful to know that Cole and his parents were sitting right behind her. They could usher her out if she started to get sick or overcome.

"Dylan?"

She looked up. Realized that Pastor Greg, and just about everyone else, was looking at her. Waiting. Expecting.

She stood, smoothed the wrinkles from her pants, and adjusted the pink scarf around her neck. It was a last-minute addition.

As soon as she'd slipped it on, she felt complete.

She walked to the podium, looked out across the audience,

and made a point to take in as many faces as possible. Dozens and dozens of funerals throughout her life, and she'd only really seen the backs of people's heads. She'd never experienced seeing their faces as they came to offer their good-byes to someone they loved or cared about.

The scene was almost too much to process.

She gulped. Looked down at her notes and then looked back up, surprised to make eye contact with Joshua. He sat toward the back with his mama. She could see his bruises even with the distance. A part of her felt pity for him, the other couldn't help but still despise him.

Poe quietly studied the audience again. Took all the time she needed. Nobody could go anywhere; they were a captive audience. She wanted to take it all in. Remember the moment so she could think back on it when their lives got back to normal, the usual gossip started flowing, and people weren't so loving.

She lowered her eyes to her notes, took a deep breath, looked up at Cole, and smiled. "She's not who we thought she was. Payton Brave."

She turned her focus to the notes in her hand. "Not that she wasn't beautiful and friendly, or smart and optimistic, because she was all those of things.

"But she was more than a socialite with great clothes and a big group of friends. Because Payton . . . the real Payton was, well . . . real. Authentic. She didn't struggle to be friendly to people, because she genuinely liked everyone. She didn't have to suck up to her teachers to get help, because they couldn't help but like her on their own. She didn't argue to make a point, because she didn't care if she was right. She needed those around her to feel special and be happy.

"She wanted to be a light in this very dark world. And even though someone tried to extinguish that light, they didn't accomplish their goal. While he may have killed her body, he didn't kill her spirit. Or the memory that we all have of her.

"I tried to be her and wore myself out doing it. But, all I came to realize is that God makes us who we are for a reason. He made Payton because we needed a Payton. He made me Dylan because you all needed a Dylan. And I believe that he created Poe because I need to live in a world where a part of me and a part of Payton can still exist together.

"So, I'm gonna stay Poe for a while. I need a little more Payton and Dylan in my life, and I hope you do to. But, today, we say good-bye. Payton's laid to rest, and now she can live in your memories and hearts.

"It's time to let her go . . . to let her soar with the angels. So, let's let her do just that.

"Soar, Payton Belle Brave, soar."